UNDISCOVERED TOMB

UNDISCOVERED TOMB

REG RAWLINS, PSYCHIC INVESTIGATOR #15

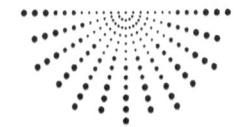

P.D. WORKMAN

 PD WORKMAN

ISBN: 9781774685013 (KDP Paperback 2 ed)
ISBN: 9781774681619 (KDP Hardcover)
ISBN: 978-1774681602 (IS Paperback)
ISBN: 9781774681626 (KDP Large Print)
ISBN: 9781774681589 (Kindle)
ISBN: 9781774681596 (ePub)

ALSO BY P.D. WORKMAN

FIND MORE BOOKS AT PDWORKMAN.COM

MYSTERY/SUSPENSE:

Reg Rawlins, Psychic Detective
Paranormal Mystery & Adventure

What the Cat Knew

A Psychic with Catitude

A Catastrophic Theft

Night of Nine Tails

Telepathy of Gardens

Delusions of the Past

Fairy Blade Unmade

Web of Nightmares

A Whisker's Breadth

Skunk Man Swamp

Magic Ain't A Game

Without Foresight

Careful of Thy Wishes

Time to Your Elf

Undiscovered Tomb

Missing Powers

Thrice Spared (Coming Soon)

Cloaked Campaign (Coming Soon)

AND MORE AT PDWORKMAN.COM

For those who are seeking homes

CHAPTER ONE

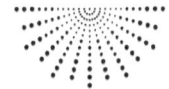

*R*eg rubbed her eyes and yawned, not particularly ready to face her day and Sarah's disapproval. The gray-haired, older woman was usually pleasant and easy to get along with. Reg's landlord, she rented out the guest cottage in her backyard at a very reasonable rate, fully furnished in a rustic Florida style, and could frequently be found stocking Reg's fridge or writing new appointments into Reg's appointment book on the kitchen island, which Reg didn't pay her to do. She was helpful and grandmotherly and had helped Reg through some difficult situations.

But Sarah did not like cats, and that was a problem. She had an African gray parrot as her familiar and bird feeders in the beautiful gardens on the property, and cats were high on her list of pests to be eliminated.

Starlight, Reg's black and white tuxedo cat with a white marking on his forehead, had been lucky to escape Sarah's wrath. Reg had adopted him before she knew of Sarah's anathema, so Sarah had overlooked Reg's not consulting her first. Sarah even fed Starlight when she popped over—which was frequently. Too much, if the truth were told.

But the recent addition of Horace was another story. Reg had not gotten permission to take in another cat and had known that Sarah was strict in her rule that Reg was not to have any more pets.

Especially cats.

Of course, Reg knew that the pure black cat was not actually the usual, run-of-the-mill domestic short hair that he appeared to be.

And she hadn't adopted him. Not intentionally, anyway.

"I can't help it that Harrison left him here," Reg told Sarah for the hundredth time. She gathered her box braids into both hands to pull them all back behind her shoulders, and let the red strands fall. "I told him not to. But he did. And it's going to take me a little time to find a new home for Horace."

"You can't keep him."

"I know that. And I'm not planning to, I told you that from the start. He's not going to stay here. But... I need to find a new home for him. And I can't just dump him on someone."

Sarah's sour look indicated that she didn't see why not. "That's what you said last week."

"I'm trying. It isn't like I can return him to his previous owner. That warlock was in Egypt, and I don't even know if he exists anymore."

It seemed like a strange thing to say about a person, and maybe it was, but Reg didn't know how else to put it. Uncle Harrison had made the warlock disappear and, whether he had used his powers as an immortal to teleport him back to his house in Egypt or had annihilated him, Reg had no idea. And she didn't really want to know. Even if she asked Harrison, he would probably give her some nonsensical answer or ask her something about the nature of human existence and she would be no closer to the truth.

"Didn't he have heirs? Maybe the cat could go to his children."

"I hope he didn't have children." Reg gave a little shudder, thinking about the evil, power-hungry warlock. "And if he did, I wouldn't give Horace to them. He wasn't happy in Egypt."

"Egypt is a wonderful place for cats. They are worshiped there," Sarah pointed out.

"They *used to be* worshiped there. That was a long time ago. Now… who knows how they treat them. Probably let them wander the streets and get eaten by dogs."

"There is a natural order of things," Sarah said with a nod, as if this were a sad truth that nothing could be done about.

"Just like cats eating birds?"

Sarah's face got red.

Not the right thing to say. Not when Reg wanted Sarah to calm down and relax about Horace being around for a few more days.

"Sorry." Reg rubbed her eyes again. "I just got up. I need my coffee. Then I'll be in a better mood. I shouldn't have said that."

"You know that I said no more cats. Even having that other one over to visit…" Sarah rolled her eyes over the concept of kitty play dates. But Starlight really did like having Nicole over. Horace's adoptive mother, Nicole was also black all over, and she and Starlight were very close.

"I know. But I didn't take in another pet. You wouldn't want me to just open the door and shoo him out, would you? Have him stalking around your garden?"

"Certainly not!" Sarah's voice got noticeably shriller. "But we do have animal shelters. You could take him to one of those."

"You want him to be put down? How is that fair? He hasn't done anything to hurt anyone. His owner turned out to be an evil warlock who should never have had a pet. Who knows what kind of abuse Horace had to put up with while he was there. You think he should just be turned out and put down for something that wasn't his fault?"

Reg's own experiences with being abused and frequently moved from home to home in foster care meant that this hit much closer to home for Reg than it did for Sarah. It wasn't Horace's fault that he had been treated that way. Harrison had rescued him from a bad situation and dumped him on Reg, believing that she would be the best person to take care of him. And in other circumstances, maybe he would have been right but, as Reg couldn't take on another pet under the current circumstances...

Reg pulled the coffee pot out from the coffee maker, even though it was still dripping a little and the drips sizzled on the hot plate and filled the room with the smell of burning coffee. She sloshed a good amount of coffee into a mug and quickly put the pot back in place.

"I'll give Francesca a call later today," she promised. "She was going to be looking for some other homes too. Okay?"

"Yes, fine," Sarah agreed grumpily. "Why doesn't she take this cat in until she can find a new home for it? She had all of the kittens before. She can easily manage two."

"I've tried to get her to take him, but she says there is too much else going on and she needs to concentrate on the others... she's worried about... things."

Reg didn't want to get into it too deeply. She too thought that Francesca should be able to take one more cat. Even if it were just short term. But Francesca's worries about Horace and his eight litter mates were serious and not something that could just be brushed off. And Reg would prefer that Francesca were the one taking on that responsibility. Reg didn't want anything else to do with the Witch Doctor and the other kattakyns.

"Just see that you deal with it soon," Sarah reiterated, looking at the black cat who, for the moment, was curled up on the cushion of the wicker sofa, looking perfectly happy and at home.

"I will," Reg promised.

But she didn't know how she could find him a home any faster than she was already trying.

Sarah did a quick flip through the date book on the island, showing that she was moving on to other things and would not stop being involved in Reg's life.

"Let me know when you do."

CHAPTER TWO

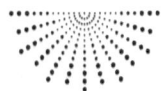

*R*eg decided to take a page out of Harrison's book and just show up at Francesca's with Horace. Maybe if Francesca actually had him in the house, and he showed how well he got along with Nicole (pronounced NEE-cole in Francesca's beautiful Haitian accent) she would let him stay there, at least until the two of them could find him another home. Then Reg didn't have to listen to Sarah's lectures three times a day and could focus on her psychic services business.

And they would find Horace another home. Eventually. Unless Francesca decided he could stay there permanently.

Francesca raised her brows when she saw Reg on her doorstep with Horace in the cat carrier. She swept long blond curls back over her ear, frowning.

"Why did you bring him here?" Francesca asked. She looked at her watch. "We did not have anything set up today."

"No, I know. But he wanted to see Nicole and has been moping around my place. So, I just took the chance that the timing would be okay. You don't need to do anything; he won't get in your way. He can just have a visit with Nicole…"

"You know I have other things to do."

"I know. You're a busy person," Reg agreed crisply. "Lots of responsibilities. I don't need to stop and visit. You can keep working on whatever…"

"I am not working on 'whatever.' I am working on preventing a disaster!"

Reg stepped toward the door and angled to get through it before Francesca decided to slam it in her face. As she expected, Francesca elected to be polite and stepped back, allowing Reg in. Reg put down the cat carrier and, as soon as Francesca closed the front door, Reg opened the carrier and let Horace out. He slunk out immediately and began smelling the floor around the carrier. He had lived there before and Reg was sure he would recognize the place and be happy to be there with his adopted mother again.

"Can you take a break from your work to have some tea?" Reg suggested.

Francesca sighed. She rubbed her forehead and nodded. "Come into the kitchen," she conceded.

Reg followed her in and sat at the kitchen table while Francesca turned the kettle on and got out cups. Bright sunlight was streaming in the kitchen windows, making the glass fronts of the cupboards sparkle.

"So, I take it things are not going as well as you would hope?" Reg hoped that sympathy would go a long way to greasing the wheels and convincing Francesca to take Horace for a few days.

"No. It is… difficult" Francesca puttered around waiting for the kettle to boil and thinking about what she wanted to say. When she sat down at the table, she was ready to talk. "This is the problem. First, we fought the Witch Doctor, who was raising draugar from the dead to do his will. Not just one or two of them, but an increasing army."

Reg nodded. "Nine zombie guys."

Francesca rolled her eyes and shook her head. But Reg's summary was correct, of course.

"We battle this immortal and together we are able to do what is not possible. With the help of Corvin and Damon, we are able to defeat him. Take most of his power away, until he flees, sending his essence into the nine draugar."

"Which have shifted form from huge zombie guys to cute little black cats."

"I use my charm to call them to me and bind them with a spell so that the being of the immortal cannot separate from the kattakyns and re-form as Samyr Destine."

"Which you figure should hold him bound for a thousand years."

"More or less," Francesca agreed. "But I did not count on any interference in the process. I thought that once we found homes for the kattakyns all around the world, we would be safe from them rediscovering each other and re-forming even when the binding spell wore off. So scattered, they would have a difficult time finding each other."

"But we sent Horace to Kareem."

Francesca sighed and nodded. She pulled a file out of a pile of papers beside her and opened it up. Reg saw the research profile she had done on Kareem before they sent Horace to him. Everything they needed to know about his background. Except for the fact that he had merely been waiting for opportunity to present itself so that he could make his grab for power. He was an older, well-respected warlock, the leader of his coven. He had recently lost his cat familiar and was looking for his replacement. They thought that he would do well with the sedate, often sleepy Horace.

But Francesca's profile had not suggested that the warlock might recognize the kattakyn for what he was and, even worse, recognize the portion of the Witch Doctor's power that had been bound to the kattakyn. And that he would have the knowledge and skill to unwind Francesca's charm and separate that piece of Samyr Destine from the creature for his own use.

"I cannot believe…" Francesca started. She stopped and shook her head sadly. "He seemed so *perfect* on paper. And I talked to him on the phone, corresponded with him in email. Everything seemed to be ideal."

"He's sneaky," Reg comforted. "He was being deliberately deceptive. How were you supposed to know that?"

"I should have sensed it. Things that he said, I should have known."

"You couldn't," Reg asserted. "Don't spend time beating yourself up. You have enough to do without that."

Francesca rubbed the bones around her eyes, looking tired. She nodded. "I know. You are right. So now... Kareem unbinds the kattakyn and takes that part of Samyr to himself. That is one thing. A powerful warlock with a portion of immortal powers— that is not good."

Reg nodded her agreement.

"But after losing that piece... *now* what are we to do?"

Reg didn't actually need a refresher on the problem. She knew that Francesca was just trying to lay it all out logically, to look at it again and find a solution they might have missed.

"It depends on where the piece went," Reg offered.

"If you are sure that Kareem no longer had it..."

"Well... yeah. Harrison wouldn't have *disappeared* him if he still had it."

"Why not?"

"Because... he and Samyr are both immortals. Harrison always follows the rule that immortals are not allowed to harm one another."

"Or so he says."

"So he says," Reg agreed. But she didn't think that Harrison would do anything to harm one of his fellows. That was one thing about him that had remained constant. Even when she had asked him for his help, he had refused to do anything that might harm another of his kind. Or even one-ninth of his kind.

"He wouldn't have done anything to Kareem if he still held a piece of the Witch Doctor."

"Not even to return him to Egypt?"

"Well... I don't know. But he said that Kareem no longer had that piece. And I believe him."

"Then explain where it went." Francesca took a sip of her tea and then folded her arms across her chest. She'd already heard the story from Reg enough times, there were no new details to give to her. They just kept going over the same facts.

"Harrison thinks that someone hid it."

"And he would not be able to sense it?" Francesca's tone was skeptical.

"He said that if it was hidden well enough, he would not be able to."

"He was able to find each of the kattakyns."

"But…" Reg struggled with magical concepts, not having been raised in a practicing home. "Were they *hidden*?"

Francesca considered. She chewed on her lip and had another sip of the tea. "I do not know how to hide something from an immortal. My skills are not in hiding."

"If Kareem could sense the piece attached to Horace, and he is just a human, just a warlock, then it couldn't have been hidden very well."

"No. Perhaps… just because I could not sense it after they were bound… that doesn't mean that *no one* could."

Reg nodded her agreement. They sat for a while, nursing their cups. Reg knew where the conversation was going next, but she really didn't want to go there. Talking about the past, about their battle with the Witch Doctor and finding the kattakyns homes; that was one thing.

Talking about what danger there might still be, a danger that was no longer a millennium away; that was something Reg didn't want to do.

"The options are very limited," Francesca said. She raised her index finger. "One, Harrison was lying, and he has the piece of Samyr."

"If he does, I'm sure it's just for safekeeping," Reg said immediately. "I explained to him how dangerous it would be for him to put the pieces of the Witch Doctor back together again. How it was dangerous to me and the whole human race."

Francesca didn't look impressed by this. Harrison was not well-known for an overwhelming concern for the human race. Reg had caught his fancy, or at least, the child that Reg had been years before when he had tried to protect her from the Witch Doctor. Reg was no longer that little girl, and she feared he might be withdrawing from her, recognizing that she was no longer an innocent little child but had powers and gifts of her own. She wasn't helpless any longer.

But against the Witch Doctor if he were re-formed and came after her? Reg shuddered at the thought of what he might do to her.

"Possibility two," Francesca raised the next finger, "Someone is hiding the piece of Samyr. Namely Corvin Hunter."

Reg nodded.

This was entirely possible. Corvin had been sucking the powers from Kareem, intent on his destruction. He might have taken the piece of the Witch Doctor during that process. And as a creature hungry for power and who already had absorbed much of the Witch Doctor's powers, he would be loath to give it up. He would hide it from Harrison and anyone else who was able to sense it. He did not have control of all the powers that he had absorbed from the artifacts and the Witch Doctor the day of their battle, but he might control enough of them to access memories and powers that would allow him to hide what he had stolen.

"Or," Reg held up three fingers, "it just dispersed out into the universe, like Corvin suggested."

Francesca shook her head. "That seems very unlikely. The more I research… the more certain I am that these final pieces of Samyr cannot be destroyed or dispersed. They must remain intact somewhere."

Reg thought of mythology stories she had heard in school. Very powerful beings were difficult to kill. Even if you cut them into little pieces, those pieces had to be scattered or burned to prevent them from resurrecting, re-forming, or reincarnating.

"It isn't like the pieces are his physical body," she countered. "His spirit or powers or whatever is left of him… it isn't like a body that has to stay the same size and shape."

"No," Francesca agreed thoughtfully. "They could be present in many different forms."

"I don't think that Corvin took that piece and hid it. I would know if he did that."

"How?"

"Because... he can't hide from me. We are connected."

"He cannot hide *anything* from you?"

"Well..." Reg wavered.

Of course he could.

Francesca read Reg's expression and nodded. "You do not even know all the powers he has absorbed. From Samyr and his artifacts and... anyone else he has drunk." She grimaced as she said it. The thought made Reg a little queasy as well. She had been one of Corvin Hunter's victims. He had charmed her and tricked her into agreeing to his proposition, which she did not realize meant taking her powers from her.

She had awakened empty and hollow, the silence as loud as a klaxon in her head. But he had returned her powers to save her from torture, and she had guarded them carefully—or *tried* to guard them carefully—ever since.

"It's either Harrison or Corvin," Francesca told her. Her lips pressed together in a line as Reg shook her head, not wanting to attribute the theft to either one of them. "If it isn't them, then the only other person who could have taken it was... you."

CHAPTER THREE

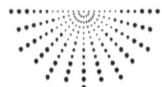

*R*eg's jaw dropped. She stared at Francesca in disbelief, trying to come up with the words to protest this accusation. The ridiculousness of it! The very suggestion that she would take a piece of the Witch Doctor and hide it from Harrison and everyone else…

Why would she even want to? She had a hard enough time controlling her own powers and learning what her abilities were, what things were dangerous, how she could defend herself without blowing anything up or burning anything down. How to avoid her siren instincts being triggered so that she wouldn't try to drown the nearest human male.

"I wouldn't—I would never!" she sputtered.

"I don't think you would. I don't think it is something that you seek. But… you have surprised me before. You have abilities and a heritage that is… suspect. You were there. You were the one who attacked Kareem."

"I defended myself; I did not attack."

Francesca shrugged. "I was not there. You and Kareem fought, did you not?"

"Yes. Because he forced the issue. He was attacking me, threatening me and my friends. Orri, the elf. I had to fight him. It wasn't my choice."

"But you did. And in that fight, you might have taken what he held."

"No."

Francesca nodded and sipped her tea. "I think not. But... if not you, then who?"

* * *

When Reg prepared to leave, Francesca didn't forget that she needed to take her furry companion with her.

"You need to take him, Reg. You cannot leave him here."

"I can't keep him at the cottage. Sarah will kick me out. She lets me stay even though I have Starlight, but if I keep another cat there, she won't let me stay."

"She can't evict you without notice. You have thirty days to find a home for him."

Reg opened her mouth to protest again. Francesca shook her head and held up her hand. "If you leave Horace here, I will take him to the animal shelter."

"What?"

"You heard me. I cannot take him."

"You had him before. You had all nine of them before, plus Nicole."

"And I cannot take him back. I simply cannot, Reg. I am sorry."

"You would take this poor, defenseless animal to the shelter."

"Yes."

"And what would happen then? You would let them put him down? He isn't even really a cat, Francesca. What would happen when they tried?"

Francesca tilted her head to the side slightly. "I do not know. Do you want to find out?"

"No." Reg stomped off to find Horace. She found him in the laundry room where Nicole's litter box and dishes were, pawing at her empty dish. Reg bent down to pick him up. "Did you eat all Nicole's food, you little pig?"

He made several noises of protest and squirmed, trying to get away from her. Reg kept away from his powerful back legs, marched back to the kitchen, and pushed him into the cat carrier.

Horace hissed and turned around to face the gate as she closed it, growling and spitting at her.

"I'm sorry. It's time to go." She felt a little bit bad for just grabbing him and shoving him into the carrier. She wouldn't have liked to be treated that way. She should have given him a warning that it was close to time to leave. And then called him and given him time to say goodbye to Nicole. Then maybe given him a treat in his carrier so that he would walk into it willingly.

She sighed. "I'm sorry, boy. I really am. I'll do better next time."

Francesca raised an eyebrow, as if she thought it was silly that Reg would apologize for her treatment of him.

"Let me know if you figure anything out," Reg told her. "About... how to keep Harrison or anyone else from unbinding the kattakyns. And maybe... about how to find the missing piece." She scratched the back of her head. "I really don't like the idea of it being out there somewhere, whether someone else has it or it's free-floating. The Witch Doctor... he's dangerous."

"And you let me know if you discover something about Corvin or Harrison. Because I can't think of anywhere else it would be."

Reg nodded. She thought they should set up another play date between Starlight and Nicole, but the timing felt wrong.

Reg stepped out the door and Francesca closed it behind her. As Reg walked down the sidewalk toward her car, she felt a heavy sense of sadness. She wasn't sure why until she put the cat carrier in the passenger seat beside her and saw Horace looking out at her from behind the bars. It was his sadness she was feeling.

"Did you think you were going to be able to stay there?" Reg asked. "With your mama cat? I'm sorry, Horace."

She poked her finger between the bars to pat his head or

scratch his ears, and he snarled and swiped at her with bared claws.

Reg jerked her finger back. "Hey. I know you're upset, but you don't have to attack me. We'll see Nicole again, okay?"

But after she said it, she regretted that she had. When was he going to see Nicole again? She had to find him a new home soon, and Nicole would not be there. Francesca wouldn't take Horace in. Horace's new owner, whoever he or she was, would probably not agree to set up play dates between Nicole and Horace on a regular basis. Or ever.

She shifted the car into drive and headed back home.

* * *

Does the cat wish to visit the garden?

Reg was a little startled by the voice in her head as she prepared to unlock her front door. She hadn't seen Forst, the garden gnome, in the yard. But then, she rarely saw him if she weren't looking for him. And even when she was, he was easy to miss despite his red cap.

Reg turned her head and saw him watching her from the corner of the house, by one of the bushes that had flourished under his care, growing thick and wild and producing beautiful pink blossoms.

Forst. Reg answered him telepathically as well. The gnomes usually spoke with each other in their "inside words" and had a difficult time with spoken communication. She looked down at Horace, looking miserable inside the cat carrier. *Maybe he would. Couldn't hurt to give it a try. I'll keep him in the carrier so he doesn't try to run away, but maybe if he can just get some fresh air and watch the birds and the bugs flying around...*

Forst nodded his agreement. *Wild things need wild places.*

Horace had been pretty wild lately. His personality had changed so much since his rescue from Kareem. He'd been so quiet before. Francesca attributed it to the fact that he had been separated from the piece of the Witch Doctor.

Reg wasn't so sure about that. She hadn't seen anything quiet or sedate about the Witch Doctor. Francesca said that everybody had sides of themselves that they hid, and it was just a side of the Witch Doctor that they hadn't seen. Reg wondered if there was more to it than that.

Reg followed Forst around the guest cottage to the back garden, where there was a fountain and a bench to sit on. She looked for just the right spot to set the cat carrier down, positioning it so that Horace could see the pool and the trees and long grasses and plants, and would get some of the light breeze that was blowing across the yard. She looked in at him to assess how he felt about it.

Horace's ears were no longer back and he wasn't hunched over in a tense, angry position. His whiskers were forward and his nose worked as he smelled everything around him, stepping forward to put his face against the grill of the carrier, as close to being free as he could be.

"How's that?" she asked softly. "You like that? Do you smell the birds?"

Sarah would probably be horrified if she realized that there was a cat in her garden. But he was safely in the carrier. He would not catch any of the colorful birds that stopped at the bird feeder.

The sadness and heaviness that she had felt from Horace as they left Francesca's house had dispersed somewhat. He was enjoying his exposure to the outdoors, even if it was through the bars. He had probably never had a chance to spend any time outside since he had been trapped in his kattakyn form. Did he remember being outside in his previous life, before he had been raised as a draugr? Had he been an outdoorsman before he had died? Had he lived other lives before then?

Reg had never thought much about reincarnation before learning that Starlight had lived other lives before he had been a cat. She didn't know whether he was reincarnated or had changed his form voluntarily or if something else had happened to him. She didn't know how prevalent reincarnation was. Had everyone lived other lives, or was it just something that happened occasion-ally? Everything she learned only prompted more questions.

She sat there, feeling Horace's emotions settle, enjoying the scent of the sea and the flowers on the wind. She closed her eyes and just rested for a while.

CHAPTER FOUR

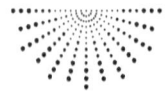

Reg could hear Forst as he dug around the bushes and flowers in the garden beds. It was just as soothing as the cool breeze and the smell of the growing things. The "living," as the gnomes described it.

You see more elven folk? Forst asked.

Reg opened her eyes and looked at him. She smiled. *No. Not since Orri appeared the last time. I don't think he will be coming back.*

They are still here, Forst observed, looking at the bushes around him.

How do you know that? Do you see signs of them?

A gnome can feel them. Sometimes hear their bells.

Reg nodded. She had seen lights in the garden and heard tinkling bells, before she had known what it meant. *It must be quite a compliment to have them living in the garden that you tend.*

Forst nodded, his rosy cheeks growing even pinker. *A great thing to have elves in your garden.* He plucked dead blossoms off a couple of plants with practiced fingers.

Are there other creatures in the garden too? Reg asked, looking around. *Orri said that we need to keep the garden protected with the wards and charms, to protect all the creatures.*

Forst spread his hands apart, indicating all the plants around them. *Plants do not live alone. They need sun and soil and water, but they also need companions. Elves and gnomen and human. And many others. Birds, bees, bugs…*

Reg nodded. *But birds and bugs don't need magical protection. Maybe there are other creatures who do.*

He smiled and nodded, but did not elaborate. Reg resolved to take it up with him again in the future.

* * *

Reg found herself getting drowsy in the warmth and peacefulness of the garden. She decided she'd better go inside before she fell asleep and fell off the bench. She picked up the cat carrier and said her goodbyes to Forst, and went back inside.

She hadn't been sleeping very well lately. Of course, when did she? It seemed like there was always something on her mind or disturbing her dreams. She had thought all of that would stop when she had a safe place to live and a regular income. But her worries had just changed from where the next meal would come from to zombies and spiders and entities like the Witch Doctor. Each time, she told herself that once the current situation was resolved, she would sleep better and wake up feeling well-rested each morning. But it didn't seem like the current situation ever resolved into a better situation, just a different one.

The voices of her foster mothers of the past were all stored in her brain, and sometimes it was hard to remember that they didn't live there like the other voices. Foster mothers had always told her that if she went to bed in good time and just lay still in her bed, that she would have a good sleep and be able to wake up well-rested in the morning and ready for school like the good kids. But it had never worked that way for Reg. She was always too restless and hypervigilant at night and couldn't settle down to sleep until the small hours of the morning which, of course, meant that she wasn't ready to get out of bed at six-thirty or seven like the *good* boys and girls. She would not be ready for school on time, would fall asleep during morning classes, and would be grumpy with her teachers.

She no longer tried to go to sleep at a decent hour. Night was a good time for psychic readings and seances. People were much more receptive and the spirits' voices were that much stronger. Reg could work at night, sleep until the late morning, and then manage to roll out of bed and start her day again.

Lately, though, she had been waking up a lot. She couldn't blame it all on Starlight and Horace, although they did make too much noise after she went to bed. Sometimes it was something else that woke her up. A dream. A noise in the night. Waking up with a feeling of dread. She would lie there awake, listening to the house around her, trying to discern whether someone or something were there. She was safe in her house; she knew that. There were plenty of charms and wards to keep away those who had evil intentions. But still…

Reg let Horace out of the cat carrier. He didn't bolt out of it and hide under the bed as she expected him to, but exited slowly, rubbed against the carrier and her leg, and wandered over to Starlight's dishes with an inquiring meow. Maybe the time in the garden had helped him to calm down and mellow out. Maybe she needed to take him out there more often. Starlight might enjoy a few excursions too. She could even get a harness and leash and take them out for walks around the garden. That would be even better than going out in the carrier.

As long as Sarah didn't freak out about it. She wouldn't like the idea of a cat in her yard, even if he were on leash.

Starlight jumped down from the bedroom window and galloped out to the kitchen to stand by his dish, shouldering Horace away. He was polite enough not to hiss and growl at Horace for getting close to his dishes, but he didn't just stand by and let him claim that space, either. He yowled loudly at Reg to hurry up and find them something good in the fridge, before both of them died of hunger.

Reg opened the fridge and looked over the numerous dishes and takeout cartons. She had tried to clean out the fridge, but it seemed like every time she turned around, there was more food in there. Some of it was from Sarah, she knew. Sarah always made too much food when she cooked, and she wanted to mother Reg and make sure that she was eating properly. Which she wasn't. Even with healthy food around, Reg always went for the junk.

"What's in here? I don't even have a clue where most of this came from."

Reg started opening containers at random, looking for something that the cats would enjoy, her own supper a secondary consideration. One smelled like tuna casserole, so Reg plopped some into a bowl from the cupboard, which she put down on the floor for Horace, and some into Starlight's dish. Both cats immediately started to chow down.

The casserole smelled good, but wasn't really what Reg was looking for. She looked through some of the takeout containers. Uncle Mike's Ribs? When had she gotten ribs? Had Sarah ordered them and not been able to finish? Reg pulled the cardboard container out, put it into the microwave, and started it warming.

Ribs were good. It had been a long time since she had gone to the little rib shack with Corvin.

CHAPTER FIVE

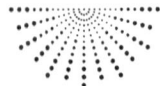

"We like ribs," Harrison commented.

Reg jumped about two feet in the air. She suppressed a shriek of surprise at his sudden appearance.

"Ah! Warn me before you do that?"

"Do what?" Harrison asked, raising an eyebrow in query.

He was a tall, thin man with a dramatic long mustache usually curled at the ends, but now drooping down. He wore a pink silk shirt and striped black and green shorts. And a perky little cap like the one from a police uniform.

"You scared me," Reg scolded. "You can't just appear out of nowhere and start talking to me. I wasn't expecting it."

"It wasn't out of nowhere."

"Well, I don't know where you were, but suddenly appearing here is startling." Reg blew her breath out, trying to calm her racing heart. The microwave beeped and she pulled the ribs container out. She got two small plates out of the cupboard and set one on the island in front of herself and one closer to Harrison. They each helped themselves to some ribs.

"We like ribs," Harrison repeated.

"Yes," Reg licked her fingers. "We do. Is that where they came from? You left them in the fridge?"

Harrison nodded. He put one of the ribs in his mouth and gnawed the meat off. "You do not need to go with the soul sucker to get them."

Reg nearly choked on her mouthful. She swallowed strenuously and filled a glass of water from the tap to wash it down.

"No," she agreed. "I could go there myself."

"Or eat with me."

Reg nodded. She watched him as she ate, looking for any sign of a change in him. He seemed eager to please her lately, looking for ways to show her that he had her welfare and happiness in mind.

"You don't like Corvin Hunter, do you?" Reg asked.

Harrison shook his head. "A spirit drinker cannot be trusted."

"He has helped me out a lot of times. I mean… I know he does it because he wants to get close to me, because he wants my powers, but… he has been helpful."

"He cannot be trusted."

"And I don't trust him. I'm always careful."

"Always?" Harrison repeated. He shook his head.

"Well, I always try…"

Harrison picked up another of the ribs and pulled the meat from it. He looked at Reg. "We do not need forks?"

"No. You can eat ribs with your fingers. It's not rude."

He continued to eat, apparently filing this information away for the future. Another of the strange quirks of human society, how some food had to be eaten with a fork and some did not.

As Reg watched him, she tried to determine if there were anything different about him. If the piece of the Witch Doctor had made Horace sleepy and sedate, would it affect an immortal in the same way? Or would he be unaffected by it because it was only a small piece of Samyr Destine and they were of the same kind? Harrison had a strong personality himself, and his own seemingly endless reservoir of powers and abilities. Too much for the Witch Doctor's spirit to affect him? Or did he just hide its influence well?

She had only Harrison's word for it that the piece of the Witch

Doctor that had been bound to Horace had disappeared. Reg didn't think that he had the guile to lie to her and hide something like that from her, but he often surprised her and she couldn't be sure.

"How have you been lately?" she asked him. "Everything… going well in your world?"

She had no idea where he was or what he did when he was away from her. Was he somewhere? Or nowhere? Or everywhere? Was he somewhere with other immortals, like Weston, or was he alone? Or were there others in the mortal world that he visited, supplying them with tasty food, protection, and extra power when they needed it?

"Everything always goes as it should."

Another of Harrison's impossible answers. Did that mean that he controlled the outcomes? Or that it was all up to fate? That everything was predesigned? Did the fact that he could travel to other times mean that he could see the future and already knew what would happen before it happened, or could he only travel to the past and not see the future? Was he subject to fate or did he control it?

"Are there a lot of immortals?" Reg asked. "I haven't met very many of you."

Harrison licked sauce from his fingers, looking remarkably like a cat as he did so. "More than you think."

"How many?"

"They are not numbered."

"Does that mean that there are more than you can count? Or what?"

Harrison shrugged. "I cannot tell you that."

"You're not allowed? Or it isn't possible?"

"Yes."

"Why do you come here if you are never going to answer my questions?"

He looked surprised. "I did answer your questions."

"But not in a way that I can understand?"

"I am not responsible for your human brain."

"Well… no. But I think you could explain better."

"Perhaps."

But he didn't make any attempt.

* * *

Reg made a stop at the Sandy Claws Thrift Shop to pick up some new items for her wardrobe. One thing about living out of a suitcase and not really having a permanent address—she hadn't had to worry before about any variety in her wardrobe. Now that she had a place of her own, and the same people were seeing her week after week, Reg felt the need to expand and diversify her clothing choices. She didn't want people to think that the options were quite as limited as they were. There were only so many different combinations and ways to accessorize her outfits. A scarf could be worn a dozen different ways, but it was still the same scarf.

She felt better after picking up a few additional items at the thrift shop. As she left, she saw Marian's store front. She also ran a psychic service business but, instead of having it out of her home like Reg, had her own little storefront where people could come for consultations. Reg could see the benefits of not running her business out of her home. Unexpected callers would be reduced. She wouldn't have to worry about having her home address on business cards. There was opportunity for walk-in traffic. And at the end of the day, Marian could just go home and relax, with a clear separation between business and non-business life.

But a storefront had to have a lot more overhead too. Reg wasn't about to lease a storefront or office space. And while Marian operated during daylight hours, Reg's late-night work would mean that she was traveling between work and home in the dark, when it was lonely and predators were more likely to be out. She would stick to her home-run business for the time being.

She decided to pay Marian a visit. While the two had started out as rivals, Reg had broken the ice a little when she had asked Marian for a consultation on the dreams and visions she had been having during one particularly difficult case. Since then, the two were nodding acquaintances. Reg didn't feel like Marian wanted to run her out of town every time they saw each other. They could at least be civil to each other.

A bell jingled as Reg pushed the door open into Marian's business. There was no one in the consultation area but, in a moment, Marian came out of the back room, a welcoming smile on her face. It wavered only slightly when she saw who it was. She was a tall woman, with a scarf turban and a sagging, pouchy, jowly face. She wore a bright skirt that made her skin look drab and colorless.

"Reg. How nice to see you."

"I was just in the area and thought I would stop by and say hi."

"Wonderful… would you like some tea? It's a few minutes before my next appointment."

"Oh, you don't need to put yourself out for me."

"I'm going to make some tea anyway."

Reg shrugged. "All right. Sure."

Marian nodded. She walked to a little nook and turned on the kettle and busied herself with the tea things. "So, how are you? Having problems?"

"No. I really didn't come here because I wanted anything. Really."

Marian pursed her lips and kept fiddling with the teabags while she waited for the kettle to boil. Reg tried to read her expression and her aura. She was very careful not to infringe on Marian's consciousness. The psychic would be sure to realize if Reg ventured where she wasn't wanted.

"Are *you* okay?"

Marian lifted her brows and nodded. "Yes. Why do you ask?"

"It's just… you seem a little sad. It isn't any of my business, of course. I just wondered whether you want to talk about it."

The kettle whistled. Marian poured the boiling water into mugs and brought them to the table with a basket containing tea bags, sugar, and powdered creamer. Reg helped herself to a generous amount of sugar, making her selection of tea almost as an afterthought.

"I don't know what you might have heard…" Marian started.

"Nothing. I just… well, I'm a little bit psychic, if you want to know," Reg offered with a laugh.

Marian chuckled, the tension easing a little. "Well… it's nothing, really. Just one of those trials that everyone goes through. A loss…"

Reg reached across the table to touch Marian's hand, trying to convey her sympathy and to push a little warmth into Marian, hoping to boost her spirits.

Marian made an expression that was part smile, part grimace. "Thank you, Reg. You're very kind. You came at a very fortuitous time."

"I want to help. Is there anything I can do?" Reg cast around for some idea. "You could come over for a movie. Or ice cream. Just hang out for a while."

"Oh, no, no. You don't need to do that. We're not used to seeing each other socially, it would be awkward."

"A drink?"

Marian gestured to their mugs. "Tea is fine. Really, this is probably better for me than anything else you could have done. Just having someone here who recognizes that I'm going through a tough time and can sympathize."

Reg quit trying to dissolve all the sugar into her tea and took a long sip. "Well, good. I'm happy to help however I can. You really helped me that day. With the visions."

Marian nodded. "I told you then… we can do things for each other. We are a community. Not everyone can understand what it is that we deal with every day, so intimately involved with others' thoughts, feelings, hopes, and dreams. It can be a burden."

"It can," Reg admitted, a little surprised. "I'm always tired after a few sessions, and I thought it was just the amount of energy that it takes to see or hear what others can't."

"It's more than that. That part probably isn't even hard for you, you're so very gifted. But taking on others' burdens, feeling their feelings, even for just a short time, does sap a lot of energy. You can't let yourself be gloomy all day just because you did a reading for someone that didn't turn out to be very positive. But when you feel what they feel…"

Reg nodded slowly. It gave her more insight into what happened inside her during those sessions with clients, helping them to make decisions, or to see a vision for their life, or to contact a loved one who had already passed death's door. Maybe it should have been clear to her without Marian's insight, but Reg had always talked to ghosts and exercised her powers without even knowing what she was doing. She hadn't had anyone to teach her about the world she was a part of. Only parents and teachers and social workers and therapists telling her that she needed to pay attention, be obedient, and at least *try* to fit in.

"Do you want—" Reg started impulsively, and then stopped herself.

Marian took another drink of her tea and shook her head. "Do I want what?"

"No, nothing. I was just thinking…"

"If you don't tell me what you were thinking, I have no idea. How do you know whether the answer is yes or no?"

"Well… okay. But you can say no."

Marian gave her a dry smile, which lifted the wrinkles on her pouchy face a little. "I am more than capable of saying no," she agreed.

"Okay…" Reg had to bite her tongue to keep from adding any other reassurances or excuses. "I wondered if… you wanted a cat."

CHAPTER SIX

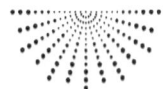

*M*arian stared at her.

Reg sipped her tea and looked away. She cleared her throat. "It's just that I have an extra cat right now… I know, it's weird to just ask you if you want one. But he's looking for a home. I can't keep him. And I thought… maybe you could use some company around the house."

"I recently lost my cat." Marian sniffed and wiped her nose. "How could you know that?"

"I didn't, exactly." Reg's spirits lifted. She could help Marian and find a new home for Horace at the same time. "He's a lovely little cat. All black, short hair. He's not a kitten anymore, and you know it's so hard to find people to adopt older cats."

"Where did he come from? How did you end up with him?"

That was a longer story that Reg wasn't willing to reveal to Marian. She didn't need to know about the zombies and the kattakyns and trying to keep the parts of the Witch Doctor away from each other.

"Do you know Francesca St. Martin? Blond hair, from Haiti?"

Marian nodded. "Not well, but I know who she is."

"She has a cat, Nicole. She had nine kittens, all pure black. We found homes for them, but Horace's new owner didn't work out.

And I ended up with him. But I can't keep another cat. I'm lucky Sarah lets me keep Starlight. She really doesn't like cats. And Francesca says that she can't take Horace on right now. Which kind of leaves me in the lurch…"

"Maybe… I could come meet him. See what I think of him."

Reg hoped that Horace would be in a quiet mood when Marian came over, not one of his crazy, knock-everything-off-the-shelves moods. "Of course. Anytime. Do you want to come over now?"

Marian looked toward the door. Reg supposed she still had clients coming in. "Well… I suppose so. I don't have anyone coming in until later. And I haven't really been feeling very well. Kind of off my game the last few days."

Reg nodded understandingly. It was hard to connect with someone and be empathetic when she was going through a crisis of her own.

"Why don't you come? I'm sure you'll like him."

Marian nodded tentatively.

"I'll give you the address." Reg dug into her shoulder bag to dig up a pen and some paper.

"I know where Sarah lives. You're just in the back, right?"

"Yes."

"Okay. I'll be a few minutes closing up here, and then I'll be over."

Reg had enough time to worry about whether things were going to work out or not. She wanted to believe that everything was falling into place for a reason and Horace was meant to be with Marian.

But there were so many things that could go wrong. She didn't want to get her hopes up and she didn't want to jinx it by believing it wouldn't work out. Why did everything have to be so complicated?

She tried to brush Horace before Marian got there so that he would look his best, but Horace objected and swiped at her hand, drawing blood when his claws snagged her wrist. Reg sucked on the wound, trying to explain to Horace how important it was.

"You want a new owner, don't you? A home where you can stay and be happy? Marian is looking for a new cat. She just lost hers. If you're a good kitty and show her your best behavior, she could be your forever home."

A wave of vertigo went through Reg, flashing back to Mrs. White, one of many social workers, trying to talk her into behaving at her new foster home. "Just be quiet and be on your best behavior. Didn't you brush your hair this morning? You have to try, Regina. This could be your forever home."

But there had never been a forever home. After a few years, Reg had stopped believing the promises. Stopped hoping for things to get better and just trying to survive until she aged out of the system and didn't have to live with anyone else and pretend to be something she was not.

She bit her lip, trying to keep herself present with the pain. She petted Horace. Long, soothing strokes to calm him down. It was okay if Marian said no. They would find him another home. She would try harder and find him the place where he belonged.

Horace purred and rolled over, offering his belly to her. Reg knew better than to be taken in and scratch it. Any cat worth his salt would just be waiting for her to fall into the cuteness trap and would attack at the first opportunity.

"Oh, no. You're not getting me with that one," Reg told him, choosing to scratch his ear instead. Horace made a low trill, enjoying the attention. Reg didn't just sit and pet him very often. She usually left him alone if he was settled down and behaving himself, and chased and scolded him when he was not. Not much of a relationship. But then, she had never intended to take him in. She didn't want to get attached and then to give him up.

The doorbell rang. Horace flipped back over and put his ears back. He looked toward the door to see who it was.

"It's going to be okay," Reg told him. "Just see whether you like her."

She opened the door and ushered Marian in, pointing her toward the couch where Horace was sitting, bunched up uncomfortably, no longer sprawled out relaxed and happy.

"Marian, this is Horace."

"Horace." Marian approached slowly, her feet quiet. She sat at the opposite end of the couch from the cat. "Hi, Horace. I'm Marian."

He watched her suspiciously. Like any cat being introduced to a stranger. They were always reserved, unless the person was allergic and didn't want a cat in her lap. Then that's where the cat would be.

They sat apart for a while. Horace's nose was twitching as he inspected the new woman sitting beside him.

"Reg told me you were looking for a new home. And I'm looking for a new cat to share mine with. Do you think you might like to come and live with me?"

Marian clearly knew cats. She talked with Horace and gave him time to get used to her. He eventually let her scratch his ears and chin and purred away while she crooned to him. She petted him and gave him a few kitty treats she had brought in her pocket, which made him crawl into her lap excitedly and snuggle and nuzzle her for more. Yes, Marian knew cats.

Reg was happy to see Horace letting go of his suspicions and becoming more natural with her, the red aura around him dissipating until she could no longer see it. She could feel warm, hopeful thoughts from him, like when they had gone over to Francesca's house.

Marian nodded to Reg. "Yes, I think this will work out. I'll take him."

"I can lend you my carrier and you can take him with you now. If you have everything you need?"

"My carrier is in the car. I didn't bring it in because…" She shrugged.

Because she didn't want to jinx it. She didn't want all of them thinking that it would work out, and then to change her mind and walk off with the empty cat carrier.

"Do you want me to go get it out?" Reg offered. "I don't want Horace to think that you're leaving without him…"

Marian chuckled. "Here we all are, all worried about how the cat will feel if he isn't chosen."

But Reg knew what it felt like not to be chosen. And she had a feeling that Marian did too. She might feel silly assigning human feelings to an animal, but with the way she had connected with Horace, Reg was sure she could feel his feelings and knew how hopeful he had become that he could go with her.

"Do you want to give me your keys?" Reg pressed.

Marian got them out of her purse, a much smaller and neater receptacle than Reg's cavernous shoulder bag. She handed them over to Reg, keeping Horace on her lap, warm and comfortable, blissful under her gentle strokes and attention.

"Thank you." Marian smiled.

Reg could feel that Marian's mood had lifted too. She had been feeling very bad when Reg had popped in to see her, but now she was happy and a bit excited, buoyed up by the new little fur person who had come into her life.

Reg hurried out to Marian's car. She unlocked it with the fob and grabbed the cat carrier from the seat. There were supplies in bags in the back seat too. Marian had obviously stopped in at the store before her arrival. She had really wanted to take Horace home with her. Reg felt light and happy. They would make such a good pair. They were already bonding.

She shut and locked the door and returned to her house with the cat carrier. Marian and Horace were right where she had left them. Reg opened the carrier and placed it on the floor near Marian.

"He's pretty good about traveling. Doesn't make a big fuss."

"That's good. It's always so distressing when they are upset and don't understand what is going on."

Reg nodded. She bent over to give Horace a final pet. He swiped at her arm and sank his teeth into her wrist.

CHAPTER SEVEN

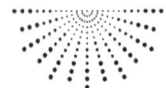

*R*eg sat bolt upright in bed, gasping from the intensity of her dream. She looked around her, disoriented at first, thinking that she was somewhere other than her own bed in her own room. But where else would she be?

Still, there were pictures in her head. Strange pictures on the wall. A long, narrow bed that was hard and cold. A woman who was angry with her.

The woman was probably some iteration of one of the foster moms. She still had nightmares about not being able to perform to their expectations. About trying to hide some disaster that she had created or the fact that she had not been able to find her classes at school. Trying to avoid punishment, whether it was a lecture or a beating. She could never tell for sure which it would be. Even the ones who seemed patient and loving when talking to the social workers could break, letting go of all the good intentions and lashing out.

Reg gulped a few times and tried to relax her body. It was just a dream. She had a lot of dreams; this was no different from any other.

Starlight jumped up onto the bed and rubbed against her, his tail tickling her nose. Reg laughed.

"What are you doing? That tickles!" She sneezed and rubbed her nose. "How are you, boy? Are you doing okay? Are you lonely now that Horace has found a new home?"

But she didn't think Starlight was lonely. He had put up with the new cat as well as he could, but they weren't best friends. They played and got into mischief together, but when it was time to sleep, they went off to opposite corners, and Reg had never seen them groom each other. A couple of guys hanging out together, but then wanting their own space to chill in after.

Starlight continued to rub against Reg and make inquiring trills.

"I'm okay," Reg assured him. "Everything is fine. Just a dream."

She rubbed her eyes and looked around the room once more to make sure that everything was where it should be and that she was alone. Although she liked Harrison, it freaked her out that he could just appear in her house, bypassing all the wards that she and Sarah had set. Sure, it was fine if all he was doing was making chocolate cake or Uncle Mike's ribs appear, but if he were angry with her or used his powers to trap her, as he had when he'd wanted her to just stay home and look after Horace, there was nothing she could do about it. Francesca was right that being as powerful as he was made him dangerous, even if he did like her and was trying to protect her. Immortals were fickle and his feelings could change in an instant. Or he could do something to her, not realizing that it could harm her. He was remarkably ignorant of many things concerning humans.

But she didn't see Harrison or any sign that he had been there. Not in her bedroom, anyway. She couldn't speak for the kitchen or living room, and she wasn't going to get up and check. She would work on the assumption that if he'd materialized in her house, it was because he wanted to talk to her, and he would have come to the bedroom to find her.

"Everything is fine," Reg repeated, rubbing her forehead.

Reg had left the closet doors open, as she usually did, and the moonlight shining into it made it look as though something was glowing. It gave Reg a weird, uncomfortable feeling. She was too tired to get up and close the doors, but she would make sure that they were closed the next time.

* * *

She tossed and turned for a while, trying to find her way back to sleep. Other people made it look so easy. She remembered other foster kids she had shared a room with. When it was bedtime, they lay down in the bed and in a few minutes were asleep. No special rituals. No lying awake for an hour or two before being able to convince their bodies to go to sleep. And that was how it was on TV too. People turned off the light, lay down in bed, and fell asleep. No fuss or drama. Sleep just stole into the room and carried them off to dreamland. And no one ever had nightmares unless it moved the plot forward.

When an hour had passed and she still had not been able to get back to sleep, Reg picked up her phone from the side table and unplugged it. She intended to just check her email and social networks until her eyelids started to get heavy again, but her fingers moved as if of their own accord, tapping and swiping to find Corvin's contact card in her list and to initiate a call.

He wasn't even on her favorites list. She had hoped that by not setting up a shortcut for him, she wouldn't be tempted to call him impulsively. Apparently, that didn't work. Her hands and brain still knew how to access his record on her phone.

"Hello?" Corvin's words were thick and drowsy. "Regina."

"Yeah. Sorry, I guess you were asleep."

He didn't point out that sleeping was what he generally did at five in the morning, or whatever time it was. Reg looked at the time on the face of her phone, then promptly ignored it.

"Yes. But I'm awake now."

"Do you ever have trouble sleeping?"

"On occasion. I could recommend a sleeping potion, if you like. There are some very good ones."

"No. I used to have to take pills to make me sleep when I was a kid. I don't like the way they make me feel."

"It wouldn't be the same. Potions don't have the same side effects as medications."

"But they still have side effects, right? I don't want to be having weird magical symptoms either."

"No. Well, sometimes a potion can have unintended consequences, but…"

"I'm bound to be one of those people who would have them. Seems like that's just the way my life works."

Corvin grunted. "Well… I suppose it's not outside of the realm of possibilities."

"And how do they affect… other species? Because with my heritage…"

"You are still more human than anything else."

She knew it was meant to reassure her, but she wasn't sure it was true, and it irritated her that he would say so.

"So, what were you doing today?" Reg asked, changing the subject. If she got him talking about himself or one of his academic projects, then it would be sure to put her to sleep…

"I don't think you're interested in any of my pet projects," Corvin dismissed.

"I am. What are you working on?"

"Nothing. Just some ancient tales and mythologies."

"Roman?" Reg asked.

"No."

"Which country?"

"I really don't see how that would be of interest to you."

"Mythology is interesting. Unless it's one of those weird ones, I kind of get lost on the Norse stuff."

"There are a lot more countries with stories to tell than just Greece and Rome."

Thinking about it, Reg realized she knew next to nothing about any of the mythologies of the Asian countries or even the Americas. How bad was it that she didn't even know the stories from the country she had grown up in? But she didn't remember their teaching that in school. Just the ones that Corvin had mentioned, Roman and Greek mythology. Maybe she could look up some of the other stuff on YouTube. There were some informative videos there. Maybe she could learn more about Bastet and the other Egyptian gods.

"Do you know much about Egyptian mythology?"

Corvin made a choking noise.

"Does that mean you don't?" Reg asked. She mentally reached out, trying to sense his mood.

"Stop doing that," Corvin ordered.

"What?"

"Reading me."

"I wasn't… I didn't do it intentionally. You said not Greek or Roman, and I was thinking about Egypt because, you know, we were just there…"

"You thought about it because that's what I was thinking about."

"Well… not on purpose. And… there are other reasons." Reg stroked Starlight, looking into his blue and green eyes.

"Your gems, you mean?"

"Oh." Reg hadn't been thinking of them. She glanced toward the closet. "Yes. That too. Sooner or later, I'm going to have to take them back to Egypt. Sooner, since the rings have been… activated."

"You know it isn't safe."

"I wouldn't be going back to see Kareem. Tourists still go to Egypt…"

"There are other dangers. I would not recommend that you go by yourself."

"If these rings are so powerful, then it shouldn't matter. I can use them to protect myself, right?"

Corvin was silent.

Reg thought about the two rings. They had just been curiosities to begin with. Most of the gems that she had been given by the fairies had been loose, cut gems. There were only a few that were set into jewelry like the rings. Reg had worn them on her last trip to Egypt, more by accident than anything else, and that had apparently not been such a good idea.

She didn't actually know what powers the gems had, or how to use a stone like that. She was still woefully uninformed about the magical world around her. For someone like Corvin, growing up in a magical home, it was second nature but, for Reg, everything was new, and people expected her to know things that she didn't.

"Have you used the rings?" Corvin asked.

Reg didn't know whether he was expecting a yes or a no answer, or what implications either would have. Would not using the rings mean that she was ignorant and uninformed? Was using them taboo?

"What difference does that make?" she hedged.

"You are playing with powers you know nothing about."

"Well, that's par for the course," Reg pointed out. "Since I hardly know anything about anything."

"You shouldn't use them without knowing their history and the proper way to use their powers. You already know that they are cursed."

Reg did know that they were cursed, but she didn't think that they were evil or would do anything to harm her. She saw the cursed gems more as being sad or broken. Like a child who had been traumatized or moved through too many different homes. Lashing out because they were hurt, not bad.

"I know. That's why I want to get them back to Egypt."

Home, where they belonged. Where they could rest. Back to the people who were supposed to own them. That was what they wanted.

CHAPTER EIGHT

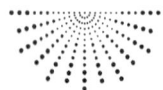

"*A*re you still there, Reg?"

Reg took a deep breath in. Her eyes were closed and she didn't open them. "Yes. I'm here."

"Thought you might have dropped off to sleep."

It sounded like a good idea. But part of Reg was too awake. Too watchful. "I don't know whether I'm going to go back to sleep tonight."

"What did you dream about?" Corvin's voice was rich and resonant. Like he was in the same room with her, leaning in to talk to her as she'd seen him do so many times. Getting just a little closer. A little too close.

She opened her eyes just a sliver to make sure that he wasn't there with her, although she knew that he couldn't be. The wards were enough to keep Corvin away. He couldn't come into the house or even into the yard without her invitation.

Or some sly trick. But Reg thought she knew all his tricks now.

Hopefully.

"What?" she said, forgetting what it was that he had just asked her.

"What were you dreaming?"

"I don't know; a lot of it has disappeared already." Reg let her eyes close all the way again and thought about it. "Um… a room. A dark, empty room. Strange pictures on the walls. An uncomfortable bed." Maybe she had been dreaming about foster care. Moving into a new room was always a little scary, everything unfamiliar when she woke up. Everything different from the last place and from what she would have liked it to be.

Or one of the institutions. They didn't usually have pictures on the walls, but some had art installations. A mural on the wall rather than pictures hung there.

Maybe that was it.

"Hm." Corvin sounded uninspired by Reg's dream. "Nothing… portentous, then."

"I'm not even sure what that means. Nothing *important.*"

"Portentous is like… ominous. An omen. A vision of something to come."

"Oh. No. I don't think so. Just… a dark dream. And when I woke up, I couldn't get back to sleep."

"So you called me."

"You said I can call you anytime," Reg reminded him. "You always look forward to my calls."

Corvin chuckled. "That sounds like something I might have said," he admitted. "But I'm afraid I'm going to have to cut it short tonight. I have a lot of work to be done tomorrow if I'm going to… get anywhere on this project. I can't let myself get sidetracked by a siren's call."

He thought he was so clever. Reg rolled her eyes.

"More work on Egyptian mythology?"

"Stay out of my head," Corvin warned. "A man's thoughts are his own. Private."

"Yeah. Well, goodnight, then. Talk to you some other *more convenient* time."

"Good," Corvin agreed. "Talk later, then."

He hung up. Reg shook her head. Corvin was in a strange mood. Usually, he was happy to hear from her, teasing and seductive. But during the call, he had been irritable and impatient.

Maybe it was just because he was tired and she had woken him up after a long day of studying.

* * *

She never did get back to sleep. Every time she started to get close, a noise would startle her awake, or she would think she saw something moving in the shadows. Or she had one of those sleep starts where she thought she was falling and her whole body clenched in panic.

Eventually, Reg got up and wandered around the house, unsure of what to do with herself. She made coffee and stood in front of the TV, flicking through channels, but there wasn't anything on that she wanted to watch, and she didn't even feel like going to YouTube to watch her favorite channels or to look up more information on Egyptian mythology.

Horace wandered over and meowed at her, looking for attention or wondering why she was standing in front of the TV instead of sitting on the couch where she could be comfortable. Reg bent over to pick him up, and then realized before she wrapped her hands around him.

"Horace? What are you doing here?"

Reg looked around the room, disoriented. Had she only dreamed that she had given the cat to Marian? Or was she dreaming that he had come back? She hated having dreams where she didn't think she was dreaming. They were the most disorienting of all.

"Horace, you can't be here. Where did you come from?"

He meowed and stood on his back legs to rub against her hand, coaxing her to pick him up. Reg did, and stood up with him in her arms, trying to figure out whether she was dreaming or awake. Nothing changed. She didn't start dreaming of something else. Horace didn't morph into Starlight or someone else in her life. She didn't dream of any unbelievable creatures. She just stood there in the living room with Horace purring in her arms.

Reg raised her phone to check the time. She didn't know what time Marian usually got up, but it was probably too early to call her to find out what was going on.

Was she losing her mind? Maybe the whole day had been a dream. Maybe she never had found a home for Horace. But now that she had thought of Marian in her dream, maybe she could contact Marian in real life and see whether she wanted a cat. And then she would probably find out that Marian didn't even like cats and certainly didn't want one in her house.

Despite Horace's contented purrs, she put him down on the floor. She went to the window and looked up at the brightening sky. Of course, there was no way to tell just by looking at the sky what day it was. She looked at her phone again and checked the date and the day of the week. But then she wasn't sure what day it was supposed to be. She often lost track of the day, so she had nothing to anchor herself to. She went over to the appointment book on the kitchen island and opened it up. Checking through the sessions, she could see which ones she had completed—or thought she had—and that it should be Thursday. She looked at her phone again to confirm that it was Thursday.

Then she hadn't dreamed an extra day. Had she dreamed that it had happened differently than it really had? Had she skipped to a parallel time, where things had unfolded differently and she hadn't given Horace away to Marian? Reg rubbed her forehead, where pain throbbed in the third eye position.

She fed the cats, moving automatically while she tried to figure everything out. They didn't usually get fed that early in the morning, but they certainly were not objecting.

"What is going on here?" Reg murmured to no one in particular. She didn't expect an answer from the cats. Though maybe Horace could tell her what was going on if he wanted to.

"It's just one of those things. It will all make sense later. It's just because I haven't slept. Because I woke up from a nightmare. Once I've been up for a while…" She trailed off, looking around. What would change? When she had been awake for a while, how was it going to make any sense?

CHAPTER NINE

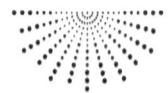

Once Reg deemed it late enough that Marian should either be getting ready for her day or already be at her storefront, she phoned for a chat. She didn't have to mention anything that had happened in the dream or the alternate reality. She would just let Marian bring it up. If she didn't, then Reg would know that it hadn't really happened.

"Reg!" Marian answered the phone almost immediately, sounding upset. "Reg, I don't know what to do. I don't know what happened!"

"What is it?"

"Horace is gone! I don't know how he could have gotten out; there wasn't a window or door left open. But I can't find him. If he's hiding in the house somewhere... I just don't know how he could be. Could he have somehow gotten into the ceiling or wall? Into a vent? He's not crying. I tried to sense him, but I can't..."

"It's okay," Reg assured her. "He's back here."

Marian was silent, too shocked to speak. Reg gave her a few minutes. Eventually, Marian spoke again.

"He's there? How did he get there? Did you come and get him? You should have told me. I've been worried sick."

"I didn't come and get him. I have no idea how he got back

here. Or into the house. No more than you know how he got out of yours."

"A cat can't just teleport himself somewhere else."

Reg thought about that. When Nicole had been taking care of the nine kattakyns, they had all disappeared more than once, reappearing in another part of the house that they couldn't logically have gotten to. There had been a wormhole between Sarah's garden and Francesca's house, some kind of passageway, and it had, Reg and Francesca had assumed, also enabled the cats to get from one part of the house to another when they shouldn't physically have been able to. Was there a similar passage between Reg's cottage and Marian's house that Horace had made use of? Or did Horace himself have the ability to make wormholes, and the passage that they had assumed had been made by Weston had actually been made by Horace?

"I don't know," she said slowly to Marian. "Maybe he has powers that we don't know of."

"You don't seriously think that he just decided to go back to your house and teleported himself there? I've heard of cats having strong gifts, but not like that. That can't be possible."

But Starlight's powers were as strong or stronger than Reg's. He had once been one of the immortals. And Horace was a kattakyn, not an actual cat. He had been bound to a piece of the Witch Doctor and maybe it had conferred some residual power on him. But Reg couldn't tell Marian that. They were being careful not to tell the kattakyn owners about the kattakyns' true origin. Which might be a bad idea, considering that Kareem had figured some of it out himself anyway and had taken advantage of the situation. Francesca had assumed that the owners would be better off not knowing the nature of the cats. Maybe she had been wrong.

"I don't know what happened," Reg told Marian. "I can only tell you that I didn't come over to your house—I don't even know where you live. And I didn't leave any doors or windows open either. But... here he is."

"You're sure it's him?"

"Who else would it be? What other black cat would suddenly appear in my house and act like he lived here? Of course I know it's Horace. I can *feel* him."

"That doesn't make any sense."

"It makes more sense that a random cat off the street showed up inside my house without any way to get in? And that Horace disappeared from your house?"

"He must be hiding here somewhere. Or else someone came here and got him."

"It wasn't me," Reg told her evenly.

But it could have been someone else. What about Harrison? He was the one who had originally brought Horace to Reg's house, telling her that she had to keep him and that was where Horace wanted to stay. And Reg *might* have promised to keep him when she had never intended to, just to get Harrison out of her house.

"Some kind of magic is at work here," Reg pointed out the obvious. "I can't explain it, but that's kind of the point of magic, isn't it? That it is things that cannot be explained?"

"I can't perform any magic. All I have is some psychic ability. Unlike *you*."

"I'm just a psychic too," Reg insisted. She'd never been able to consider herself anything else, despite what others had said. All of her gifts were just an extension of her psychic gifts.

Except that her mother was part siren. And her father, if Weston really was her father, was an immortal. And psychics didn't have firecasting abilities. That was a witch craft.

Still…

"You're not fooling anyone but yourself," Marian snapped. "You're playing cards from all the decks."

Reg shrugged uncomfortably, a gesture that Marian couldn't see. "The question is… what do we do now? Do you want to try again?"

"Would you let me?" Marian asked, surprised. "I thought that…"

"I didn't come and get him back. I can't keep him here; I told you that. I need to find him a new home. If we have to take him to your house a few times before he gets used to the idea… then let's do that. Sooner or later, he'll figure out that he's supposed to stay there, right?"

"It's worth a try," Marian conceded. "But… I'm a little bit worried about taking on a cat who apparently has such strong gifts. I can't control them."

"Um… I don't know anything about that. Maybe you could talk to Sarah about it. Maybe she would have some ideas. I know she doesn't like cats, but it must be something that witches deal with. You can't be the first person to end up with a cat with stronger powers than she has."

"I suppose. Maybe I can find something on the internet."

How exactly did someone search for that? *My cat has magical powers; what should I do?*

"Okay. So, do you want me to bring him over? Are you going to be home for a while, or do you have to go open your shop?"

"I don't normally open for a couple of hours yet. People don't like to see psychics first thing in the morning for some reason."

"Great. I'll put him in Starlight's carrier and bring him over. What's your address?"

Marian gave it to her, sounding slightly surprised and suspicious, as if she still believed that Reg was gaslighting her and had come to her house in the middle of the night to get Horace after all.

* * *

Reg waited for the cats to finish eating and then, as the two of them were completing their after-breakfast baths, got out the cat carrier. Starlight eyed it and then looked at Reg.

"Not for you this time," Reg explained. "I'm just going to take Horace back to his new owner."

Horace stopped licking and stared at Reg, one hind foot still raised in the air.

"Yes, that's right. You need to stay at Marian's. You can't keep coming back here. I can't keep you."

He stared at her for a minute longer, then resumed his ablutions.

When he was finished, Reg showed him a treat and put it inside the carrier. Horace was not fooled. He knew exactly why she wanted him to go into the carrier. He'd done it enough times to recognize what was going on.

"Come on," Reg coaxed. "I'll take you to the garden for a few minutes first. Then just a short ride over to Marian's. It's not very far, you know. I can come over and visit you sometimes, if that would help you to make the transition."

She didn't think he was really attached to her, though. He'd wanted to stay with Nicole, not with Reg and Starlight. Which made Reg all the more suspicious that Harrison was behind Horace's return to Reg's house. Horace hadn't done it himself.

Eventually, she coaxed Horace into the cat carrier and shut the gate. She said goodbye to Starlight and, as she had promised, took Horace into the garden for a few minutes. He definitely found the garden calming. His body language started to relax as he sniffed the air and sat in the green grass and leaves, even if he had to be inside a cat carrier to do it. It was like a little cave in the wilderness. Other than the bars on the door.

CHAPTER TEN

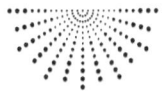

*A*fter returning Horace to Marian and staying with them for a few minutes to make sure that Horace was settled and would not immediately vanish, Reg stopped in at Witches' Brew, a coffee shop she and Corvin had previously visited. She really needed a large mug of very hot, very good, very caffeinated coffee. The stuff from the machine at home would just not cut it after the day and night she'd had.

A cat that could jump from one location to another that was a great distance away was definitely a problem. They had thought to be able to keep all the kattakyns apart, and thus prevent the Witch Doctor from re-forming again for hundreds of years. But if the kattakyns could jump from one side of the country to the other, or one side of the world to the other, then it would be impossible to keep them from visiting each other and gathering in one location.

Reg had no idea what to do about it.

Was there a way to stop a creature from teleporting from one location to another? Was there a way to stop Harrison from gathering up all the kattakyns if he decided to do so? He said that he had been trying to keep Horace safe and to get him away from the warlock in Egypt, not that he had been trying to gather the pieces of the Witch Doctor to re-form him. But Reg wasn't sure she believed that.

Not sure at all.

"Reg? I don't think I've seen you here before!"

Reg turned her head to look at Detective Marta Jessup.

Dang.

She had not intended to run into anyone at the coffee shop. Least of all Detective Jessup.

They had been friends. Or building a friendship. They had done a few things together like friends. But after Jessup's suspicions had fallen more than once upon Reg for a crime, and she hadn't believed Reg or protected her from a police investigation, Reg had started to avoid her. A friendship between a con and a police officer was not really a good idea, no matter how many fun TV movies they made about it. And while Reg was currently running a legitimate "entertainment" business and was not trying to con anyone out of their money, Reg wasn't prepared to say that she never would. If she were desperate, or the right opportunity presented itself, she might take the chance.

A person didn't simply move to Florida and go legit, giving up a life of crime forever.

"Hi," Reg greeted. She sipped her coffee, holding the large mug in front of her face so that she didn't have to meet Jessup's eyes, hoping that the woman would just get the hint and move on. Get her coffee and be on her way.

But Jessup did not take the hint. She smiled, her pretty Asian features softening a little. Her *friendly* face. The one she used when talking to her friend Reg, rather than the suspect, Miss Rawlins. But Reg would not take the bait. Jessup had proven that she wasn't willing to overlook indiscretions on Reg's part, that she was quick to suspect her when things looked bad, and Reg could not let herself be taken in by a friendly word and smile.

After Jessup placed her coffee order, she sat down next to Reg without an invitation.

"It seems like forever since we saw each other. I really miss our talks."

Reg had never treated her as a confidante, so Reg wasn't sure where Jessup was getting this script.

"Things have been busy," she said tersely.

"Yeah. For me too. It seems like things just never stop happening, do they? You think that you'll be able to get together after this particular case is resolved or crisis is past, and then something else pops up in its place." Jessup laughed. "But that never happens."

Reg said nothing. She kept her mug in front of her face and didn't look Jessup in the eye.

"So... how did that thing with the gems end up?"

Reg had been trying to get rid of the cursed gems. But that hadn't worked out too well when she had been caught on several surveillance cameras dumping them. As people had turned the gems in to the police, they had identified Reg as the rightful owner, and Jessup had dumped them all back on Reg's doorstep when she had refused to go to the police station to claim her property.

"Nothing to tell."

Jessup fished for more information. "I never could figure out why you did that... it was crazy. And why everyone turned the gems in. If you'd asked me what percentage of people would turn gemstones in to the police instead of keeping them and cashing in... the number would have been very low. But so many people brought them in... it must have been pretty close to a hundred percent."

It had, in fact, been more than a hundred percent. Somehow, Reg had ended up with more cursed gems than she had "lost" in the first place.

"Yup. People are more honest than you think," Reg said, getting in a little dig. Friends should believe each other. Especially when friends were telling the truth and hadn't had anything to do with a murder. No matter how bad it looked.

Jessup shifted and sipped from her large travel cup. "We should get together again sometime. Make some time."

P.D. WORKMAN

Reg didn't respond. A friendship with a cop had been a bad idea from the start. She had thought that maybe in her new life it was something that could work out, but that had been a fantasy. She shouldn't have even considered it. It was too much of a risk.

Jessup tried a couple more times to convince Reg that nothing had changed and the two of them were buddies. Reg concentrated on remembering how confrontational Jessup had been the first time they had met, and how she had threatened to bust Reg for fraud for running a psychic consulting service. All Reg's literature and the sign on her table said, "for entertainment purposes only," so it wasn't like Jessup could have followed through on that. And then there had been the trouble with Sarah's stolen emerald necklace. And the dead man in the cemetery. She needed to stay focused on Jessup's track record, not on the possibility of having a friend to hang out with.

* * *

She should have been in a good place mentally and emotionally when she got home. She had taken care of the problem with Horace. She'd had a really good cup of coffee, and caffeine usually settled her nerves. She had been firm in not letting herself be pulled back into a relationship with someone who could be a danger to her. Unlike with Corvin, she wasn't psychically connected with Jessup and Jessup didn't exercise any magical influence over her, so it was just a matter of setting boundaries.

All of that meant that she should have been calm and focused when she got home. Not unsettled.

Starlight met her at the door, meowing and rubbing against her legs. Reg put the cat carrier down, and he sniffed it.

"Horace has gone back to Marian's," Reg told him. "Hopefully... permanently this time. You don't know how he got back here, do you?" She focused on the white spot on Starlight's forehead and reached out to him. "You didn't have anything to do with him being able to come back here?"

As far as she knew, Starlight could not teleport himself back and forth through space. But he had helped her to call or to jump on more than one occasion, so she couldn't discount the possibility that he had the power to do so on his own.

She got only warm feelings of concern from Starlight, not an explanation of how Horace had come back. No vision or sudden insight.

"Well, I don't know either. Probably Harrison. Was Harrison here last night?"

Again, no emotional response from Starlight. Starlight liked Harrison, so she figured she would get something from him if Harrison had been there. But did Harrison need to actually physically appear in Reg's house to transport Horace from Marian's house? Reg suspected not. He could make food from Uncle Mike's Ribs appear in her kitchen in an instant. He didn't seem to go there and bring them back in his hands. Julian had said that what Harrison did to make food or other objects appear out of thin air was impossible, against the laws of physics, and yet he did it. As far as Reg could tell, their human understanding of natural laws didn't apply to magic or immortals.

Reg heard a fluttering noise and looked around the room. What was that? A fly that had gotten in when she had opened the door? Some other bug or creature? She didn't see anything when she looked around, which made her a little nervous. Her cottage was supposed to be her safe place, protected by the wards. She hoped it wasn't the beginning of another series of visions. She'd had visions of spiders and of snakes previously, and they freaked her out. Especially when actual live spiders or snakes put in an appearance.

She walked through the house, looking and listening. The noise seemed to be coming from the bedroom but, when she entered and looked around, she couldn't see or hear anything out of place. No bugs or flying critters.

Reg went to the closet to move the clothes around and make sure that nothing had landed on them and was just hiding from her. Nothing flew out. Reg looked down at the small wooden box that held the gems. Sarah had told her repeatedly that she needed to put them into a safety deposit box at the bank, but Reg hadn't. She couldn't countenance being separated from them like that. She needed them close by so she had them when she needed them. A person never knew when she would have to move at a moment's notice. She didn't want to be tied down to bank hours to make her escape if something happened.

She knelt down and picked up the box. She also had to make sure that they were safe. Storing the precious stones in the cottage, she could check on them at any time to be sure that they were all there and... settled. She couldn't think of another word for the feeling she got knowing that they were safely stored in the box, "tucked in" like a child going to sleep.

But when she opened the box, she didn't get that calm feeling of reassurance. Instead, she felt anxiety and uncertainty. She ran her fingers restlessly over the bags of gems, grouped together by the country or area from which they had originated. The Egyptian gems and rings, which Corvin had told her had been activated when she took them with her to Egypt in the hopes of finding their rightful owner, gave her an unsettled, hollow feeling.

"Hey. It's okay," Reg murmured, handling the bag and studying them through the plastic. "I'm going to go back. We'll find out where you belong. Soon."

How soon?

She acted as if she didn't care when Corvin told her that it wasn't safe for her to go to Egypt alone, but she was a little worried about it. She had been on the streets enough to know how dangerous it could be for an unaccompanied woman in the good old USA; she really had no idea what other dangers she might be up against in Egypt. She had been nervous when she had gone with Corvin. And of course, dealing with Kareem hadn't turned out at all as she had planned. He had been dangerous. And she'd been told he was well-respected. How would a rogue warlock or a street thug act?

She had powers to protect herself, but Egypt was an ancient land, rife with magic. Maybe stuff she'd never seen or heard of before. Which wasn't hard, considering her lack of experience.

Maybe she should ask someone to go with her. Davyn? She and Damon weren't really seeing each other, so she couldn't ask him. And Corvin... he would be eager to go, which was part of the reason she wouldn't want to go with him.

Soon.

CHAPTER ELEVEN

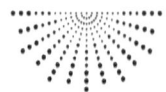

*R*eg's phone rang. She kept her fingers resting on top of the gems. Of course she knew who it was.

Even people who didn't consider themselves psychic still had experiences when they thought about someone, and then that person called or got into contact with them. If they were not practitioners, they just laughed and brushed it off as a coincidence.

But Reg and Corvin were closely connected and it wasn't hard to figure out that if the phone rang as she was thinking of him, it would be Corvin on the other end.

She let it ring for a minute or two and go to voicemail. Maybe he would think that she was with a client and would just leave her alone.

But her phone buzzed with a voicemail or text message. Reluctantly, Reg picked it up. A text message.

Where are you?

Reg breathed slowly, thinking about it. He wouldn't give up. He might wait half an hour in case she had an appointment, but then he would call again. Text again. Maybe show up at the gate, demanding to be let in. He really could be annoyingly persistent.

Obsessive, even.

She chewed on her lip for a minute, then swiped the missed call to dial him back.

"Regina." Normally, he breathed her name, laying on the charm. This time, he sounded anxious and distracted, as if she had pulled him away from something, when he was the one who had called her.

"I missed your call."

"Where are you?"

"At home."

"I'll come over there. We need to talk."

"You're not coming here," Regina told him firmly.

"Don't start that nonsense with me again. We both know very well that you're perfectly capable of protecting yourself."

"No. Not here."

"This is getting tiresome."

"You called me. I'm not playing games with you. You're the one who wants to get together. It has to be on my terms."

"You can't tell me you're not playing games."

"I can hang up. What's gotten into you today?"

"I didn't exactly sleep well."

"Well, neither did I. Sorry, next time I won't bother to call you."

There was a pause as Corvin considered that; then his voice was a little softer the next time he spoke.

"No... I don't mean that. I enjoy our late-night talks. *So what if you woke me up one night?* I just got up on the wrong side of the bed. It's not your fault."

"Because if you don't want me to..."

"I do want you to."

Reg was silent. She let him consider his next move. Eventually, he continued.

"I suppose we could go out for dinner. That would suit you better than meeting at your house?"

"Yes."

"A private room this time."

"Still no."

He grumbled under his breath, not loud enough for her to hear his complaint. Better if he kept it to himself.

"Where do you want to go?" he asked.

"The Crystal Bowl?"

"It's not exactly quiet there."

Reg shrugged. She liked the Crystal Bowl. It was a pub and restaurant and was more her kind of place. Corvin liked his fancy club, but it always made her uncomfortable. She didn't like the way that the hostesses fawned over Corvin and that everybody watched them. At the Crystal Bowl, where it was busy and noisy, she didn't feel as though everyone was watching them and listening in on their conversation. And the waitresses were too busy to do anything more than smile stupidly at Corvin.

"I like it. It's my kind of place."

Corvin grunted, but didn't come back with an insulting retort, so he was obviously trying to keep himself under control.

"Six?" Corvin suggested.

"Sure. That should give me time to get back to my clients."

"Can't you clear your calendar for one night so that we could... spend more time together?"

"No."

"You are impossible."

"Then why don't you give up? There are plenty of fish in the sea. You could ensorcel a dozen women in the time you've taken to pursue me."

"I don't want them." His mouth was close to the microphone on his phone, maybe touching it. "I want you."

"You want my powers. It's not exactly the same thing."

"Your powers are part of you. The most—one of the most important parts of you. The way that you grew up, that your personality was formed, the person you turned out to be. They were all influenced by your gifts."

"They are because of my history," Reg disagreed. "My mother being killed when I was four. Growing up in foster care. Sure, some of what I became was because of the way they tried to keep me from talking to ghosts. Trying to convince me that I couldn't see what I could or that there was something wrong with me. But there were a lot of other things going on in my life."

She reminded herself that her mother, Norma Jean, had not died in the current timeline. Even though that was what she remembered, everything had changed when Weston returned. Single events, even ones that she thought were life-defining moments, apparently didn't have as much effect on a person's destiny as she would have believed.

"Suffice to say, I am still interested in more than just your powers," Corvin assured her.

But she doubted it was true.

He might believe it, but she didn't.

"I'll see you at six at the Crystal Bowl?" Corvin asked, filling the awkward space.

"Yeah. Six o'clock. And I do have clients later in the evening, so don't even bother asking about having a nightcap or coming back here after. Not that it would do you any good anyway."

CHAPTER TWELVE

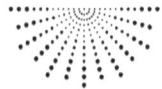

*I*n person, Corvin was just as he had sounded over the phone. Moving around restlessly, his eyes darting back and forth while he and Reg talked rather than staying focused on her as they normally did. He was irritable, quick to snap or to disagree with her. She wanted to ask him what was going on, why he was being so difficult, but she held her tongue. He'd already said that he'd gotten up on the wrong side of the bed. Best to leave it at that. She hated it when she was having problems and people tried to dig down into her psyche, insisting that they had to know what was going on with her. People's thoughts were private and, even if she and Corvin did have a strong psychic connection, that didn't give Reg the right to know everything that was going on in his head.

Corvin flicked through the menu. Which he probably didn't need to do. He'd lived there longer than Reg, and she already knew everything good on the menu at the Crystal Bowl. It wasn't exactly a wide range of cuisines. Corvin would probably have preferred a thick, rare steak at his club, but he would have to settle on a burger, roast beef sandwich, or fish fillet. She'd seen what the Crystal Bowl served as steak, and he might as well chew on his shoes.

"Where are the kattakyns?" Corvin asked, leaning forward as he grumpily tossed the menu to the side.

"They all have new homes." Reg was a little surprised at the question. He already knew that.

"I know that. But where?"

"All over the world."

Corvin rolled his eyes and shook his head. "Are you being deliberately thick? Where? Where is each one?"

"I don't know," Reg evaded. "I don't have all that information at my fingertips. Francesca was in charge of that. I just helped out a little when she wanted advice as to which cats to place with which people."

"And look how well that turned out," he said with a sarcastic snarl.

"Francesca was the one who picked people out and screened them. I didn't have anything to do with that. All I did was try to match the personalities of the cats with the personalities of the witches and warlocks and their needs."

"You must remember where they are. Most of them, at least."

Reg shook her head. "It isn't like I knew addresses. Maybe countries. But I don't know that I could even give you those. You should talk to Francesca. She could tell you all the details."

Corvin shook his head. The waitress approached and took their orders. Corvin tapped his glass impatiently. "And a refill. I've been waiting."

She nodded politely and removed the empty glass from the table. Corvin was usually very gracious and friendly with the staff. He wasn't the kind who raised a ruckus if there were a problem with his meal or he had waited for too long.

Corvin turned his attention back to Reg. His eyes were weird. Bright and fixed on her, but easily distracted. Like he was high on something.

"I don't know where they all are," Reg said with a shrug. "Sorry."

"Horace was in Egypt," Corvin said. "Nico is with the dwarfs."

"Yes."

"Where else did they go?"

"There was one to China." Reg shook her head, unable to remember which kattakyn it was or what city she had been sent to. But there were too many holes in her memory still. Things had been disrupted and misfiled during some of her recent experiences. She knew she should be able to remember more, but she couldn't bring the memories up. Trauma could do that, cause all kinds of memory issues. She had been very scattered and unpredictable as a child. Her grades had been awful and teachers were always complaining that she couldn't attend to the work or to remember what she had been told just five minutes before. And recently she hadn't just been traumatized; she'd actually had to live with someone else in her head, and that wasn't nearly as much fun as it sounded like.

Meaning not at all.

"Yes…?"

"And I think, one to South America."

"Only one? Which country?"

"I don't know. Honestly, Corvin. You need to talk to Francesca, not to me. I don't remember much about it, and I didn't know a lot at the time. I was just a sounding board. Giving her my thoughts on some of the different applicants."

Corvin's mouth was a thin, downturned line. He was still incredibly handsome, but the sour look did something to him. It made him feel like a different person to her. Someone dangerous. He'd never seemed dangerous before, even though she had known that he was.

The waitress returned with a glass, which she set in front of Corvin without a word. Then she turned and walked away without so much as an acknowledgment by him.

Reg looked at Corvin with sudden understanding. "You've already talked to Francesca."

Corvin just stared back at her, his dark eyes glittering.

"And she wouldn't tell you anything," Reg guessed.

Francesca didn't trust Corvin. Of course, she was right not to, but Reg was still surprised. Corvin had a very strong effect on most women.

"*You* can tell me," Corvin said firmly.

She could feel his charms working on her. Waves of warmth flowing over her, the scent of roses making her giddy. Corvin moved his hand over hers and the buzz of electricity sent her heart racing.

"Back off," Reg told him weakly. "We haven't even eaten yet."

Corvin smiled, looking like his old self for a moment. He withdrew his hand.

"Just tell me everything you know about where the kattakyns are. It's important, Reg."

"Why?"

"Why? You know why. Because if anyone can get to all the kattakyns, they might be able to unravel Francesca's charm and bring the Witch Doctor back."

He leaned forward.

"You know how bad that would be. All the work we did before... destroyed. The Witch Doctor back among us, raising havoc. Raising draugar, smuggling, slaving, killing. He will stop at *nothing*."

He withdrew slightly, watching her face.

"And he knows you. He knows you from when you were a child. Do you think that he won't come back looking for you? He knows that you are one of the humans who overcame him. He may not know who the rest of us are, but he knows *you*."

Reg felt a chill.

She had known this. But she had avoided thinking about it. It was just a hypothetical. No one had unbound the other parts of the Witch Doctor, so he couldn't return. It was something that could happen, but not necessarily something that would happen. And if it did, it might be long after she had died.

She had not wanted to think about what impact it would have on her personally. Maybe he would go somewhere else. He wouldn't necessarily come back to where he had died. In fact, since it would bring back bad memories, he would probably avoid it, wouldn't he?

But Corvin was right. He knew that Reg had been involved in his downfall. The first thing he would probably do would be to come after her.

Reg felt suddenly exposed. She had hidden from the Witch Doctor in the Crystal Bowl once before, under Corvin's protection spell. But when that spell had broken, the Witch Doctor had seen her.

He knew that she had been there. He could come back. If anyone released him, he would come after her, and he knew where to go.

She drew back from Corvin and looked around. "Maybe we should go somewhere else."

"You're the one who suggested the place," Corvin reminded her. "Now you'll have to at least wait until we've been served. I'm not leaving without my dinner."

"But what if he comes back here?"

"It's not going to happen before dessert."

It was a process. It would take time for anyone to find and release all the kattakyns. So far, the only one that had been compromised was Horace. And no one but Francesca knew where the kattakyns all were.

"You think it's good that only one person knows?" Corvin asked. "What if something happened to her? How could you be sure that the kattakyns were all safe? You wouldn't even know where to start."

"But if I don't know, no one can come after me for the information. I can't give them anything. I can't give *you* anything, no matter how hard you try to charm me. Because I don't know."

"I think you do know."

CHAPTER THIRTEEN

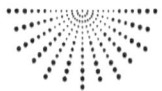

"$\mathcal{I}$ told you I don't," Reg told him firmly.

"You can't remember. That's not the same as not knowing."

Reg shook her head. "I don't see how. If I don't remember it, I don't know it."

"No. If you don't remember it—and I'm not sure you're not just withholding it—that just means that you can't currently access it. It doesn't mean that the information isn't there. In your mind."

Reg immediately saw where this conversation was going and tried to slam shut the doors to her mind. But her experiences with Corvin had bound them together so closely that she could not keep him out entirely. No matter how hard she tried, he could still worm his way in.

"I can help you, Reg. I can access the information."

"No, you can't. If I can't access it, then neither can you. It's just not available."

"You're just muddled. That doesn't mean that I can't find it with some diligent searching. Maybe it's misfiled. Maybe it is blocked. Either way, I *can* bring it to light. It just takes a little patience and someone who is truly motivated."

"No. You can't."

"Don't make this harder on yourself, Regina. We both have the same goals in mind. You don't want the Witch Doctor returning any more than I do. You're the one who stands to lose the most."

But Reg saw for a moment, just the briefest of flashes, that she wasn't the one who had the most to lose. Yes, she could lose her life to the Witch Doctor. She was a fragile human being without the ability to fight an immortal by herself. But Corvin, he was the one who had stored up all the Witch Doctor's powers. He was the one who had a massive treasure trove of magical gifts that he hadn't even begun to delve into. If the Witch Doctor stole *that*, Corvin would be empty.

And as someone who had been empty before, he did not want to be put into that position again.

Reg just stared at him. Corvin looked away, avoiding her searching gaze, his eyes flitting around the room. He was looking for danger, perpetually vigilant in a way that she had never seen him before. Corvin was always cool and relaxed. They had fought together; she had seen passion and intensity from him before, but he wasn't a worrier. The new vigilance was concerning.

The waitress arrived with their meals.

Reg was no longer hungry. It was time for her to eat. If she didn't, she would end up famished later. She couldn't let a good meal go to waste. But she was worried about Corvin's words and behavior.

She picked up her sandwich and held it in front of her face, breathing in the hearty, spicy smell and hoping that would do the trick and change the heaviness in her belly into hunger.

Corvin took a few bites of his burger and looked at her. "I just want to do what's best for everyone."

As usual, what Corvin wanted was what was best for himself. But he was right in one thing; their interests were aligned. She didn't want the Witch Doctor to rise up again in power any more than he did.

Reg toyed with her food. The more she thought about it, the

less appetite she had. She wanted to go home, where she was safe. Corvin couldn't do anything to her there.

But he had been able to sense her thoughts when he had called her when she was thinking about him. That might have been unconscious, but it still showed that he had access to her mind while they were apart, and she was in a place that was supposed to be protected.

She could use a psychic shield to keep him out. But that required energy and she could not keep it up all day long or while she slept. Sooner or later, she would have to let it go, and when she did... he would have access to her thoughts, her dreams, her memories. He could search for the answers he wanted. And if he were patient enough, he could find them.

She thought about the rings she had left at home with the gems from Egypt. A lot of good they did her sealed up in a plastic bag in a wooden box in the closet. Or under the bed, which was where she generally moved it when she started to think that the closet wasn't a safe enough hiding place for them.

With a powerful ring, she could protect herself from Corvin. She had not been trained in using the rings, but she had worn them for a short time, and she knew that they would help her to keep Corvin out of her head. They could provide a shield around her that she didn't need to consciously maintain and that didn't draw power from her all the time.

Why had she left them at home and not brought them with her? It was ridiculous. She should be using the tools available to her, not hiding them in the closet.

"I have to go."

Corvin's eyes met hers. He frowned, looking at her meal, barely touched.

"Uh, to the restroom," Reg said. She stood up. Maybe if she stood up, got some air, had a chance to think on her feet for a few minutes...

Corvin stood as well, a gentleman as always, standing when she stood, helping her with her chair, taking her by the arm.

Reg jerked away from him. It wasn't as though she needed to

be escorted to the bathroom. He wanted to hold on to her, to make sure that he didn't lose her, but she would not put up with his attempts to control the situation. She was strong too. She could be the one in control. As long as she thought things through and didn't act impulsively.

"Thank you," she said sweetly. "I'll be right back."

She headed to the restaurant's ladies' room. She looked back over her shoulder at Corvin once, feeling his gaze on her. His eyes were glued to her. He would not glance away so that she could slip out one of the other doors instead of into the bathroom.

Reg went into the bathroom. At least farther away from him she could think more clearly. She didn't need his pheromones muddling up her thoughts and his own psychic powers trying to break down the barriers of her mind to access the information that he needed.

She paced up and down the aisle in front of the stalls a couple of times, too agitated to sit down. She needed to keep moving to get her brain working.

Reg hadn't thought to put the rings on or even just to bring them in her purse. That had been a mistake. Knowing that the rings had power, she should have put some thought into how to handle them and what they could do for her.

But what if she could call them? She had been able to see and call Calliopia and Ruan from across the country. That had to be far more difficult than a ring or two. They were such small objects and she knew exactly where they were. She could envision them even without any psychic knowledge. They were hers, so she should be able to call them to her at any time.

Reg closed her eyes and stood still. She thought about the rings in the box. They weren't far away. She remembered how they had felt on her fingers. The smoothness of the insides of the bands. The shine of the gems. They had fit her fingers perfectly. Was that because of her magic? She imagined that rings of power would have been made for a man, not a woman, and would have been far too large for her fingers.

She ran her thumb over the bands, feeling how they fit her so perfectly. As if they had been made just for her.

Reg opened her eyes and looked down at them. There was no feeling of having exerted power, and she had not seen or felt them flying through space to her. When she called a person, she experienced the sensations that they did. With the ring, there was no outward sensation. Just *not there*, and then *there*.

She studied them for a long time, gazing into the crystalline depths of the gemstones. One ring was carved into the shape of a beetle, with the gemstone the main part of the beetle's body.

"Are you okay?"

Reg was still standing in front of the stalls, staring down at her hand. A woman stood in the doorway looking at her uncertainly.

"Oh." Reg forced herself to move. She looked around the room and decided she should get out of the way. "Yeah. Sorry."

"It's okay, I just wondered whether there was something wrong."

They passed each other. Despite her words, the woman gave Reg a look that suggested she wondered what substance Reg had retreated to the bathroom to get high on.

Reg's face got hot, but she didn't say anything to defend herself. A person could go to the bathroom to have the peace and quiet she needed for a few minutes to get over an upsetting conversation or event. People did it all the time.

She put her hands over her cheeks, waiting for the flush to subside before going back to talk to Corvin. He would tease her and want to know what was wrong.

Finally, Reg took a few steadying breaths and went back to their table. Her dinner was still there, largely untouched. Corvin was nearly finished his, though he laid down the remainder of the burger when she approached, and he rose to pull out her chair for her.

"You don't need to do that," Reg told him irritably.

"I know I don't need to. But I want to do things for you." He leaned close while she sat down, so close that she could feel his breath on her neck.

"Well, don't. It's annoying and it attracts attention." Reg looked around at the other patrons. They weren't exactly staring, but they were watching Corvin and Reg with interest. It was better if they didn't do anything to attract attention to themselves.

"Are you unwell?" Corvin asked, returning to his own seat. He nodded to her plate. "You've hardly eaten anything. And you spent quite a bit of time in there."

"I just needed to think for a few minutes. Where... you weren't."

"Fair enough." Corvin picked up his burger. "And what did you decide?"

"Nothing. Like I said, I don't know anything about the kattakyns. And you know that you're supposed to stay out of other people's heads. If you're going to go where you're not wanted, I'll tell Davyn. What do you think that will do to your reinstatement application?"

Corvin's face flushed red. The waves of heat that poured off him were not enticements this time, but a warning to stay back or she would get hurt.

"You don't have any right to interfere with my relations with the coven."

"Oh, no? Davyn asked me for my input. Considering that it was because of your previous assaults on me that you were shunned by the coven, I think it would be of great interest to him that you were trespassing on my mind." Reg forced a smile. She didn't want to betray how anxious his rage made her.

Show no fear.

"I haven't done anything against the rules. And Davyn knows that we are... intertwined. That the nature of our relationship means that the psychic connection between us can't be broken by will."

"If you do what you said, trying to go through my memories and find the ones that will help you find the kattakyns, I will report you."

His anger was so great that he couldn't even speak to her immediately. Reg could see a black, shadowy aura around him.

She was dealing with a dangerous warlock. She both knew and didn't know how great his powers were. She knew that he didn't respect boundaries and had no compunctions about flouting the laws that were imposed on him when it suited his purposes. Would that extend to forceful intrusion on her mind?

There was a knot in Reg's stomach. She was already dealing with the aftereffects of having had someone else possessing her mind. The fractured and misfiled memories were just one of the consequences. She didn't need to be dealing with even more damage from an attack by Corvin.

CHAPTER FOURTEEN

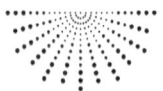

The beetle ring was warm on Reg's finger, growing hotter and demanding her attention. As a firecaster, heat was unlikely to hurt her, but she did notice it. She touched the band with her thumb, feeling the smoothness of it, stroking it. Her thoughts became clearer. The anxiety eased. She was not as worried about Corvin's anger. Yes, he was powerful, but so was she. She had immortal blood in her veins. She already knew that her touch as a siren could enchant Corvin. He couldn't do anything she didn't want him to.

Corvin's gaze dropped to Reg's hand. He looked at the two rings, his brows drawing down.

"Where did those come from?"

Reg raised her eyebrows. "Egypt."

Corvin grunted in irritation. "Clearly. I mean how did you come to be wearing them now? I thought you had decided not to use the rings."

Reg shrugged. She didn't owe him any explanation. She could do what she wanted to. Change her mind. Wear the rings. Use the rings against him if he decided to make good on his threat to invade her psyche.

"You weren't wearing them when you arrived here."

"How could you be sure? You just didn't notice them."

"Didn't notice them? How could I help but notice them? They are like beacons."

Reg looked down at them. If she thought about it and used all of her senses, she could see the glow that emanated from the gemstones. Corvin was right, they were pretty bright, hard to ignore. Was Corvin able to see power all the time, like a cat was able to see in the dark? It would make sense that a power drinker, would be able to quickly identify any sources of power that came into his presence.

"Maybe they were in my bag."

"I would still have been able to feel them." Corvin shook his head. "Did someone bring them to you? They were already here? I don't understand how you came to hold them."

Reg didn't enlighten him any further. If he thought about it, he would probably realize that she had been able to call them to her.

Reg looked down at them. They were old and plain, not like some of the modern jewelry she had seen. The carving was fairly primitive. But she was drawn to them like a moth to a flame.

"Do you like them?" she asked. "The little beetle is cute."

"A scarab," Corvin corrected. "It is a powerful symbol of power in Egypt, not just 'cute.'"

"But it's cute too."

Corvin rolled his eyes. His rage seemed to be settling as they talked about other things. It had gotten away from him momentarily, but he was doing better now, back under control.

"Do you know anything about Egypt?" Corvin demanded. "You can't just go back there without knowing anything about the place. It's an ancient land, full of magic and power."

"I know it's hot and sandy," Reg offered flippantly, which she figured would probably set him off in another rocket-blast of rage.

Corvin suppressed his reaction, grimacing, but keeping his eyes steadily on hers. "Yes, it's hot and sandy," he agreed. "And it's full of unknown and unknowable dangers. You don't have a clue what you're going to find there."

"Well... I have a clue. Several clues. But I don't see what any of this has to do with you."

"You can't go there alone."

"I think I can. But I'm not going to today. So you can relax."

"Does that mean... that you have set a time? You are making your plans?"

"No. I just have other things going on tonight." Reg waited several beats. "Do you know much about Egypt?"

"Do I—? Of course I do! I have always been interested in the ancient lands and legends. And since we came back from there, I have been studying, trying to work everything out in my mind..."

"About what?"

Corvin pointed to the rings on Reg's fingers. "These rings, for one thing. Do you have any idea how old they are?"

Reg used her thumb to spin the smaller one around her finger. "No. What difference does that make? Because it will be so hard to find out who the rightful owner is?"

"I have been looking through all the literature, everything I can find about early Egyptian jewelry discoveries. These would appear to be contemporary with rings that have been dated to 2500 BC." He stared at Reg, his eyes drilling into hers. "That makes them more than four thousand years old."

Reg gazed down at the rings, raising her eyebrows. "Wow. I don't know whether I've ever even *seen* anything that old."

Corvin nodded. "A find like this is almost unheard of. I don't know where the fairies got it from or how long they had it. But actually getting something like this into your hands... they are priceless, Reg. And not just because of how ancient they are."

Reg glanced around her at the other restaurant patrons. Their eyes were no longer on Reg and Corvin, but she wanted to be sure that no one would overhear the conversation. She knew what could happen when the right—or wrong—person overhead infor- mation like that. She would be in constant danger of having the rings stolen. And of possibly being killed herself in the process. It would be a thief's dream, getting his hands on something so rare, priceless, and untraceable.

"What do you know about them? Other than the fact that they are old?"

"Not much without examining them, maybe taking them to some experts. May I...?" Corvin made a gesture toward the rings, opening his hand for Reg to give them to him.

"No." Reg shook her head. "You can look, but that's all." She put her hand a little closer to Corvin, with her knuckles up so that he could see the faces of the rings. She watched Corvin carefully. He could grab her hand and pull them off. Leave town or just deny to the police that he'd ever seen them or knew what Reg was talking about. As long as he had a place to hide them for a few months, any investigation into the theft would peter out. The police had better things to do than to search for lost jewelry. Especially when Reg couldn't prove she'd had them—or that they were rightfully hers—in the first place.

But Corvin put his hand down and didn't grab Reg or try to take the rings by force. She could feel his disappointment that she didn't trust him enough to hand them over, but he probably recognized that in her position, he would never have let them out of his hand either.

He leaned closer to look at the rings. He also glanced around to make sure that no one was paying too much attention to them. But no one appeared to have noticed his intense interest in Reg's jewelry.

"When you brought me the gems before, you had a magnifying glass."

Reg pulled her bag closer to dig around in it, looking for the tool. She really did need to clean out her purse of everything but the essentials. The trouble was that to her, everything was essential. She needed to have things with her, within reach, in case something happened. If she had to run or wasn't able to get home for some reason, she would be starting over with nothing but what she had on her. Just like when she had gone to a new foster home as a child.

After a few minutes, she found the jeweler's loupe and handed it across to Corvin. He held it above the rings, studying them closely. Then Reg saw his eyes close to slits and knew that he was feeling the power the rings emanated. He could pull power from artifacts, so she watched him carefully and kept herself attuned to the rings in case he tried to pull from them.

"I see Egypt," Corvin said in a murmur. "Egypt as it was, long before cars and phones and men with white skin. They have been through many hands. Men who wielded their power, even when they had not earned it."

Reg nodded. His words resonated with her. The rings responded to his acknowledgment. *Yes. Yes, there had been many unworthy hands.*

"I want to take them back," she said. "I know they need to go back there. They won't rest until they are back there."

Corvin shook his head. "You don't feel the curse."

"I know they're cursed," Reg said. "Or what you call cursed. But I don't think it feels the same for me as it does for you and the others who have examined the stones. They don't feel… malevolent."

Reg gazed down at the rings, feeling the stones and connecting with them. They wanted her attention. They wanted her to hold them and to put them on her fingers and to use them. And they wanted her to take them back to Egypt. Reg touched each stone with her thumb, gently.

"You treat them more like a dwarf would," Corvin told her. "You will hear them talking about gems like they are their children. As if they have personalities and feelings and preferences. And you don't want to admit how powerful and dangerous they are."

"They're not dangerous to me."

"Until they are."

"They don't feel that way toward me," Reg insisted. She closed her eyes, focused on the stones. "I understand them."

"You don't know anything about them. How can you understand them?"

"I don't need to know everything about them."

"You should know *something*. It's very irresponsible to meddle with things that you don't know anything about."

"Who is meddling? How is it meddling to take them back to where they belong?"

"Why did you bring them here? And *how* did you bring them here? I don't think you are taking this seriously. You didn't have any idea how old they are. You don't know anything about who owned them or the history behind them. What they were used for, what the symbols signify. There is so much to learn about them, and you don't seem at all interested."

"And... why do you care? Why does it matter to you where they came from or who owned them before? They aren't yours. What I do or don't do doesn't have anything to do with you."

"I'm coming with you to Egypt. So of course it makes a difference whether I know about them or not."

"Oh. You're coming to Egypt." Reg shook her head. "We've never discussed that."

"We don't need to. It's the only sensible thing to do."

"What if I don't want you along?"

"You need someone to go with you. You can't go alone."

Reg rolled her eyes. She picked up her sandwich. She was starting to relax and feel better. Corvin couldn't do anything to her while she wore the rings. She should have realized that when she had been in Egypt, under attack by Kareem. He couldn't really have done anything to her while she wore the rings.

Reg's appetite returned as she relaxed. She took a big bite of the sandwich and chewed, thinking about Egypt.

It was more than hot and sandy. With the rings on her fingers, she could see and feel a much richer tapestry woven by the history, the people, and the buildings. There was a deep spiritual undercurrent to everything. Ancient, running through the blood over everyone who had come through that stock, permeating everything.

The sandwich was really not that good. Not when she was dreaming of the richness of Egypt. Soft white bread, limp lettuce, bland tasting fillings. Not like the food that had been grown there anciently or was now sold on street corners all over the country. Spicy and hearty and rich.

Reg ate it anyway. She wasn't into Egyptian food.

CHAPTER FIFTEEN

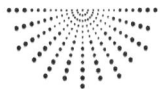

"I don't know what I'm going to do with this cat!" Marian complained. "I've had cats before and they were always pretty quiet and kept to themselves. Horace is… different."

"He just needs some time to settle in," Reg assured her. "He's only been there for a day. It might be a while before he gets used to it. We don't have any idea what it was like for him in—at his last owner's. It was probably very different from the way that you live."

"He's always underfoot. I've almost fallen flat on my face a few times when he has tripped me up. Except for when I'm looking for him. If I want him for something, then he's gone. Hides and won't come out when I call or even when I shake his treats. He just tucks himself away somewhere and won't come out. I keep thinking that he's gone back to your place again, without me realizing it."

Reg looked around her, verifying that there was no pure black cat hanging out there again. "Nope. I haven't seen him again."

"No, he's still here, I just keep thinking that he must have somehow escaped."

Reg wondered if Marian were exaggerating. She'd had cats

before; she must know how they could behave when they got in the mood. Underfoot or racing around the house like they were on crack. Cute and cuddly one moment, and then trying to take your hand off the next.

"So... other than that, has he been okay?"

It had only been a day, and Marian had probably been working for half of it. How could she make any judgment based on a few hours? Horace hadn't had any time to get acclimated. It wasn't really fair to judge him based on a few hours.

"He's pushed things off my shelves. Must have gotten behind my books to push them all off onto the floor. He dumped his water bowl across the kitchen floor. Why would he do that? Did he object to the water or just do it out of general principle?"

"It probably wasn't on purpose."

"Did he drink out of a water bowl at your house?"

"Well... yes."

"And he must have drunk out of one wherever he was before that. Then why tip it over at my house?"

"I don't know... maybe it was a different kind of bowl? Or something scared him? Maybe he was just racing around and bumped into it. Cats can be clumsy sometimes."

Starlight, who had been kneading the couch cushion in front of him with his eyes closed while he settled in for a nap, opened his eyes and looked at Reg. She mouthed "sorry" to him. She wasn't saying that he was clumsy. Just that cats were not always the graceful creatures they were portrayed to be on TV and in poetry. Sometimes they ran into things, fell off of things, or fell over in the middle of having a bath.

"Maybe," Marian conceded. "It's just that with everything else..."

"What else? Just with him disappearing last night?"

"No, not just that. He practically ripped my easy chair to shreds. I don't know how he could be so destructive in just one day."

Maybe Reg should have found somewhere the owner would be home for most of the day. A retired person or someone who worked from home like she did. She hadn't thought about Marian being at her shop and leaving Horace home alone all day. He might have felt bored or abandoned, suddenly all alone for hours on end.

"Well… I hope you'll give him a little longer to see if he can settle in. Once he adjusts to your schedule and his surroundings…"

Marian sighed. "Yes, I'm not going to just bring him back to you after one day. But I'm not very happy with him so far. I may not be able to keep him if things keep going like they are."

Reg thought of all the families who hadn't wanted her. All the supposedly experienced foster parents who had declared her too much of a handful, or not a good match, or disruptive to the rest of their family. She had known after a few homes that no matter what the social worker said, she was not going to find her forever home someday.

"Let's give him some time. I'll come over tomorrow and see how he's doing… see if I can make him understand that he's safe there and that he can calm down."

Marian was silent for a few moments. "Of course he's safe."

"He might not feel as if he is, though. Moving around might be making him anxious. And he wasn't… it was a little traumatic for him, the last home he was in. The warlock that couldn't take care of him anymore… Horace probably doesn't understand what happened and why he had to leave."

"You're being very cryptic."

"You don't think he's scared?" Reg asked. "What is he feeling?"

"Well, I don't know. How am I supposed to be able to tell that? It isn't like he can tell me."

"But you're a psychic."

"I'm not a *cat* psychic."

Reg blinked. She looked at the phone, then over at Starlight. He had stopped kneading and was just watching her.

Couldn't all psychics read cats just as well as humans? It wasn't exactly the same, of course. There weren't words to describe what was going on in a cat's head. But there were auras and feelings.

"You can't tell what he's feeling at all?"

"No, Reg. I've never had a gift with animals."

"Oh. Okay. Well. I'll come over and see him. Maybe I'll be able to help him understand what's going on. Or find out why he's acting the way he is. Maybe he's not feeling well. If he can't communicate with you, he might do things that don't make sense."

"We'll set up a time, then. In the evening tomorrow?" Marian sighed. "If my whole house hasn't been ruined by that time. Giving that animal free rein for another full day…"

"Give him some attention tonight. Maybe if he can spend some time with you, things will work themselves out. He'll be able to relax."

* * *

Reg had clients to deal with until the early morning, so she didn't give much more thought to Horace and the problems he was causing for Marian. After the last client was gone, she opened the fridge to look for something good to eat.

Although she had lectured herself several times about needing to start a diet and quit eating all the junk food and sugary treats she could get her hands on, the first thing her eyes landed on was a cake. A big, luscious-looking black forest cake. Reg pulled it carefully out of the fridge. There was one slice taken out of it. Had Sarah had a craving for chocolate cake but had only been able to buy a whole cake when all she wanted was one slice? Or had she planned to hold coven at her house and no one had been able to come? A failed book club meeting?

Reg cut a larger slice than she really needed and put it onto a plate. She put the rest back into the fridge. Sarah really was not helping her to keep her diet goals. Reg couldn't eat an entire cake by herself without putting on a few extra pounds. And her impulse control was not good enough to ignore the fact that there was a big cake topped with creamy white icing and cherries in her fridge. Willpower was not her strong suit.

Starlight complained that he didn't get anything to eat, forcing Reg to go back to the fridge to look for something that was good for him. Not chocolate cake. He might like the thick piles of buttery icing, but it wouldn't be good for him. Not that it was good for her either.

She managed to find some leftover roast beef that must also have come from Sarah, and chopped some up for Starlight. "There you go. Now let me eat my snack in peace. Neither of us should really be eating right before bed."

But Starlight was already noisily digging into the dish and ignored her advice.

* * *

In the morning, Reg woke up with a cat snuggled on either side of her. She looked in dismay at Horace, who looked peaceful and angelic curled up in a ball against her.

"What are you doing here again?"

Horace snoozed heavily. Reg poked him to try to wake him up. He started purring, but didn't open his eyes. Reg petted him and scratched his chin and ears. He purred away, a picture of happy contentment. Reg turned to Starlight on her other side.

"How did he get back here? Can you tell me that?"

Starlight opened his blue eye and looked at her.

"Was it you?" Reg asked. "Do you know how to call him here? Or how to make a wormhole for him to go through?"

The membrane of Starlight's inner eye slid back over his eye before he closed it all the way.

"Hey!" Reg scratched his ear, unable to help herself even if she were trying to get answers from the two of them. He was just so cute and cuddly. "I'm talking to you. Was it Harrison, then? Did he bring Horace back here again?"

Starlight began to purr. Reg was trapped there, between the two purring cats, not wanting to wake either of them up. If she did, then they would just be demanding breakfast in loud voices and wrapping themselves around her legs until she complied.

Reg grabbed the phone from her side table and pulled off the charge cable. She dialed Marian's number.

"Reg. Well, I did like you said and gave him some treats and cuddled with him last night, hoping he'd feel more at home and not act out today. But this morning, he was hiding again. I couldn't find him before I left for work. I left him food and water, of course, but he's sleeping behind the furniture or in some closet somewhere. I couldn't look everywhere before I left the house. I had appointments."

"He's back here again."

"He's back there? How did he get back there?" Marian sounded just as astonished as she had been the first day. Hadn't she at least suspected that Horace might have found his way back to Reg's house again, since it had already happened once?

"I have no idea how he's doing it. Or I have some ideas, but I don't have any proof yet as to how he's doing it or who is transporting him."

"I don't know how long I can put up with this. It might be best just to leave him at your house. I'm sorry, I was willing to help, but…"

"Can we give it one more try?" Reg coaxed. "I'll bring him back once you're home from work, and I'll explain it to him. If I keep bringing him back there, then he'll get the idea sooner or later, won't he?"

"Hmmph. You tell me. It seems to me that he knows exactly where it is he wants to be."

"But he can't stay here," Reg said firmly. She understood Marian's frustration; she was feeling it too. "Sarah will not let me stay here with another cat. If I can't find a new home for Horace where he'll stay, then I'm going to have to move out. And if it turns out that he's attached to the cottage instead of me, I'm still going to have some explaining to do!"

"Bring him back tonight. But I can't keep going on this way."

"Okay," Reg agreed with a sigh. "Maybe just one more time will do it."

But she was worried that it wouldn't.

CHAPTER SIXTEEN

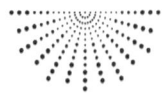

*R*eg eventually managed to tear herself away from the purring cats in order to go to the bathroom and afterward find some coffee. It was earlier than she usually was up, and she thought she might want to just go straight back to bed, but her need for the coffee was strong, so she would try breakfast first.

With the cats meowing around her feet, Reg was just getting the coffee on when Sarah's key turned in the lock of the front door and she let herself in.

"Well, you're up early. I wasn't expecting to see you yet."

Reg nodded. She looked down at Horace guiltily. Sarah's eyes followed her gaze.

"Reg! I thought you had found a home for that cat."

"I did... Marian took him. But... there's just one small problem."

"What? If Marian took him, then what is he doing back here?"

"He... keeps showing up again. I'm going to take him back tonight when she is off work. But..."

"Why is she letting him out? Tell her to keep him inside the house. At least until he gets used to it there."

"She isn't letting him out. He's... letting himself out."

Sarah rolled her eyes. "A cat can't get out of the house all by himself. They don't have fingers, Reg."

Reg's face got hot. She shook her head and punched the start button on the coffee maker much harder than she needed to. "I know that. And don't ask me how he's getting out and getting back here, because neither of us knows that right now. I talked to Marian before I went to bed last night, and he was fine. She gave him some extra kitty treats and tried to make him at home. But this morning, Horace was back on the bed next to me."

"He can't just materialize there."

"Well... it seems like that's what he's doing. I can't explain it. I guess he has some powers that we don't know about. How do you *know* that cats can't have... the power to teleport themselves somewhere else?"

"I think that we would know if they did. Cats and humans have been living together side by side for thousands of years. If they could teleport, we might have noticed that by now."

Except that Horace was not a normal cat. He was a kattakyn. And that might be completely different.

"I've already talked to Marian and told him that he can't stay here," Reg said, hoping to head off any further lecture. "She knows that, and I'll take him back there after she is finished at work. He's not staying here."

Sarah considered this, her mouth turned down, displeased. But there wasn't much point in continuing to tell Reg what she had already acknowledged, so she gave a stiff nod. "I hope this will be worked out soon."

"Me too!" Reg sighed. "I like the little guy, but having two of them around here, especially when he gets wild, is too much for me to handle."

After Sarah had gone, Reg fed the cats.

"You really can't stay here," she told Horace sternly. "This isn't your home. Marian wants you to stay at her house now. You have the whole place to yourself; she'll make sure that you get enough to eat and have your own place to sleep and a clean litter box. I'm sure she has some sunny windows, and she'll play with you. What more could a cat want?"

Horace continued to eat his breakfast, ignoring her. Reg knew that he could hear what she was saying. But he didn't like it.

"What is it that keeps you coming back here? Is it because you like to play with Starlight? I can bring him over for a play date now and then. And Francesca can bring Nicole, too. Just because you're the only cat living there, that doesn't mean you have to be lonely."

Starlight looked up from his bowl briefly. Reg sipped her coffee, even though it was still too hot.

Reg fingered the rings she wore. Could they really be as ancient as Corvin had suggested? Or was he just trying to make her believe that they were more precious than they were or that he knew more about jewelry and ancient Egypt than she did? He might have just been showing off, hoping that it would ensure his place at her side when she went back to Egypt to return the gems.

The scarab ring was hot. Horace looked up from his bowl and stared at her, his pupils getting big and black like they did when he wanted to chase something.

"No," Reg warned. "You aren't going to attack me."

He stayed where he was, staring at her, his eyes big and round. Starlight looked from his bowl to Horace's and, seeing that his was all gone and Horace still had some left, moved toward it to help himself. Horace hissed and swiped at Starlight.

"Horace!" Reg warned. "And Starlight, you have your own dish, leave Horace's alone."

Starlight looked at Horace and growled. The two had gotten along before, so Reg was a little thrown by the sudden animosity between the two. But Horace was just protecting his food dish. Reg bent down to move Starlight's dish farther away from Horace's. She could add a few kibble to keep Starlight happy and away from Horace's food.

But as soon as she reached down to move the dish, Horace's paw flashed out like lightning, and he ripped several bloody red lines across Reg's skin.

"Oh! Ow!" Reg brought her hand up to her mouth and sucked on the deepest cut. "No, Horace! Bad boy! Ow!"

He crouched down closer to his dish, eyeing her.

"I was just going to move Starlight's dish farther away," Reg told him. She nudged Starlight's bowl with her toe, separating it from Horace's. "Ouch. That was nasty. Bad cat!"

She looked down at her hand, the stripes welling up with beads of blood. He'd gotten her really good, and she'd let him, not expecting any trouble.

"No scratching. Sheesh. Ouch."

Starlight followed his bowl as Reg pushed it farther away. She used her good hand to scoop a little kibble from the bag of dry food and scattered it into his bowl. Starlight bent over the dish to eat. Horace looked up from his dish to Starlight's, his green eyes alert. He looked at Reg and meowed.

"You still have food in your dish."

He looked down at his, and then over at Starlight's.

"No," Reg told him sternly. "You're not being very nice. You finish what you've got. I'm not going to give you more."

He went back to eating, emanating resentment that she would give Starlight a treat and not him. Reg didn't try to point out again that there was food in his dish already and that she wasn't showing favoritism. But that was a bit abstract for a cat to be expected to understand, even if he was a kattakyn. He no longer had the Witch Doctor's consciousness to help him to evaluate a situation. He was all on his own.

Reg ran cold water over the back of her hand to wash away the blood and ease the stinging of the scratches. It was a good thing that Horace was just a small domestic cat rather than a panther or something bigger and more dangerous. He could have done some real damage. As it was, those scratches would take days to heal. They were pretty deep. As she thought of a panther, she pictured Horace as one, remembering the one she had run across in the Everglades. He had, luckily, been on her side and had helped her rather than stalking her.

Horace as a panther… she was glad that he wasn't any bigger

than he was. That was when she had a flashback to the draugrs when they had been in their other form. When they had been giants. Huge, hulking black man shapes in the shadows and darkness, full of malevolence, stinking of rot. She shuddered at the memory. It was a good thing that Francesca had bound them in their much cuter kattakyn form.

CHAPTER SEVENTEEN

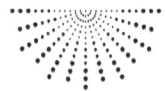

G W orrying over finding Horace an appropriate home if
Marian didn't work out, Reg's mind was drawn to
Nico. It had been a while since she had seen him. She missed him,
even though he had raised havoc when he had been around.
Horace was nothing compared to Nico. Nico had been the type to
climb the curtains, to hide under the furniture in order to jump
out at Reg and attack her, had knocked down and broken things
way more than Horace, and had clawed, scratched, and bitten her
at the least provocation, or even without a reason, as far as Reg
could tell.

He had seemed unplaceable, and yet, the dwarfs had been
delighted with him. They had not coddled him and tried to
explain to him, as Reg had, that he was safe and didn't need to
attack her. She had told him he needed to settle down so that they
could find an appropriate home for him. Instead, the dwarfs had
been pleased with his nature. Gwythr had declared him a rare
warrior cat. They had made cat-sized armor for him and had
trained with him, teaching him how to fight in battle.

Reg wasn't quite sure how useful a cat would be in battle. It
seemed like it would be too much of a distraction and not really
be able to cause any damage. The dwarfs would have to watch him

and protect him, because a cat would be vulnerable to swords, spears, arrows, and other weaponry. Even with his armor on, they would still have to protect him rather than his being an asset.

But that was their business. Just because Reg didn't understand how a cat would participate in battle, that didn't mean they were wrong about Nico or shouldn't take him. However warlike the dwarfs were, she didn't think they were actually going to go to battle with anyone. They had rallied their troops to fight Harrison in case he should come and try to take Nico away from them, but Reg didn't think they stood a chance against an immortal. And she didn't know of anyone else who would go against the dwarfs to battle.

But it might be a good idea to check in anyway.

Reg found Gwythr's name in her contact list and tapped it to call him. The call started to ring through, and Reg waited for him to pick up.

"Reg Rawlins!" Gwythr greeted heartily. "Great sorceress! You honor us with your call."

"Uh... hi, Gwythr. I'm just wondering how things are going. With Nico. Whether there have been any issues."

"Nico is well. Grown very large, into a formidable opponent. You would be very proud."

Reg thought again of the panther. Just how large did kattakyns grow? She had always assumed that he would stay the size of a domestic house cat, but maybe that wasn't true. She couldn't be sure.

"I am proud," she assured Gwythr. "And... I might come see him one of these days."

Having learned how to use her gifts to transport herself from one place to another, Reg didn't have to worry about what a long drive it was to the Blue Ridge Mountains. She could jump herself to just outside the dwarf kingdom's doors, make sure everything was good with Nico, and then jump back home again, all within the space of minutes instead of having to cover the distance by car as they had the last time.

"Reg Rawlins will come here?" Gwythr asked, his voice

cautious.

"Maybe. If that would be okay. I don't want to put you out."

"Of course not." But his voice was reserved, not inviting her to immediately come and have a feast with them.

"I wouldn't take him away from you," Reg assured them. "I would never do that. I just want to see for myself how things are going. Make sure there aren't any problems."

"Gwythr would tell thee if there were problems."

"Probably," Reg agreed lightly. "But I would be more reassured if I could see for myself."

"*Far* has not been to see him the last few days. The ancient one has not been here."

Far was the name that Gwythr told her the dwarfs had for Harrison.

"And Nico... nothing has changed? I mean... his personality? His behavior?"

"No, the warrior cat is fine, Reg Rawlins."

"Good. I'm glad. I would like to see him one of these days. He must really have grown since I saw him last."

"Very much," Gwythr agreed. "And perhaps you would like to continue our discussion of the stones of power you wish to sell. It has been some time since I last heard from you."

"Oh." Reg chewed on her lip. "I communicated last with Brimir. I sent a counter to his offer."

"Brimir," Gwythr repeated, sounding surprised. "Why would you have talked to Brimir?"

The son of King Fraeg had taken over the negotiations on the stones the last Reg heard. Reg shifted uneasily. "He told me to deal with him. That he spoke on behalf of the king..."

"He has no right to negotiate for the gems you offered me," Gwythr growled. "Why would you go to him?"

"I didn't. He... answered your phone. He said that he was the one I was supposed to deal with, that you were busy looking after the war preparations against Harrison—Far, I mean. He said... I'm sorry, I didn't realize he was trying to scoop you."

Though Reg had wondered at the time. She didn't understand

all the politics that went on in the dwarf kingdom, but it had not been hard to discern the tension between the chief of the smithies and the prince. Gwythr had withdrawn when Brimir had taken over the negotiations on Calliopia's fairy blade, and so Reg had assumed that he'd had the authority to take over on the negotiations for the gems as well. But she'd had a feeling…

"I'm sorry," she repeated.

Gwythr grunted. "You knew not. I understand. Are your negotiations with Brimir binding?"

"Uh… no, I don't think so. I haven't… signed anything. We haven't come to a landing on price, so I could pull out at any time, right? I don't really know about your legal system, so I don't want to say something that isn't true. I don't think I've said or done anything that was binding."

"Good. When he contacts you next, tell him you have changed your mind. He does not need to know why. You can continue to talk to me. What was his offer?"

Reg hesitated for only a moment before quoting him Brimir's first offer.

"It is low." Gwythr said immediately. "I will send you better."

"Okay. Thanks. And I am sorry, I thought that he was the one I was supposed to talk to."

"He is devious. I do not think he will live long enough to take the throne."

Reg worried that Gwythr's words might be treasonous. Was he making a threat on the life of the prince? Or just observing where his underhanded ways might take him? She didn't want Gwythr to get in trouble or for Brimir to get killed over something she had done. If she had misjudged the situation and somebody got killed for it… Reg did not want to bear the responsibility for something like that.

"I look forward to receiving your offer," Reg said neutrally. "Thank you. And… let me know if anything happens with Nico. If you have any worries about him… let me know. If Far shows up again. Or if there is something wrong. When we talked before…"

"I recall," Gwythr agreed. "We will protect him with our lives.

It will not be easy for even one such as Far to take any part from him."

"Thanks. Hopefully... it won't come to that."

CHAPTER EIGHTEEN

*R*eg checked her date book and noted that she had a firecaster training session with Davyn in the afternoon. Davyn was the only other firecaster that Reg knew, and he was the head of Corvin's coven. One of the people who would be dealing with Corvin's reinstatement decision. Something that Reg did not want to talk to him about.

But she was eager for another training session. She was getting better about handling fire, and Davyn was allowing her to attempt more difficult tasks in spaces that were not enclosed and controlled like her cottage. It was more dangerous, of course because, if Reg let her fire get away from her, she could do real damage. She was strong, and if things got out of control, it would be more difficult for Davyn to deal with.

But Reg knew that she could handle it. She was up to the task. Davyn had really put her through the paces the last time and, while she probably couldn't say that she had passed with flying colors, she had done reasonably well. She would do even better as she continued to improve her control.

Davyn had said that he would meet Reg at the cottage, and then they could go somewhere else for the training session. Reg was watching for him and opened the door before he reached it, eager to be on her way.

Davyn smiled. "Good to see you, Reg. How are you feeling today?"

"Good. Ready to get started."

"Well rested?"

Reg hesitated. "Well… sleep is not exactly something I have mastered."

Davyn chuckled. "You're going to need good control today. Strong focus. Do you think you can manage that?"

"Yes."

"No distractions?"

"There are always distractions. You don't exactly try to eliminate them."

They both laughed. On the contrary, Davyn did the opposite, trying to provoke Reg by bringing up things that might upset her to see whether he could break her focus. Things he knew would make her angry or upset or that would tempt her to let her fire burn hotter. That was how he built up her resistance.

Horace jumped down from the couch, where he had been sleeping in the sun earlier. The patch of sunshine had since moved on. He yawned and stretched his front legs and then his back legs and arched his back, quivering all over. He started off in Reg's direction but, before she could call his name or reach out to pet him, his head snapped around to look at Davyn. He stopped, frozen, for a moment, looking at the stranger.

"It's okay," Reg told him, amused. "Davyn's just here to help me. We'll be gone in a minute."

"I don't know this one," Davyn commented. He reached out a hand toward Horace. "Kitty, kitty?"

"This is Horace."

"Funny name for a cat."

He continued to reach his hand out to the motionless cat.

Then in an instant, Horace broke free of his inertia. He dashed toward Davyn, then leapt into the air and fastened claws and teeth into the outstretched hand. Davyn was too slow to avoid the attack. He gave a howl as Horace chomped down on his hand.

Reg dashed in to save him. She grabbed Horace around the middle and tried to pull him away.

"No, no! Bad kitty! Let him go, Horace!"

Horace writhed, his hard muscles snakelike under his fur and skin. Reg could barely hold on to him. He was heavy in her grip and felt more like a crocodile or fighting fish than a pussycat. Reg separated the two with difficulty. Once Horace was free of Davyn, she let him go. But instead of running away, retreating to hide under the bed like Reg expected him to, he went for Davyn again, attacking his legs this time. Reg dove in and again grabbed him and pulled him back. "No! No, Horace!"

She couldn't hold him for long, but dashed toward the bedroom to put him down somewhere she could lock him up. He escaped her grasp before she managed to get him there. Reg kept between him and Davyn, with her arms out, trying to herd him backward into the bedroom. Eventually, Horace gave a huff and a growl and slunk into the bedroom. Reg shut the door.

"I'm so sorry! He's never done anything like that!"

Reg looked with dismay at Davyn's arms, where Horace had raked him with powerful back legs. They were ripped and bloody.

"I don't know what happened. He's never attacked anyone."

Davyn was pale, looking down at the bloody shreds.

"Sit down," Reg told him, pulling a chair away from the kitchen table and shoving it behind Davyn, so that he was forced to fall into the seat. "Can I try healing? Is that okay?"

Davyn had taught her the basics of pushing heat into someone to speed the healing process. She'd been allowed to use the technique even when he was away from her, as long as she only used her heat and didn't directly kindle fire.

Davyn nodded his mute agreement.

"I'm so sorry," Reg repeated. She rubbed her hands together briskly, feeling the warmth of the friction to start with, and then the growing heat of her internal fire. She held her hands a foot apart, like she was holding a basketball between them. A small ball of fire started to form, and she extinguished it. Just the heat. Not the fire itself. Though perhaps with Davyn, the fire would be okay. She couldn't light him on fire, being a firecaster himself.

Reg traced a path above Davyn's arms, hovering just an inch or a fraction of an inch away from his skin, pouring healing heat into him. She didn't need to worry about it being too hot for him to take, so she pushed more than she normally would have been able to. She watched as the cuts stopped bleeding, sealed, scabbed over, then started to fade. She wasn't able to completely eliminate the lines where Horace had scratched him, but the scars that were left were faint and would probably disappear over time. They didn't look painful anymore. Reg pulled another chair away from the table and sank down into it, looking at Davyn's hands and arms.

"I can't believe he did that. I don't know why he would do such a thing."

If it had been Starlight, she would have been suspicious. Starlight tended to be quite intuitive about people, not trusting people who intended harm to her, scratching or biting in order to protect her. Not like that, though. Just a quick nip and then running away to evaluate the response.

"Where did you get him?" Davyn asked, sounding breathless. "Do I need to get a rabies shot?"

"No. No, he doesn't have rabies." At least that would be an explanation. "He's—" She had been about to say that he wasn't a real cat, but didn't want to explain that. "He's up to date on all his shots."

"Thank goodness for that." Davyn ran his fingertips over the healed scratches. "He's very… strong."

"Yeah. I've never had him react that way before. When I've picked him up, he's always been pretty chill, even when I put him in the carrier. Today…" She recalled the feeling of Horace's muscles and his sudden weight. That hadn't been the cat she knew. Even when he had been racing around the house knocking things down, he hadn't been like that with her. She shuddered. It was like trying to hold a demon or Tasmanian devil.

She remembered how it had felt to try to hold on to a pixie, when she had first met Ruan. The inhuman strength in his deceptively thin limbs. Was Horace something other than a cat? Even as she asked herself, she shook her head at the ridiculous question. Of course he was something other than a cat. She had known that from the start.

But why had he attacked Davyn without any provocation? He had never behaved that way before.

"Maybe he doesn't like men," Davyn suggested. "Has he been around other men?"

Reg considered the question. "Well… no, not a lot. Mostly me and Francesca and Marian. His last owner was a man, but…"

Maybe that was it. Maybe Horace had remembered something that Kareem had done to him while he was living there, or as he had removed the piece of the Witch Doctor bound to him. Having something that was bound to him torn away must have been traumatic, even if Kareem had been an ideal owner otherwise. And he had been bounced around from one home to another; to Francesca's, then Kareem's, then Reg's, then back to Francesca's for a visit, then Marian's. Too many homes in too short a time. It was disruptive.

"We had to remove him from his last home," she explained to Davyn, trying to give him a coherent explanation for what had happened. "It was with a man… he might have been abusive. I never thought…"

"Well, cats don't normally behave that way when they don't like someone," Davyn conceded. "Normally, they run away and hide. You had no way of knowing. But… you'd better be careful after this. Maybe shut him away if you are expecting company. You can't let him savage your guests. Even if you can heal someone afterward," Davyn looked down at the pink marks on his arms again, "You don't need anyone suing you or passing it around town that you own a dangerous animal."

"He's not even supposed to be here. He's not really mine."

Davyn shook his head. "And I suppose I should be more careful about trying to make friends with unfamiliar felines. I must have done something that made him feel threatened."

Reg was relieved that he wasn't ranting about how she needed to keep her cat under control or threatening to call animal control and have Horace put down.

"Thanks for understanding. I'll be really careful. It won't happen again."

Davyn nodded. He took a deep breath in and out. "Okay. Are you still up to training, or did that take all your energy?"

"I still want to go. If you're okay with that. If you want to go home and rest, I'll understand…"

"I don't need to rest. I'm fine. You didn't use any of my energy for the healing. You're sure you still have enough?"

"Yeah. I'm fine. It was just…" Reg shrugged. "Just the skin, mostly. It wasn't really deep. Not like when Calliopia was injured."

CHAPTER NINETEEN

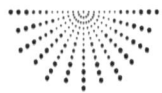

*D*avyn drove Reg out to a remote location for their training. Not the same dilapidated property that he had previously taken her to. There were skeletons of some old buildings on the land, but mostly it was just open fields filled with weeds and trees. Or what Reg assumed were weeds, since they grew there by themselves without any cultivation.

"Let's do a couple of practice exercises first, just to make sure you're in the right frame of mind and not having any trouble focusing," Davyn suggested.

Reg stifled a groan. She hated the basic exercises that they had been working on over the preceding weeks. She felt so constrained. So held back. She wanted to burn things. To really "play with fire," as Davyn put it.

But she didn't argue with him. She needed to be on her best behavior after the attack by Horace. She didn't want Davyn to be reluctant to return, thinking there was no point if she wouldn't do what she was told and he had to worry about being attacked by an insane cat. She went through the basic exercises with him, one step at a time, showing that she was ready and would do what she was told.

"Okay," Davyn agreed, nodding. "We worked on a campfire

last time. That was pretty easy stuff. Something a little more challenging today. I want to see a grass fire, but kept confined within
the boundaries that I set."

Reg knew how easily grass fires could get out of control. She
bit her lip. Was he really going to trust her to do that? What if she
lit half of Florida on fire?

"I can help contain it, but I will set my boundaries outside of
yours," Davyn explained. "A safety fence, if you like. But I still
need you to be focused. This kind of burn can very easily get out
of control."

Reg nodded.

Davyn gave her step-by-step instructions and pointed to
each of the boundaries that he wanted Reg to keep the fire
within. Reg started the fire. Though the area was green, there
was a lot of drier grass under the fresh growth, and it went up
quickly. Reg focused, trying to keep it from getting too high,
which might allow it to skip over the boundaries she was
keeping.

"Has your new cat ever met Corvin?" Davyn asked.

Reg knew it was an intentional distraction. One that she was
expecting. Davyn often asked her about Corvin.

"Um, not for very long. A couple of quick meetings. But there
were other things going on and... Horace certainly never attacked
him."

"That honor belongs to me."

"Yeah. He's never done it to anyone else." Reg was happy to
see that she was able to keep her fire low and under control, still
within the set boundaries.

"I don't suppose Corvin called him or tried to get close to
him, though."

"No," Reg agreed with a laugh. Corvin didn't like cats. He still
referred to Starlight as "the cat" without calling him by name. If
Horace had attacked him... Reg wasn't sure what would have
happened. Corvin had quite a bit of power. He probably would
have used a magical attack on Horace without even thinking
about it. "He and Sarah are both like that. They like birds but not

cats. Is everyone like that? They like one particular kind of animal over another?"

"I think it is pretty common to like one kind over another… but some people like all animals… or don't like any."

"And it's the same in the magical world? I thought that witches were supposed to like cats and use them as familiars. I never heard of them having any other kind of animal instead."

Though Erin's friend Adele, who had warned Reg against playing with powers that she knew nothing about, had had a bird. A big black bird that was always close by. They hadn't told Reg that Adele was a witch, but she thought it was pretty obvious. Who else but a witch would have warned her about using her powers without understanding them?

"That's just popular media," Davyn said. "You know you can't believe everything you see or hear on TV."

"Yeah, I know. They don't get it right."

"You know that we're considering Corvin's application for reinstatement."

He would not throw her off with any mention of Corvin this time. Not even about his being reinstated into his coven. They'd already talked about it before. What difference did it make to Reg whether his discipline was terminated? She wasn't the one who had charged him in the first place for what he had done. Maybe if he had someone other than her to talk to, he wouldn't be calling her at all hours.

Though Reg knew that the last call had been from her, not him.

"Is he… stressed out about the application?" Reg ventured.

"Stressed out? I don't think so. Corvin usually keeps a pretty cool head about things. Outwardly, at least. Why do you ask?"

"It's just that he seems a little different lately. More irritable." She remembered his threatening to read her mind, going through all of her memories to find the information he wanted, without her permission. "And… I don't know. Acting differently than usual. Not so… charming. More serious and… what's the word when someone gets angry easily?"

Davyn considered, his expression serious. "Volatile?"

Reg nodded. It was a good word. One that could refer to fire as well as to people. Reg couldn't help liking a word that meant something that caught fire easily. Davyn grinned, clearly thinking the same thing.

"Volatile. Yeah. I mean, I've seen him angry before, but it seems like he's really on edge, and doing things... he normally would not."

Davyn's smile was gone again. "About anything in particular? I know that he sometimes gets that way when he's... hungry."

Reg's fire flared. Corvin's hunger was something she had experience with. Both because he had taken from her, and because he had put his hunger into her mind to demonstrate what it was like for him. That painful, hollow feeling was not something she wanted to feel again. She tamped down her emotions and managed to keep the fire controlled.

"I don't know. Maybe. How could I tell?"

"Aside from asking him, I don't know. The two of you are connected, so maybe you could notice some sign if you were thinking about it. Of course, he may show increased... hunting behavior."

Reg nodded slowly. Corvin had not been trying harder than usual to charm her at the restaurant. On the contrary, he had seemed more interested in other things. In the kattakyns and in her rings. She hadn't had to fight him quite as much as usual, and he hadn't been showing the waitresses the attention he usually did.

"It didn't seem like that. More like he was off his game. Anxious. Maybe he's not sleeping very well."

"It's possible. Maybe he *is* worried about his application. It is something that has a fairly large impact on his life. Who he can associate with, his business, his mental state."

"Yeah. Well, I hope it doesn't take too long. I never thought I'd say this, but I prefer his old charming self to this new version."

"I'm sure everything will go back to normal fairly quickly once we've heard his case."

CHAPTER TWENTY

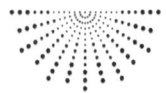

*R*eg knew she'd made a mistake as soon as she stepped in the door. She could hear Horace yowling in the bedroom, where she had shut him in after detaching him from Davyn.

"Dang. I'm sorry, Horace!" Reg hurried to open the door and let him out.

Starlight was in the bedroom as well, but he sat on the windowsill and acted as if he didn't even know that the door had been closed. Horace streaked out of the room immediately and bounded around the cottage, meowing at her several times to express his displeasure.

Reg set her jaw. "I'm sorry you didn't like being shut in, but if you're going to attack guests like that, you're going to have to be shut away where you can't hurt anyone."

He stopped running and licked his back several times, as if she had petted him and gotten his fur fluffed up. He glared at her.

"You can't attack people. You really hurt Davyn. He was bleeding. I had to heal him."

Horace licked his back a couple more times. The feelings she was getting from him when he resumed glaring at her were a mishmash of negatives. Angry, anxious, upset that she'd locked him up and then left the house.

Obviously, he couldn't teleport himself from one place to another, or he would have transported himself out of the room while she was gone. Maybe even out of the house. Someone else must be involved in his reappearances.

Harrison.

Reg decided that the best course of action was to just give Horace some space. He'd settle down once he'd had a chance to move around a bit and seen that everything was back to normal. She wasn't going to shut him back in the bedroom or leave.

"I'm going to clean out the fridge," Reg decided aloud. Every time she had opened it lately, it seemed to be stuffed to the gills. She blamed Sarah, who was always bringing her food, but Sarah had been irritated with her for not leaving any space for healthy dinners. Would she be irritated if she were the one who had filled it in the first place?

Maybe she would. Maybe it was irritation over Reg not eating everything she had brought over, but leaving it in the fridge to go bad. Or maybe she was getting forgetful and didn't remember that she was the one who had put all that food there to begin with.

Whatever the reason, the fridge was full, and Reg figured she'd better thin it out before things went bad and she had to deal with moldy, stinky, rotting food. She thought she and Harrison had finished the ribs the other day, but there was a pretty hefty takeout box from Uncle Mike's Ribs still in the fridge. And that chocolate cake that she had started on. It had been pretty good too.

Surprisingly, most of the things in the fridge were Reg's favorite foods. Usually, the offerings from Sarah took up most of the space and were things that she either threw out or gave to the cats. She could have ribs for supper and the cake for dessert. Though what would go really nicely with the cake would be some ice cream…

Reg opened the freezer door to see whether she had anything left. There were several boxes and tubs of ice cream in varying flavors. Reg looked through them and pulled one out. The freezer was too full too. She would need to clean it out. Finish off one or two boxes of the ice cream.

"We like ice cream," Harrison announced from behind her.

Reg jumped and nearly dropped the box of Cookies & Cream ice cream she had chosen.

"Crap! You scared me!"

Harrison looked at her steadily, unapologetic. "You like that kind?" He nodded to the box in her hands.

"Yes, I like that kind. This kind."

Harrison nodded. He looked at the other containers that she had pulled out of the fridge. But she wasn't eating those, she had gone straight for the ice cream. Reg's face warmed. But what did Harrison care? He wasn't worried about following human conventions and probably had no idea that she should eat dinner before dessert.

"Do you want some?" she offered.

Harrison nodded. "Yes." As an afterthought, he tacked on, "Please."

Maybe he was starting to better understand human interactions. Though by the looks of his clothing… Reg turned away from him before rolling her eyes at the horizontal black and white stripes on his shirt and breezy paisley pantaloons.

She got out a couple of bowls. They would eat like civilized people instead of straight out of the carton standing in front of the fridge. Harrison watched her prepare the two bowls of ice cream. She put a spoon in each and passed a bowl to Harrison.

"Do you remember ice cream?" Harrison asked as he took the bowl from her. He took a large bite of ice cream that would have given Reg an instant headache, and looked at her, waiting for a response.

"Do I remember ice cream? What do you mean? Of course I remember ice cream." He had mentioned her memory more than once lately. Reg knew it had been bad since the possession, but it hadn't been that bad. Of course she knew what ice cream was.

"Little Reg," Harrison explained. "Do you remember little Reg liked ice cream?"

Reg took a small bite of her ice cream and swirled it around her tongue. She tried to remember when she was younger and Harrison had come to visit her when she was living with Norma Jean or one of her early foster families. Ice cream? She could remember hiding under the table or in the cupboard, licking ice cream from her spoon. Making it last as long as she could. She remembered Harrison sitting with her, apparently not visible to the others, laughing and stirring his melting ice cream with a spoon, making a soupy mess.

"Yes. You brought me ice cream when I was hungry."

Harrison gave a delighted smile. "I did!" he agreed. "We like ice cream. And cake." He looked at the fridge, anxious for Reg to open it and serve him a piece of cake as well. Reg did so. Why not? She shouldn't eat the whole thing herself. She had put on enough weight without eating whole chocolate cakes.

Harrison mixed ice cream and cake together and put a big spoonful into his mouth, closing his eyes and savoring it.

"Are you the one who has been filling my fridge?" Reg asked.

"I do not want you to go hungry."

"I don't think there's any danger of that. It isn't like when I was little and Norma Jean spent all her money on drugs and didn't have anything to feed me. Between what I buy and what Sarah puts in here, I'm pretty well-fed."

He frowned a little, nodding.

"Now that I'm grown up, you don't have to worry about me as much. When I was little and you had to protect me from the Witch Doctor and my mother and other foster kids and parents. Now..."

"There are still dangers," Harrison pointed out. "The soul drinker. Sirens. Witches and warlocks. Other creatures."

Reg had to admit that she had faced a lot of challenges since moving to Black Sands. Things that she had never anticipated dealing with. She no longer had to scrounge from one day to the next, wondering where her next meal might be coming from, so it didn't feel like as much of a struggle. But she'd never faced so many things that wanted to kill her. Or at least, she didn't think so. She didn't remember all of what had happened when she was with Norma Jean.

"Well, you don't need to give me quite so much food. It will go bad before I can eat it all. And I should be eating stuff that's good for me, not all ice cream and cake and Uncle Mike's ribs."

"They *are* good."

"They taste good, and I really like them. But I need to eat things that my body needs too. Vegetables and stuff that isn't full of sugar."

Though Reg's brain rebelled against this idea. She *liked* foods that were full of sugar. She did not like vegetables. She shook her head at the unruly child that still lived in her head, despite her best efforts to act like a grown up.

"He is not polite," Harrison said.

Reg blinked at him, trying to figure out what he was talking about. Corvin? The Witch Doctor? She followed Harrison's gaze to Horace, who was creeping around the corner, watching them.

"Horace isn't polite? How is he not polite?"

Of course he *wasn't*. It certainly wasn't polite to go around mangling Reg's guests. She wouldn't be able to have him out when her clients showed up for their appointments. And he wouldn't like being locked up again. But maybe that would encourage him to stay at Marian's instead of returning to Reg's house.

"Did you bring him back here?" she asked. "Something keeps returning him here when I take him to his new home. If it's you, you need to stop so he can get used to Marian's house."

"He likes it here."

"I know he does. But he can't stay here. My landlord won't allow it."

"Because he did *that*?"

"What are you talking about?" Reg frowned, looking at Horace and trying to figure out what Harrison was trying to tell her. "He did what?"

Horace was sitting in the middle of the floor having a bath. Which was something cats did. They weren't embarrassed about licking their toes or backsides around other people.

Harrison gestured, not at Horace, but farther away. Reg looked past Horace into the living room, at something dark on the floor. She put her ice cream down and went a few steps closer for a better look. The odor hit her. Reg wrinkled her nose and looked at the black cat.

"Horace! Tell me you didn't!"

Horace continued to lick, unconcerned with what she thought about his behavior. Or maybe secretly happy to have put her in her place. Reg got closer and gagged.

"You know how to use the litter box! Oh, yuck!"

Reg tried not to breathe through her nose as she gathered the supplies she would need to clean up after Horace. When she looked around, Harrison was gone.

CHAPTER TWENTY-ONE

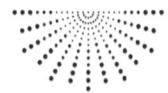

*A*fter she had finished cleaning up, Reg put Horace into the cat carrier and called Marian to see what time she would be home.

"I'll be closing up soon," Marian assured her. "I'll let you know what time I'm at home so you can bring Horace back over. I hope he's settled down…"

"Well, he's been kind of a pain while he's been here." Reg didn't want to tell Marian about any of the worst behavior, in case Marian decided not to take Horace back. Maybe he would behave better at Marian's. "I think maybe he's ready to go back to your house."

Marian laughed. "I wouldn't count on it. He hasn't been there long enough to miss it. He just keeps going back to you. If you didn't have to worry about being kicked out…"

Earlier in the day, Reg might have had a difficult time saying no to Horace if Marian wouldn't take him and Sarah wasn't an issue. Even though she hadn't gone looking for a second cat, it might be nice to have two of them around the house to keep each other company. And two cats weren't that much harder to take care of than one. Until they started behaving the way Horace did.

"Maybe he's sick," Reg suggested. "Sometimes kids act out when they're not feeling well."

"It's possible, I suppose," Marian said. "But I haven't seen anything to indicate that he isn't feeling well."

Reg had done a couple of searches on her phone that suggested one reason that cats sometimes stopped using their litter boxes was because they were sick.

"Keep an eye on him, just in case. Maybe I'm wrong. But if he is sick, then we should get him looked at sooner rather than later."

"Yes," Marian agreed, her voice a little wistful.

Reg had forgotten that Marian had just lost another cat. She didn't want to make her sad by suggesting that they could lose Horace too.

"I'm sure it's nothing. I'm wrong. It isn't like he's just been lying around not doing anything. He has… lots of energy."

"That's one way to put it," Marian laughed. "In fact, I could do with a little less energy, if you could somehow manage that."

"I don't think so. He hasn't exactly been quiet here."

* * *

Reg wasn't sure how long it would be until Marian was actually home. She said she was closing up the shop, but Reg had worked a few retail jobs and knew that closing procedures could take a long time. And Marian might need to run some errands or pick up supper before she went home, too. "Soon" might be a few hours away. She already had Horace in the cat carrier and had nowhere to take him.

"We could go visit the dwarfs."

Horace lifted his head and looked at her. Reg was pretty sure that he hadn't understood what she had said and was just responding to her voice or her mood.

"Would you like that? Would you like to go to the mountains and see the dwarfs for a few minutes? I could check on Nico. Do you remember Nico?"

Horace bumped his face against the barred gate of the cat

carrier. He emitted a low yowl. Not surprising that he didn't like to be penned up in the cage. Reg wouldn't like it either. But she couldn't risk what he might choose to do next. She had clients coming later and her house needed to be in good enough shape to receive company. And that meant that all the furniture and decor were intact and there weren't little kitty surprises left in strategic places for someone to step in.

"Yeah, let's go," Reg agreed. She called Starlight with a kissy sound. "Starlight? Do you want to go visit Nico?"

There was no answering thump as Starlight jumped to the floor. Reg waited for a minute to see whether he would come out, then went to the bedroom to look for him. He was curled up on the bed and lifted his head just enough to look at her through one eye as she approached.

"We're going to the dwarf mountain," Reg told him. "Where Nico is. Do you want to go with us?"

He put his head down and closed his eye.

"You sure? You liked it there. The dwarfs were pretty good to you."

Starlight didn't get up or acknowledge her. Reg shook her head and sighed. "Fine, then. Your loss. Just don't get mad at me for not bringing you along."

He didn't look like he was going to. It wasn't like Reg would be there for long or would be doing anything exciting. Just seeing a few dwarfs. And Nico. And to touch base with Gwythr on the gems. There was no reason, given her skills, that she couldn't pop in and visit them for a few minutes, just as if they were staying next door.

Reg went back out to the living room where the cat carrier was. She picked it up and closed her eyes.

She thought about the dwarf mountain and all she had seen there. All of the dwarfs; men, women, and children. Dressed in cartoon and superhero t-shirts and children's pants, their long beards incongruous with the popular media images they wore. She thought of the smell of the food in the cafeteria they referred to as their feast hall, and the heat of the forge where she had fired

Calliopia's necklace. In a few breaths, she opened her eyes and looked around her, recognizing a change in the atmosphere around her.

She had, unsurprisingly, materialized in the crafting room that the forge was in. That was the place she had the strongest sensory memories of. She had not thought to ever go back there again, but there she was. The air was heavy and warm, and she was surrounded by the crafting tables of the dwarfs who were crafting jewelry and mementos for sale on Etsy. There was a kanban board on the wall showing various projects and what stages they were in.

The room was unnaturally quiet. The dwarfs, who should have been busy working away and chattering with each other, were all looking at her, silent and still. Of course they were. Reg had jumped directly into the middle of the kingdom with no warning or permission. That wasn't something that people normally did. She stood there with her cat carrier in her hand, trying to think of what to say to them to break the ice. *Hello? I was just in the neighborhood?*

"Intruder!" someone across the room shrilled, and he must have pulled an alarm, because a klaxon immediately began to blare, so loud that it hurt Reg's ears. She looked down at Horace, feeling sorry for him and his extra-sensitive cat hearing. And Nico, wherever he was.

"No," Reg said, holding up her hand, trying to reassure them. "I don't mean any harm. I just stopped in for a visit…"

Dwarf crafters streamed to the doors, casting frightened looks over their shoulders at Reg. Others turned toward her, baring their sword-hilts or pulling weapons free of their scabbards.

"I'm not here to hurt anyone!"

"No one may appear in the dwarf kingdom without leave," said a dwarf woman with a clipboard, staring sternly at Reg like the meanest librarian she'd ever crossed.

"No. I'm sorry. I should have called ahead…"

"Put down the cage," one of the older men ordered.

Reg bent down and set the carrier carefully on the floor. She raised her hands to her shoulders, hoping that they would not attack without provocation.

"It's a cat," one of the other dwarfs reported, bending down to examine Horace in the cat carrier. "Kitty, kitty, kitty?"

"Careful—" Reg warned as he stuck his finger into the carrier to scratch Horace's ears.

With a snarl, Horace attacked the offending digit, making the dwarf holler and jerk his hand back, finger bleeding. He put it into his mouth, his eyes wide.

"A formidable foe!" he exclaimed around the finger.

"Yes, please be careful, I don't want anyone to get hurt. I can heal that for you..."

The dwarf shook his head, taking his finger out of his mouth to study it. "It is a battle scar!"

"Um... okay. If you want."

Reg could hear the pounding of approaching feet over the sound of the alarm. A lot of approaching feet.

"Oh, man. I didn't mean to cause any trouble. Please tell the others—I'm not here to do any harm!"

A contingent of dwarfs streamed into the cavernous room, spreading out in formation, surrounding Reg on all sides. Swords flashed in the light of the forge. Reg was anxious, and she had forgotten how the forge pulled her, calling to her inner fire. She was sweating, not because of the heat, but because of the effort to stand there, unmoving, and not release her fire.

"Halt!" One of the dwarfs who had just arrived, a helmet of iron obscuring his features, called out and held up his hand. "It is Reg Rawlins, great sorceress!"

They all stopped and looked at each other. Reg waited, wondering what the protocol was. Was she off the hook because they had recognized her? Or would she be taken before the king or even thrown into prison?

She should have known better than to appear there. She had badly miscalculated.

The dwarf removed his helmet, revealing long hair and a familiar face.

"Gwythr!"

"Hail, Reg Rawlins." He spoke stiffly. "How came you here without permission?"

"I'm sorry. I didn't even think about it. I just wanted to come and see Nico, and to see you. I didn't mean to cause a whole…" Reg gestured at the army around her and the blaring klaxon, and the dwarf woman with the official schedule clipboard.

"A friend of the kingdom may approach the outside door and request entry," Gwythr advised. "And it is best if you arrange something ahead and get onto our Google calendar. Appearing inside is…" He shook his head somberly. "It is a great breach of etiquette."

CHAPTER TWENTY-TWO

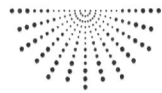

*R*eg bowed her head, trying to look suitably humbled. "I'm so sorry. It was stupid. I should have known that."

"Reg Rawlins is a great sorceress, and oftentimes a sorceress does not think she needs to follow the rules like everyone else."

"It wasn't that. I'm just... inexperienced. I was so over-whelmed with your hospitality the last time that it didn't even occur to me that you would need some notice that I was coming, and security checks and all that."

"You said you would visit," Gwythr said, acknowledging that Reg had mentioned it in their last call. "I should have told you the proper procedure then. I did not think that you would just... appear. We would normally... have several discussions first to make the arrangements."

Reg nodded. "I'm sorry."

Gwythr made an expansive gesture. "It was an oversight." He gave several sharp commands to the rest of the dwarfs in his contingent. They stood down, lowering their weapons, taking off their helmets or raising their visors, and relaxing.

Reg breathed a deep sigh of relief.

Gwythr came closer and peered into the cat carrier. "You have brought us another warrior cat?" he asked eagerly.

"No, not this time. I just thought he might like to see Nico. They are litter mates."

"Ah. Is this the one who..." Gwythr trailed off and didn't finish the question. He raised his brows questioningly. Reg had talked to him about what had happened to Horace in broad terms, though she hadn't expected at that point to take him there to see the dwarfs.

"Yes. This is the one," she said in a quiet tone that she hoped would not carry.

"Poor creature." Gwythr patted the top of the cage and was not silly enough to stick his finger between the bars.

Reg picked up the carrier. "I shouldn't be in here," she said, looking toward the forge, which was still trying to draw her in. "Can we go somewhere that is more private to visit? And to see Nico, if he's not too busy?"

She had no idea whether they had him on a training regimen or whether he was allowed to nap on his own schedule. She hoped that he would not have forgotten her already, but he had probably been very busy and had a lot of interesting experiences since he had joined the dwarfs.

"Come," Gwythr agreed. He led the way toward the door. The dwarf warriors parted in front of him and Reg was able to walk through without jostling any of them. They watched her with curious eyes, some of them whispering to each other. Maybe explaining who she was to anyone who hadn't seen her the last time she had been there.

She felt awkward walking with all of their eyes on her. She didn't want to trip in front of them and make a fool of herself. She really didn't like to be the center of attention.

She followed Gwythr through a few tunnels before she recognized the route to the feast hall. They cut through it to get to a cluster of meeting rooms on the other side where she had previously met with her company while they waited for the dwarfs to formulate a plan to unmake Calliopia's blade.

"Have a seat," Gwythr invited, motioning to the chairs around the table. "Would you like a beverage? Water? Ale?"

"Just water is great, thanks." Reg could tell that she had expended energy just trying not to be drawn into releasing her fire. She was learning that she needed to monitor her hydration level. Too much firecasting would leave her dehydrated and unable to function. Drinking too much water would quench her firecasting ability. She supposed it was the same with athletes. They needed to drink enough to operate at peak levels, but not so much that it weighed them down.

Gwythr went to the mini fridge and pulled out a bottle of water for her and a tall silver can for himself. She glanced at the label as he placed it on the table. *Dwarf Ale straight from the mountain*, it proclaimed in big, old-style lettering.

"Good product," Gwythr told her, following her eyes. "We have a campaign running right now to target D&D players. They love this kind of thing."

He sat down on one of the chairs and pumped a lever on the side to raise himself closer to Reg's level.

"I didn't offer anything to the cat. Should we let him out?"

"Uh... not a good idea to let him have free rein in the kingdom. We can shut the door, maybe, and just let him walk around in here. Maybe if Nico comes...?"

Gwythr hadn't made any effort to arrange for Nico to be brought. He leaned forward, ignoring her comment, eyeing the rings on her fingers.

"Whence came these?" He asked, eyes glittering. "You did not tell me you had anything like this."

"I can't sell these ones. They are cursed. They need to be cleansed before they can be sold. They don't rightfully belong to me."

"No," he agreed. "Egyptian. Very ancient."

"That's what Corvin said. He said maybe five thousand years old."

Gwythr nodded his agreement. "And how came they into your hands?"

"I can't really talk about that. I'm not here to trade them. I just wanted… to keep them close. I can't leave them unattended. Someone might try to steal them."

"Indeed."

"I did bring these, though," Reg offered. She reached into her pocket and pulled out the gems that she had previously offered to him via email.

"Ah!" Gwythr's eyes lit up and he picked up the plastic bag that held them. He fingered them through the plastic and held them up to the light. "They are beautiful, are they not? See how they sparkle."

Reg smiled at his obvious delight. It would be hard for him to be parted from them now that he'd held them in his hands. Negotiations should go much more quickly. He wouldn't want to stretch them out and have her go home with the gems still in her possession.

Gwythr caught her look. "Oh, you are a canny negotiator. Very smart, Reg Rawlins."

She smiled innocently.

Gwythr attempted to hand the gems back to her, but she didn't take them, waiting for him to take the next step.

"You were modest in your description. The assessments were…" Gwythr searched for an appropriate word. "They were technically correct."

Was he going to play hardball now? Pretend that she was asking too much or that they were dealing with a hardship that would prevent them from paying as much as she would like?

"There is a word we have," Gwythr said. "I do not know if there is an English word for it." He said the word in dwarfish, a sort of a guttural clicking. "Human assessors do not account for it when they are examining gems. It is a combination of the gem's history and power… its *personality*. The closest that I can think of in English would be… flavor?" His dark eyes bored into Reg's, trying to see if she understood his meaning. "These gems have a very rich, deep flavor. Is that right?"

Reg knew a bit about valuing gemstones, but only in the technical aspects that Gwythr had mentioned. Size, cut, clarity. She had never heard of this other aspect, but it made sense to her. There was something about the gems when she held them or was near them. Not just warmth or power, but a feeling of wholeness and rightness.

When she held the cursed gems, the feeling was different. She could still sense their power, but there was something unsettled and fractured about them. A need to be filled. While some of the gems could be cleansed using other methods, some of them could only be cleansed by returning them to the source they had come from. To the people who were the rightful owners. Only the rightful owners could give or trade the gems without a curse accompanying them. Then they were transformed, and she could feel that fullness again. She thought that Gwythr was right, but in her mind, she identified two separate qualifications, not just one. The flavor of the gems, the power and history and personality, but also the wholeness of them, the fullness.

"Yes... I guess flavor makes sense," she agreed.

"As such, these gems are worth more than... some of the flavorless pap that you find in human markets. Especially the grown gems."

At Reg's questioning look, he clarified. "The ones created in labs?"

"Oh." Reg nodded. She didn't have much experience in that regard, though she had heard of such a thing.

"They can be technically perfect, but worthless."

"Because they were made artificially."

"They do not have any soul."

Reg nodded again. All this was leading up to something, but she wasn't sure what.

"I must revise my offer for these gems," Gwythr concluded finally. Reg had been expecting this. "It is not high enough."

CHAPTER TWENTY-THREE

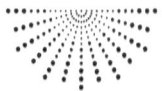

*S*he looked at him, his words clicking through to her brain, but unable to decide what he meant. She was expecting him to bargain harder, to tell her that she had over-priced them and that they could not be expected to pay so much. She had not been expecting to be told that they were worth more than he had previously offered for them.

"You're... *increasing* your offer?"

He nodded. "Dwarfs can be cunning too. And we always like a bargain. But if I were to give you too low a price, it would be robbery, and it would hurt my reputation. I must pay a fair price."

"Oh. Okay. Well then... do you have a price in mind, or do you have to think about it?"

"I will need to look over my accounts, talk to some others, and get back to you." Gwythr laid the baggie of gems down on the table reluctantly, eyes shining as he looked at them. "I will be as quick as possible."

Reg could tell that he didn't want to leave them behind. Hope-fully, that meant that they could come to a landing before she had to go home.

"And can you... see if you can find Nico? I'd like to see him."

Gwythr looked around. "He comes."

Reg looked out the door and saw a dark shape approaching.

"Nico?" she asked uncertainly.

The proportions of the rooms in the dwarf mountain distorted Reg's sense of size. Tall ceilinged rooms with smaller furniture than she was used to as a human threw off her ability to judge scale. The shape approaching the room looked disproportionately large, and she was sure it would resolve when he got closer.

But the cat shape that came through the door was not small like the kattakyn she had left with the dwarfs. It was not the size of Horace, who had grown and put on weight while he had been with Kareem. It was the size of a panther or a small bear. Armor plates protected his body and long spikes protruded along the spine, making him look even larger.

Nico gave a trill of recognition and galloped toward Reg. She gasped as he leaped toward her, putting out her hands to stop him and protect herself. But he stopped with his front paws on the table in front of her, powerful hind legs planted firmly on the floor.

"Nico!" Reg was relieved and flabbergasted. What had the dwarfs done to make Nico grow to such proportions? Horace was the shape of a normal cat, and Francesca had not said that any of the other kattakyn owners thought that they were too large or had strange qualities. They all thought that they owned normal house cats, which would not be the case if they were as big as Nico. "Look at you! My goodness!"

Gwythr smiled as he slid down from his chair. "He is a warrior," he informed Reg, slapping Nico's armored side. "You are impressed?"

"Wow. Am I ever. What are you feeding this guy? It must be the big spiders down here."

He laughed heartily. "We know how to take care of a warrior cat."

"I guess so. Are you in charge of him, or does someone else take care of him and do his training?"

"I am responsible for him, but there are many who are involved in his care and training. As Chief of the Smithies, I do not have the ability to put all my time into his care. And there are others better suited to train him in combat."

"Yeah, I guess your calendar must be pretty full." She remembered the way he had entered the forge when the alarm bell rang. "You command part of the dwarf army too?"

Gwythr gave a little bow. "Only the protectors of the forge. As Chief of the Smithies, that duty falls to me."

"Wow. You really must be busy. I had no idea how much being the Chief of the Smithies entailed."

"Time blocking," Gwythr said. "That is the way to ensure you get things done when you have so many responsibilities." He assessed Reg's blank look. "On your calendar. Blocking off specific times for different tasks."

And he probably hadn't expected the interruption of whatever he was currently supposed to be doing, dealing with a breach of security and Reg showing up with her gemstones.

"And here I am interrupting you. I'm sorry about that. I wasn't thinking."

"It is an honor to be able to visit Reg Rawlins. But I do have other things to do… and I will need to revise my bid for you quickly, before you have to leave. Will you be here for a little longer?" He looked at Nico and gave him another ringing pat. "You will want to visit with Nico and give him a chance to see his litter mate."

"Yeah. I guess. I'll be here for a while longer."

"Good. I will do my best to work within your time frame."

* * *

Gwythr left, pulling the door shut behind him so that Reg would be able to let Horace out of his carrier.

But Reg wasn't so sure that was a good idea now. Horace was much smaller than Nico. What if Nico decided that he was a rat or some other kind of prey? She couldn't imagine how he had gotten so large. Was it something they were feeding him? A spell? Gwythr didn't seem to think that it was anything unusual.

From the beginning, they had seemed to recognize him as something different, but familiar. Had they once had kattakyns in the dwarf kingdom? It seemed unlikely. But by now she should be used to dealing with things that were unlikely.

Reg reached her hand out to Nico tentatively. She remembered how he had often slashed at her or fought back against her before she had brought him to the dwarfs. If he were to slash her now with those bear-like claws, the results would be far worse. A scratch from a kitten was something she could handle. Considering the injury, she would get from Nico now was sobering.

"Hi, Nico. Do you remember me? Remember how I used to feed you treats and how I brought you to the mountain?" Hopefully, these happy memories would make him well-disposed to her and he wouldn't be thinking of the way that she had yelled at him when he had intentionally knocked things down or broken something of hers.

Nico sniffed her hand and rubbed his jaw against it, his rough fur brushing it gently. Reg scratched tentatively, and he started a loud, rumbling purr, rubbing his face, cheeks, and ears against her like a kitten.

"Yeah? You remember me?"

He gave her hand a brief lick with his long, rasping tongue.

"Yeah, you're a good boy. Gwythr says that you are a very good warrior cat. He is very pleased with you. And look at how big you have gotten."

Nico continued to rub against her and purr. He even flopped onto his side and lifted his front leg for her to rub his belly, but Reg knew that trick. He might enjoy having his belly rubbed for a minute, but then he would attack, and she did not want those big, powerful back legs raking down her arm. Ouch.

"You're just a big kitten, aren't you? Do you want to see Horace? Do you remember your brother?"

Reg tapped the cat carrier, and Nico turned his attention to it. He sniffed the carrier and shuffled closer to it, looking in through the grill on the front. Reg couldn't see Horace, but could hear him snuffling inside the carrier as well. Was he afraid of Nico? Or was he just interested? Did he recognize his fellow kattakyn? Since he no longer bore a piece of the Witch Doctor, was there a relationship between them? Or was Horace just like any cat Nico might meet in an alley?

"Nico and Horace," Reg said softly. "Two kattakyns from the same litter. Do you remember?"

She wondered if it was right to call them littermates, since they weren't actually kittens born to the same mother. She had called them that to Gwythr to avoid having to explain where they had come from. Keep the story simple. But was that the word she should use when she talked to the kattakyns?

They were draugrs raised from the dead by the Witch Doctor to serve him. Comrades in arms? That might be closer.

Nico nosed against the grill of the carrier and turned to look at her, waiting for her to open it. Reg read him the best she could. He didn't seem angry or as though he wanted to hunt. He seemed friendly enough toward Horace. Gwythr hadn't seemed to be worried that he might attack Horace. It seemed natural to him that they would want to visit and that Reg would let Horace out of his cage once Nico arrived.

"You want me to open it?"

He moved over, rubbing against her hand again, nudging her toward the carrier.

"And you're going to be nice? You're not going to do anything to hurt Horace, right?"

He purred loudly, still encouraging her. Finally, Reg nodded. She released the catch on the front of the carrier and carefully swung the door open. She could see Horace's black, furry face, but he didn't dart out once he had the opportunity. He sat hunched over where he was, watching Reg and looking past her to Nico.

"Do you want to come out and see Nico? Do you remember you used to play together? When you lived with Francesca?"

Horace's eyes went from Reg to Nico and back again, looking remarkably like a worried child.

"It's okay," Reg assured him. "He's not going to hurt you."

And she really hoped that she was right. They would get along just fine together. They were happy to see each other and would play together and renew their acquaintance, just like when Starlight and Nicole got to have a play date.

Horace's nose wiggled and his nostrils flared as he sniffed and sniffed, gathering all the information he could from the air in the room. Reg had often wondered what it would be like to be an animal, able to sense danger by the smell, able to seek out even the smallest scent trails to track down what they were looking for. Smelling the grass where other animals had been and knowing all about them just from their smell.

But Reg had also lived with Erin, the super-smeller, and had quickly learned that being able to smell things that no one else could was not a superpower. Erin was always the first one to get sick around a putrid smell. She would be running to the bathroom to throw up before anyone else was even aware of something nasty. And that did not impress Reg as a talent she wanted. Better to have a gift like hers, being able to cold read people and make quick judgments about them. That was far more beneficial than being able to follow a scent trail.

CHAPTER TWENTY-FOUR

*H*orace poked his face out from the carrier. He and Nico touched noses. Reg felt suddenly dizzy and had to hold on to the chair to keep from tipping over. She sat very straight, trying to keep herself focused on the two kattakyns. But both of them seemed to be vibrating, blurring in front of her eyes.

Reg shook her head. She closed her eyes for a few seconds and then opened them, hoping her vision would clear. What was wrong? Had she expended too much energy without realizing it? Let herself get dehydrated? She had eaten before she had jumped to the dwarf mountain, so she should have been just fine. Maybe she was coming down with something.

She rubbed her eyes and looked at the kattakyns again, wanting to keep an eye on them and make sure that everything was okay. If Nico showed any signs of bullying or stalking Horace, or if Horace looked afraid, she needed to be able to react, not to be swooning in her seat.

Horace's fur was puffed out. Reg reached down to touch him. "Are you okay, Horace?"

He turned his head to look at her, but did not lay his ears back or look upset. He just looked puffier than usual. But when Reg touched him, his fur did not seem to be standing up, but was lying flat as usual.

"You're okay, then?"

He made a soft noise in his throat that Reg thought was meant to reassure her. She withdrew her hand and left him alone so that he and Nico could get reacquainted. There was a lot of sniffing, and some meowing and licking. The two of them seemed to be getting along together just fine. Reg relaxed. It was okay. Nico hadn't become a monster during his time with the dwarfs. He had grown bigger, but he didn't appear to have become vicious. Maybe he was even calmer than he had been when he'd been living with her. He'd had some quiet moments with Starlight in the days that he had spent at Reg's house, but most of the time he'd been climbing the walls. Or the curtains. Or the bookshelf. Or Reg's leg.

He was a little large to be climbing up her leg now!

Maybe the training regimen with the dwarfs had calmed him down, had allowed him to work out his energy and aggression in an acceptable way so that he could be calm the rest of the time.

"You're just a big pussycat now, aren't you?" Reg asked him.

Nico shot her a look. Big pussycat was clearly not the way that he preferred to be addressed.

Reg giggled.

Horace was sniffing the floor and starting to explore the room, apparently having completed the prolonged greeting ritual with Nico. Just two tomcats out having a good time. He stepped on her foot as he went by her, and Reg pushed him away and pulled her foot back.

"Ouch! You're heavier than you look. Watch where you're going."

Horace didn't even look at her. Reg looked at him and looked at the carrier. She had been holding the carrier not an hour earlier. She knew how heavy he was. He was a large cat, but he wasn't that big. Not like Nico. But his weight when he had stepped on her seemed disproportionate to how much he had weighed when she was holding the cat carrier. And looking at him, she wasn't even sure whether he would fit back into the carrier again when it was time to go.

"Did you *grow?*" Reg demanded, having difficulty believing what she was seeing. Horace wasn't a kitten anymore. He was a full-grown cat. He shouldn't still be growing. And he certainly shouldn't be growing fast enough for Reg to notice a difference from one moment to the next.

But surely he was bigger than he had been just a few minutes earlier. Was it something about the dwarf mountain? Starlight hadn't gotten any bigger when he had visited. Horace hadn't eaten or drunk anything, so it wasn't something he had consumed. He had just made friends with Nico, a very large warrior cat. Had they put a spell on him that was affecting Horace? Maybe he was radioactive. Reg couldn't think of any other explanation for what she was seeing.

Hopefully, Gwythr would be back before Horace got so large that he would not fit back in the carrier again.

* * *

Reg's phone rang. She looked at the caller ID. Marian. Reg swallowed, thinking about what she would say. She answered the call and sounded as casual as possible.

"Hi, Marian."

"I'm home now, Reg. You can bring Horace over any time."

"Great. He and Starlight are just playing right now, so I'll wait until they're done. Better if he gets plenty of exercise before coming over to your house. Then maybe he'll be quiet tonight. And I don't want to take him away in the middle of their game. I think Horace is already having enough trouble with the back-and-forth without making it worse by interrupting him in the middle of something."

"That's fine," Marian agreed. "Anytime is fine, as long as I can still get to sleep in good time to get up in the morning."

Reg was sure that Marian didn't sleep as long as she did. Not when she opened her store in the morning, even if it were late morning. "Yeah. What time is bedtime for you?" She did a quick check-in with herself. Were the dwarf mountain and Black Sands both in the same time zone? She was pretty sure that they were.

"Say... eleven o'clock?" Marian suggested. "You won't have any trouble getting here before then, will you? I thought when we talked the last time that you were in a hurry."

"I guess I was. But things have settled down since then and the cats are having a good time, so I'm more relaxed. I can have him there by eleven o'clock. No problem. I have clients coming before then anyway."

"Okay. See you in a while."

* * *

Gwythr had said that he would get back to her as quickly as he could, so Reg wasn't too worried that he would keep her for hours. He wanted the gems in his hand again by the time that she left. If the way that Reg felt about water and fire were at all similar to the way that dwarfs felt about gemstones, the gems would be calling to him now. He would be intent on making sure that she did not leave before he could negotiate a fair payment between them.

She watched the kattakyns. They didn't do anything else of concern. She swiped on her phone and scrolled through videos, looking for something to entertain herself until Gwythr's return.

Eventually, the door opened and Gwythr entered. He looked at the cats and nodded. He took his seat at the table again, and slid a stapled stack of papers over to Reg.

She looked down at it and flipped past the cover page and table of contents, looking for the bottom line. On the third page was a bold number in a box, with details around it. Reg blinked at the number and read the words above it. It was, in fact, Gwythr's offer for the gems.

"Is this right?" she asked, pointing to it.

Gwythr nodded. "As you can see, the flavor of the gems did increase the offer significantly. I can't afford to go too high. I can't jeopardize my family's wealth for one purchase. But I hoped that this would be enough to… keep you interested."

Reg nodded. She feigned a frown, pushing her brows down as she studied the paperwork. She flipped through the pages slowly but wasn't actually reading anything else. This part was all for show. She would take the amount that he had offered in an instant. It was significantly higher than the jeweler she had gone to had appraised the gems at.

Gwythr made comments as she looked through the details of the offer, pointing out similar transactions that he had reviewed, as much as he could discern about the origins of the gems, their powers and personalities.

"How long will it take you to get this much together?" Reg asked eventually. He would need to at least make a deposit before she would leave the gems with him. Even a deposit would be a nice little injection into her bank account.

"My sons are getting it together now." Gwythr pulled out his phone and looked at the face. "I think… another twenty minutes or so. You will excuse them if it takes a little longer… I do not wish to keep you here longer than you intended…"

"Twenty minutes is fine."

He was going to give her the entire amount right away? Reg's face flushed. She'd never had a windfall like that before. It was one thing to receive the gems from the fairies. It had been pretty exciting once she had realized that they were real gems and not just glass. But she had discovered that having the gems wasn't nearly as beneficial as actually being able to do something with them. Merely owning them and keeping them hidden in her closet or under her bed didn't bestow any advantages. They didn't pay the bills.

CHAPTER TWENTY-FIVE

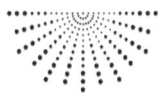

*A*fter Reg signed the formal document accepting his offer, Gwythr's gaze wandered to the cats. He watched them interacting with each other. Like Reg, he looked at the cat carrier and then back at Horace. He frowned.

"Your new cat..."

"Horace."

"Horace. He has... has he grown?"

Reg nodded. "Yeah. I was wondering about that. I thought that maybe it was something to do with Nico, with whatever it was that made him grow so big."

Gwythr considered this thoughtfully. "I am not sure... it does not usually work this way. It takes time and training for a warrior cat to grow."

"But you must have done something to make Nico grow so large, and that somehow... rubbed off on Horace?"

"It is very strange."

Gwythr watched Horace for a while. He looked at Reg, and she caught him staring at her rings again.

"Do you want to see them?" Reg asked. He was obviously curious about them. But maybe handing such a thing to a dwarf would not be a good idea. Gwythr had been fair with her about the gems, giving her more than they had been appraised at, but that was no guarantee that he wouldn't try to take the rings from her on some pretext. If she handed them over and he took off with them, there wasn't much she would be able to do about it. With so many armored dwarfs at Gwythr's command, and who knew how many others in the mountain, she didn't stand much of a chance, even if she used her powers.

Gwythr made a motion for her to keep them to herself. "They would be difficult to resist," he informed her. "Difficult for any dwarf."

"I'm not trying to tempt you. But I couldn't really leave them at home."

"No. You could not leave something so valuable so vulnerable to thieves." His eyes were fixed on the rings. "Though, I am not sure that they are safe on thy fingers, either."

Reg squirmed at this observation. What could she do if someone did try to steal them? She had powers. She could not be overcome by just anyone. But if she were taken unaware? If someone attacked her before she knew what was happening, they might be able to kill her or make off with the rings. And if there were more than one attacker, that was another possibility. She couldn't be sure of being able to fight off a physical or magical attack if there were enough attackers banded together, like the dwarf army or a few magical beings allied together, as when she and Corvin, Damon, and Francesca had fought the Witch Doctor. Several kinds of powers originating from several different directions... There was definitely a danger in being overwhelmed.

"I'm going to Egypt soon," she explained. "To return them to their rightful owners. Until then... I think this is where they are safest, even if it isn't ideal."

"You know to whom they belonged?"

"Well... no. I hope to find out once I get there."

Gwythr opened his mouth and closed it again. Reg had a pretty good idea what he was thinking. "I know... I should plan better. Be less impulsive. Get someone to do the research before I go over there..."

"Perhaps," he agreed with a nod. "But it is thy choice. They are powerful. They will call to someone." He stroked his long beard. "Hopefully... not a *lot* of people. It could be very difficult if there are many people who would claim them. And with symbols so ancient and powerful... there may be many who feel their pull."

Reg hadn't thought very much about what would happen when she got back to Egypt. She hoped that by using the rings and the gems to jump her there, that she would land in the right location. The proper owners of the treasure would be close at hand and it would be quick to complete their transaction. In and out in just a few hours, like Reg's trip to the dwarf mountain to see Nico and talk to Gwythr about the stones.

"Take care," Gwythr warned. "One must take great care in a case such as this."

"I will," Reg agreed. But was she? Or was she expecting the universe to come to her aid again? Harrison appearing and taking over if she were attacked. Friends helping her and advising her, knowing what she needed to know at just the right moment. Inspiration in the face of danger.

She wasn't exactly well-known for carefully planning things out ahead of time.

* * *

Before they could get too deeply into the conversation about avoiding dangers in Egypt, there was a soft knock on the door.

"Enter, my sons," Gwythr called.

Two men entered. They were noticeably younger than Gwythr, but Reg wasn't sure of his age or theirs. Gwythr's beard was long and gray, and his two sons had shorter, black beards. They were trimmed and groomed, and it would be some time before they could grow beards as long as their father. They stepped into the room and bowed formally to Reg.

"The great Reg Rawlins," one of them intoned in a serious voice.

Reg rolled her eyes but didn't correct them. While she didn't like to be addressed in such honorifics, she was getting used to it. And she supposed that knowing her gave Gwythr and his sons a good rep with the other dwarfs, so she was careful not to disparage the title. She gave them each a nod, hoping that was enough.

"I'm... honored to meet you," she told them, stumbling a little. "Your father is a very great dwarf."

Their eyes shone at this and smiles twitched under their beards. They stepped forward in unison, each bearing a business envelope on outstretched hand. Reg glanced at Gwythr, and took both envelopes, keeping an eye on each dwarf to make sure she did not misstep.

One envelope was thinner, and she opened that one first. It was a certified check in her name. The numbers on it didn't quite match the offer she had signed, but there was the second envelope.

"Banks sometimes hold funds such as this for ten business days to make sure that it clears," Gwythr explained. "Even though the funds have been certified."

Reg nodded. She'd never had a check for so much money before, but she had heard of things like that. Anti-fraud measures. She opened the second envelope, which was filled with hundred-dollar bills.

"The cash portion, as per our agreement." Gwythr nodded toward the offer that Reg had signed, apparently agreeing to the payment being split between cash and certified check. "It is our practice to always make sure that part of the payment is liquid and can be used immediately."

Reg folded the cash and the check and put them into opposite pockets in her skirt. "That's very thoughtful. Thank you."

"There are often expenses that must be paid. We do not agree with banks holding money that has been certified, but that is the world we live in. So we try to reduce the inconvenience."

"Very wise," Reg agreed. "It has been a pleasure working with you."

"I hope that Reg Rawlins will come to us again, if she needs to liquidate more gems such as these."

The two sons nodded their agreement. Reg smiled and let out

a slight chuckle. "I might have others. But this will keep me afloat for quite a while."

She let her mind wander to the number on the check. She hadn't thought about what she would do with a windfall like that. Buy a house of her own? A new car? Invest in something that would bring in even more money later? She'd never been in a position before to consider long-term savings and investments. When she got the gems, she had started to dream of world travel. Not just going back to see Erin if everything seemed to be quiet in Tennessee, but maybe going on a cruise or a flight around the world taking her to far-flung destinations she had only heard of before. Or maybe a few that she had never heard of, seeing sights that she had never imagined. With the addition of magical species, the world was even bigger and more interesting than she had thought. She had gotten a very small taste of that in Black Sands and at the Spring Games.

"You will keep us in mind," Gwythr said with another bow.

Reg nodded. She stood. "Now… I'd better get this cat back in the box."

CHAPTER TWENTY-SIX

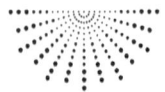

They all looked at Horace. Reg hoped that he only looked so large because of his fluffiness. She didn't want to have to actually squeeze him into the carrier.

"Another warrior cat?" one of the sons asked.

"I think he was just influenced a bit by Nico," Reg explained.

"And the power of your ring," he commented, nodding to Reg's hand.

"Shh." The quick warning came from Gwythr like the air escaping from a bike tire when Reg pulled the pump from the valve. A sharp hissing sound, quickly cut off.

The dwarf who had spoken turned red. Reg looked at him and then at Gwythr.

"*What* about my ring?"

"It is very poor manners," Gwythr said, shooting a glance at the offender.

"I want to hear anyway. You think it is my ring that made Horace grow?"

Gwythr looked uncomfortable. "These rings are powerful. They might magnify the magic of another spell."

"What spell? Whatever made Nico grow so big?"

"It would not be usual…" Gwythr shook his head, looking at

the two cats. "A spell does not expand or rub off on another crea-ture. But... perhaps. Your cats are... unusual, and the rings are very powerful. Ancient magic... the curse upon the rings... They can behave unpredictably. Perhaps in ways that we are not familiar with."

So he had noticed that the cats were *unusual*.

Not just two identical black cats from the same litter, but something unexpected and different. He hadn't asked her what that was. Perhaps that would have been poor manners. But it was clear from his words and his glances toward the cats that he knew there was something going on that she hadn't told him about.

"Can you tell me anything about the rings?" Reg asked, holding her hand toward Gwythr so that he could examine them again if he needed to refresh his memory. "Other than the fact that they are ancient and from Egypt?"

He took her hand gently in his strong, roughened fingers, but didn't touch the rings. His lips twitched as he studied them care-fully. He raised his eyes to her face and didn't let go of her hand.

"They are powerful. The coronation rings of a ruler. A symbol of his office. When whole, they will do the bidding of their owner. But cursed as they are, I would not try to wield them."

"Does that mean I shouldn't wear them? Or just that I shouldn't... try to make them do anything? I don't even know how you command a ring."

He chuckled softly. "You know much more than you think you do, Reg Rawlins. Or else you toy with me."

"But I can wear them? That isn't a danger?"

"As you said, it would be more of a danger to leave them somewhere unprotected. But you need to be cautious. They will enhance your powers, which are already great. And you may find them doing things... that you do not wish." He looked down at Horace again.

Reg sighed. She knew she needed to get to Egypt as soon as she could. Before the rings disrupted anything else. Who knew what else they could do? If they could take the magic that had been used on Nico to make Horace grow, what might they do with Corvin's power? Or Harrison's, the next time he came to visit her? Filling her fridge with cake and ice cream was one thing. But Harrison's powers extended far beyond that. She didn't want to inadvertently use his power to go back in time, put a curse on someone or make them disappear, or any of the other powers she had seen Harrison exercise. He might play the fool sometimes, but he was cunning and knew and understood far more than he pretended to.

"Thank you. You've been really helpful."

"I look forward to doing business again in the future," Gwythr agreed with a bow.

Reg stood up. She bent down to pet Horace. "Did you have a nice visit? It was nice to see Nico again, wasn't it?" She extended her fingers to Nico and, when he sniffed them and then rubbed against them, she scratched his ears. "I'm glad to see how well you're doing here," Reg told him. "You are so big and strong, and you look great in that armor. The dwarfs must be very proud of you."

Nico purred loudly.

"Now, let's go home," Reg told Horace. She pressed his side, directing him back toward the cat carrier. He resisted, which didn't surprise her. Of course he didn't want to go back inside the little cage when he had grown so much. It would be very tight quarters. "It's just for a short trip," Reg encouraged. "Just to make sure that you can't get lost along the way. I would not want anything to happen to you."

He yowled at her, not pleased. Reg pressed him again, alert and ready for him to try to bite or claw her. He might not be as big as Nico, but he still had larger than usual teeth and claws, and she wasn't in any mood to find out if they were proportionally sharper and more powerful.

"Come on, Horace. Just hop back inside for a few minutes."

One of the rings on Reg's finger grew warm and Horace's coat crackled with static electricity. Horace gave a sharp yap that sounded more like a dog than a cat, and he allowed himself to be herded into the carrier. Reg shut and latched the door.

He was too large to turn around inside the carrier to face the door, as he had done earlier. She hoped that he didn't feel too claustrophobic. But she didn't want to try transporting him without the carrier. If he got it into his head to cause mischief, he could do a lot of damage in a very short period of time.

"Good boy," she told him. "Thank you. That's very good."

Horace sneezed.

Reg patted Nico on the side, thumping his armor. "Bye, Nico. Be good and listen to the dwarfs."

She bent over to pick up the cat carrier, which was much heavier than it had been since the last time she had held it. She hoped that everything was well-constructed so that the bottom would not separate from the top. She braced the muscles in her arm. She closed her eyes, and pictured being home.

CHAPTER TWENTY-SEVEN

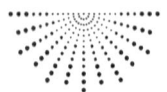

*R*eg opened her eyes and looked around her cottage with satisfaction. Traveling by magic was so much easier than having to drive for hours on end. It took a little of her energy, but not enough that she felt weak or wanted to sleep. Just a bit of fatigue, as if she'd been lifting weights and then stopped.

Speaking of lifting weights...

Reg put the cat carrier down and stretched her arms and shoulders. Horace definitely was not all fluff. While she could have jumped directly over to Marian's house, Reg didn't think it would be advisable. Just as she didn't know all the proper etiquette for dealing with dwarfs, she didn't know what the unwritten rules were about appearing in someone else's house, even if Marian had told Reg to come over any time. She had meant to come over in the car, not magically. Reg didn't particularly like the fact that the immortals could appear in her house without warning, despite the protective wards. She assumed that Marian would feel the same about Reg using her powers to get into her house.

After resting her arms for a few minutes, Reg picked up Horace's carrier with the opposite hand. It felt even heavier on that side. Taking quick, short steps, Reg went to the door and let herself out. She put the carrier down to lock the door, then picked it up again and headed to her car.

She didn't make it.

The carrier was very heavy, and Reg had to stop to put it down and take another break. She was doing the best that she could, but it was a much more difficult job than it had been the last time she had taken Horace to Marian's.

"Where are you going?"

Reg startled at the voice that came from the gathering shadows. She instantly thought of the Witch Doctor, Wilson, Weston, and finally settled on Corvin. Of course Corvin. Lurking around her yard, hoping to be able to sneak past the wards or catch a glimpse of her.

"Don't you know how to use the phone?" Reg snapped. "You're not supposed to be around here."

"I wanted to see you."

"I have things to do. As you can see."

They both looked down at the cat carrier.

"Where are you taking him?" Corvin asked, stepping out of the shadows. He picked up the carrier and started to walk toward Reg's car. "Did you find him a new home?"

"To Marian's. She's agreed to take him... but he keeps coming back."

"Like a bad penny," Corvin said. He switched the carrier from one hand to the other and marched more deliberately toward Reg's car. "Good grief, what are you feeding this guy, Regina?"

Reg didn't try to explain. She didn't understand well enough herself what was going on with Horace. If the dwarfs, who could grow humongous cats, did not understand what was going on, then how was she supposed to know?

They reached the car and Corvin put the carrier down on the sidewalk beside it.

"Are you going to Egypt?" he asked suspiciously.

"Yes. Oh, you mean now? Not now. Just to Marian's right now."

He eyed her as though he didn't believe it for a moment. He

knew that she must be trying to pull something over on him. Reg looked directly back into his eyes, challengingly.

"I told you where I'm going. If you don't like it or don't believe me, that's your problem. Not mine."

"Do you have any other luggage?" Corvin looked around.

Reg offered her empty hands. She had only the big purse over her shoulder. "Do you see any?"

"You might have already sent it on ahead. Or you might think that you won't be in Egypt long enough to need anything but your shoulder bag. Which looks suspiciously hefty…"

Reg straightened a turn in the strap of the purse so that it lay flat on her shoulder. She didn't like the look in his eye, the suggestion that he would dig into her purse and find out the truth. Just as he had said he would search through her memories to find what he wanted.

"You're not welcome here," she told him sternly. "Go back to your own house or I'll call the police."

"You wouldn't call the police."

"I could."

Corvin shrugged. "I could do a lot of things. I could be on the next flight to the moon. But you know what? I'm not. Just like you won't call the police on me."

He looked very sure of himself. Reg was tempted to call the police just to prove him wrong and to show that she didn't have to do anything he said. But she held herself back.

"Thank you for helping me with the cat."

She picked up the carrier and put it onto the front passenger seat. It would be too awkward to wrap the seatbelt around it. She would have to just be a careful driver and make sure she didn't make any sudden starts or stops that might make it slide on the seat.

"You should put it in the back," Corvin advised. "On the floor behind one of the seats. That would be safer."

"It's fine there," Reg told him. "There isn't space behind the seats."

"It could slide off the seat."

She glared at him. What business was it of his? He just wanted to tell her what to do.

"Okay, okay," he held his hands up. "No need to freak out about it. Just trying to help."

"I didn't ask for your help, okay? I'm just fine how I am. You're not supposed to be hanging out in my yard waiting to ambush me. You're supposed to be at your house, doing whatever it is that you do."

"I wanted to talk to you about Egypt."

"I'm not talking to you about it. You just get all controlling."

"I do not," Corvin protested haughtily.

"You're always telling me what to do. I'm not taking you. It doesn't have anything to do with you."

"But your safety is important to me. The only reason I want to come is—"

"I'm not sure why you think you should come along with me, but I know it's not because you want to keep me safe."

"Regina." He used that hurt-puppy look and injured voice that she hated. She knew that she hadn't hurt him. His ego didn't depend on her strokes. She knew that he was lying about just wanting to keep her safe, and so did he. She shouldn't have to act as if she believed his lies.

Reg stepped back from the car and slammed the door. "I'm leaving. Goodbye. Take yourself home. You'd better not still be here when I get back."

"Maybe I could help you. Escort you to Marian's."

"You are *not* escorting me," Reg snapped. He just wanted an excuse to keep an eye on her, and she'd had enough. He didn't need to know what she was doing every minute of the day. And he didn't need to go to Egypt with her.

Reg went around to the driver's side, slid into her seat, and slammed that door too, eliminating the possibility of any further discussion. She started the engine, then made sure that the cat carrier was all the way back on the seat before putting the car into drive. As irritated as she was by Corvin's appearance, she drove slowly and carefully. She didn't want to make it any more stressful on Horace than it had to be. She certainly didn't want to get into an accident where he could be injured.

They made it safely to Marian's house. Reg sat there for a few minutes, just breathing and trying to slow her rapidly beating heart and calm herself down.

Horace gave a low meow. He wanted out. Hadn't he spent enough time in the cramped carrier already? Reg had said it would only be for a few minutes and it had been longer than that.

"Yes. I'm ready. Let's go inside."

Motion-activated lights went on as they walked up the sidewalk to Marian's front door, and she opened the door shortly after Reg rang the doorbell. Though Reg still had to wait a minute and put the carrier down to ease the muscle fatigue she was getting from carrying it. Marian obviously wasn't standing at the door watching for her.

"Come in." Marian watched Reg pick up the carrier again and bring it inside. "How has this little beggar been behaving?"

"He's fine," Reg assured her. "Everything is just fine."

She opened the cage and, since Horace did not have the space to turn around, he backed out.

"Well, he'd better stay here now. This is where he is supposed to be. If he keeps disappearing… I won't be responsible for him."

"I'm sure he'll be okay now."

"Reg… what happened to this cat?"

Reg looked at Horace, trying to think of something to say. Something funny like that he had shrunk in the wash. But of course, he had gotten bigger, and she couldn't think of an appropriate joke to say for that.

"He's… uh… put on a little weight."

"In a *day?*"

"Yes."

"This is not Horace," Marian insisted. "It couldn't be."

"Check for yourself," Reg suggested.

"How am I supposed to tell him apart from any other black cat? I know because he doesn't look the same. He's huge."

"You can feel that he's the same cat, can't you?" Reg suggested. "Use your psychic senses and you'll recognize him."

"I can't do that. My gift does not extend to cats."

Not that Horace was a cat. But she wasn't about to tell Marian that.

"Then you'll have to trust me. He is the same cat."

Marian shook her head, looking at Horace.

"He's the same cat," Reg insisted.

"Then how did he get so big?"

Reg floundered for an explanation. "Have you ever heard of a warrior cat?"

"A warrior cat? No. Are you trying to tell me that he is one?"

Reg hesitated before shaking her head. It would make sense. It would be a good explanation. But Reg didn't really want Marian asking questions about dwarfs and cats and finding out that Reg wasn't exactly telling the truth.

"No, but he was visiting one today. And they think that... some of the magic that they use when training Nico might have accidentally rubbed off on him while they were visiting."

"Who is *they*? And Nico? I thought you were at your house; you said he was playing with Starlight."

"He was... but earlier, we went to visit Nico. I thought they might have some answers about Horace's behavior," Reg lied. It might not have been a bad idea to ask, but then she would have had to explain about the kattakyns and what if they said that they wouldn't keep Nico? She couldn't exactly take him back. Especially now that he was so large.

"They?" Marian prompted again.

"Oh. The dwarfs."

"The dwarfs," Marian repeated in a tone of disbelief. "There are no dwarfs around here."

Reg shrugged and didn't try to give an explanation. If she said that they had gone to the Blue Ridge Mountains and back, then Marian would think she was crazy or lying. Or else she would have to explain about her ability to magically transport from one location to the another. And she really didn't want to explain all of that. Marian was already somewhat jealous of Reg's gifts. She didn't need to know how much more there was to it that she hadn't been told about.

"Are you hungry?" Marian asked Horace.

Horace's ears perked up and he looked at Marian eagerly.

"Let's go get some dinner," she told him.

Horace trotted ahead of Marian toward the kitchen where his food bowl was located. Marian shot a glance toward Reg. That was, at least, one sign that Horace was who Reg said he was. Of course, any cat might find his way to the kitchen by smell, but Horace plopped his wide behind down next to his food bowl and waited expectantly. Reg smiled.

"You see? It is Horace."

"That being the case," Marian looked at him. "I'm not sure he needs anything else to eat."

Horace let out a mournful howl. Reg laughed. "He didn't get big from eating too much. It isn't his fault."

Horace meowed, looking at Marian and licking his lips.

Marian gave in and put some food in Horace's bowl. He chowed down immediately.

"I have a feeling he is going to be expensive to feed," Marian commented, hands on her hips, looking down at him.

"He'll probably be extra hungry for a few days and then settle down," Reg suggested. "You know, like a kid going through a growth spurt."

She spoke this as if she were an expert in giant cats and raising children, when she didn't have experience with either one. Marian eyed her, but didn't point out this fact. But Reg couldn't help feeling Marian's doubt and her reluctance to take Horace back. It was, Reg suspected, the last time she would be able to take Horace back. If he came back to her one more time, Marian would say no. She'd had enough.

"Thank you for taking him," Reg told her. "I really appreciate it. I know it hasn't been easy."

"No, it hasn't. He'd better be on his best behavior tonight."

Thinking about the mess outside of the litter box earlier, Reg couldn't help but be anxious about how it would work out. Where was she going to take Horace if Marian wouldn't keep him? And what was she going to do if he kept reappearing in her cottage? How exactly was she going to explain that to Sarah? And how could she stop him from returning?

How was it she could fight immortals and other beings with great powers, but she couldn't persuade one black cat to stay at his new home and stop reappearing in hers?

CHAPTER TWENTY-EIGHT

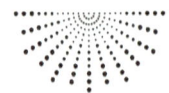

*I*t had been a long day. After everything else, she'd had several readings and a seance to lead, so it wasn't until early in the morning she could relax and make her way to bed. It took a while for her to unwind, and she knew it would be getting light out just as she was falling asleep.

But that was fine. She wouldn't have any more meetings until the next evening. She could sleep however long she wanted. She didn't have to get up for Starlight or Sarah or anyone else who thought there was something wrong with her sleep schedule. It was what worked for her and that was all there was to it.

She tossed and turned restlessly for some time, halfway between dreams and waking. She sank deeper into the dreams, trying to make sense of them. She recognized the funny looking script on the signs. That and the piles of garbage in the street and the dress of the people around her told her that she was back in Egypt. That was good. She had known that she needed to go back to Egypt to find the rightful owner of the gems. Now she was there. A tall Black man with a turban wrapped around his head walked beside her, just slightly in front of her, leading the way through the crowds. Reg didn't like having so many people around her. She had never had a problem with crowds or claustrophobia, but she couldn't shake the feeling that they were watching her. They were all watching her.

Why? They too could sense the gems. They knew she was carrying something valuable. Even with the rings turned in toward her palm so that no one could see the gems in the settings, she knew they still shone like a beacon, calling out to any magical practitioners in the immediate area.

They were all just watching for the opportunity to take the gems and the rings from her. Waiting for her to get distracted. Lying in wait. They were all around her, knowing who she was and what she carried, knowing that when she found the rightful owner of the gems, she would give them away. *Give them away. Something as precious as that. Who would do such a thing?*

"They aren't mine," Reg explained to the people hemming her in. "I am just holding them temporarily. They were stolen, taken away from their rightful owners. They can't be used by anyone else. They are cursed!"

It felt like the rings were writhing on her fingers, trying to work themselves loose. Reg closed her hands into fists, trying to hold on to them.

There were so many people, they were kicking up the dust and breathing all the oxygen. Reg couldn't seem to catch her breath.

"Come on. Give me some space," she puffed. "I can't breathe."

Still the crowds pressed in on her. Reg put her hand on her chest, straining. There was a dull ache spreading across her chest. Was she having a heart attack?

"Can't... help?"

There was a caterwaul in response, startling Reg out of her sleep. She took a huge breath in, but still couldn't seem to get any air. The pressure on her chest grew.

More cat voices. It sounded like a fight. Two cats arguing over territory.

Then the pressure was suddenly gone. Reg sat up. She panted, getting as much air in as quickly as she could. There were a few more yowls, not as angry, and then they tapered off. Starlight jumped up on the bed and nosed at her.

"Hey, Star," Reg puffed. "How are you, bud?"

She was dizzy and lightheaded, black spots dancing before her eyes. But she would be okay in a few minutes. It was just a bad reaction to a nightmare.

Starlight rubbed against her and pushed his way into her lap so that she would hold him and pet him.

Sunlight was streaming in through the window. It would make sense for Reg to get blackout blinds, considering that most of the time she spent in bed it was light outside. But she didn't like to block out the sun. And Starlight wouldn't like it if she blocked the sunbeams he liked to sleep in.

Reg startled when one of the shadows in the closet moved.

"What? What's that?"

Starlight put his ears back, looking at the shape, and gave a low growl in his throat, reminding Reg of the caterwauling she had heard as she woke up from the dream.

"Was that you growling? Is there something in here?"

The shape moved again, and Reg laughed in relief. It was Horace. Horace had come back yet again, and was sniffing around the closet, probably looking for somewhere dark to hide and get some sleep. With Reg talking or shouting out in her dreams, she was probably keeping him awake.

"Horace! What are you doing here? I told you that you were supposed to stay at Marian's. That is your home now, not here."

He meowed in response. A soft, almost kitten-like mew. Reg tried to analyze it, reaching for his feelings.

They were unexpected. Shame, fear, a restlessness and sadness that nearly broke her heart. *Didn't anyone want him? Why couldn't he stay where he wanted to?*

But he couldn't. That was Sarah's decision, not Reg's.

"Come here, Horace. Come get some pets and cuddles. I'm sorry you can't stay here. You need to stop coming back in the night. It isn't because I don't like you, just that I'm not allowed to keep you here. Harrison shouldn't have brought you here to begin with."

After a bit more coaxing, Horace jumped up onto the bed.

Reg laughed at the way that it shook when he jumped up. Starlight watched the other cat with suspicion. He knew, of course, that Horace was not an ordinary cat. Horace tried to crawl into Reg's lap like Starlight, but he was too big. He was no lightweight, either. He was good, solid muscle.

She remembered the dream she'd had when they were trying to figure out what the Witch Doctor was doing. Corvin had told Reg about the draugrs, but she didn't really understand what he was talking about. And he hadn't told her everything he knew, just hit a few of the high points.

He had explained to her that the dead that the Witch Doctor raised to become zombies could grow into giants or could shrink down into cats. They could look like a man, or be indistinguishable from any of the other stray cats out there.

Reg didn't know whether the draugr cats—the kattakyns—came in colors other than black. All the ones that the Witch Doctor had created had been pure black, but that didn't mean that other practitioners of the dark arts couldn't give them other markings, like Starlight's tuxedo, socks, and star. Or like a tabby cat. Or maybe they could be ginger cats or calicos instead of black.

She'd had a dream about one of the kattakyns. In the dream, it had lain on her chest. That was fine when it was the size of a small house cat. But as it had lain there, it had grown heavier and heavier, and Reg had experienced that same shortness of breath as in the Egypt dream. Until Starlight had attacked and chased the kattakyn in her dream away.

Others had not been so lucky. There had been several reports of people who had died in their sleep behind locked doors from asphyxia and crush injuries. Reg had been the one to suggest that the draugr cats might have done it, as one had tried to do to her. Corvin had confirmed the legends that the draugrs could kill that way, and that was all the proof that Reg needed. Her own experience, backed up by Corvin's studies.

Reg scratched Horace's ears, looking at him with fresh eyes. Had he been lying on her while she slept and dreamed of Egypt? She petted him in long, even strokes, thinking about it. While he was calming as she petted him, his foremost emotion was still the same.

Shame.

Why shame?

Because he had lain on her and cut off her breath? Because he had put her life in danger until Starlight had chased him off?

"Is that what happened?" Reg asked softly.

How could a creature who seemed so harmless do anything to hurt her? She understood that he was scared and wanted to stay with her, but why hurt her? He might have killed her if Starlight hadn't intervened. Just like those other people had been killed.

Horace buried his nose in Reg's palm and continued to rub against her, purring and drinking up the attention. Reg's eyes burned. What was she going to do with him? How could she manage such a creature?

Draugrs could enter a house through someone's dreams. That must have been how Horace had returned to her night after night when there was no physical way into the house.

She had completely forgotten all of that. Francesca had bound them into their cat form so that they could not shift into the giant draugrs. But none of them had considered that the kattakyns themselves might be dangerous. They were not just cats. Even though they might look like and act like cats, there was another side to them.

And Horace had been unbound. They had all focused on how that meant that a piece of the Witch Doctor was out there, maybe held in the hands of someone who meant to gather all the pieces back together and re-form the Witch Doctor. They had talked about the changes in Horace's behavior.

But they hadn't talked about the fact that he might no longer be bound to his kattakyn form. What if as well as being able to smother her, he could now shift into giant form? Was his growth —and Nico's, for that matter—an indication that he still had some power to shift his form? Or was it just dwarf magic and the power of her rings?

"This is not good," Reg murmured. She continued to pet and

cuddle with Horace, trying to give him all the love and assurance she could. It wasn't his fault. He hadn't chosen his nature any more than she had chosen her parentage or Corvin had chosen his condition.

But what were they going to do if Horace were a dangerous draugr? And what about the rest of them?

CHAPTER TWENTY-NINE

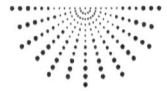

*O*nce both cats were reassured, fed, and snoozing on the bed, Reg started making her plans.

She put aside her worries about the kattakyn, focusing instead on Egypt. She had been promising herself and the gems that she would take them back to Egypt at the earliest possible opportunity, but she kept putting it off. Now she was going to get down to business.

It wasn't because she was avoiding the question of what to do about Horace. She'd been planning to go back to Egypt again for a while. It wasn't anything to do with avoiding more immediate, unpleasant responsibilities.

She wasn't sure how long her trip to Egypt would be. The travel itself was instantaneous, but she didn't know how long she would need to be there to find the rightful owners of the gems. It could be a few days, so she needed to be prepared for that instead of assuming, as she had before, that she would be back in time for supper. She needed to consider food, clothing, and how she would get lodging. She didn't know exactly where she was going, so she couldn't make a hotel reservation ahead of time. But maybe she should at least go to the bank and get some Egyptian money. She wouldn't be able to liquidate any gems on her arrival. She would need cash for food and lodgings. It would be too dangerous to just sleep on the street or find a shelter.

As she packed items into a bag, her phone vibrated in her pocket. Reg considered ignoring it, then decided it might be important and slid it out of her pocket.

Corvin. Of course.

"Hi."

"Regina."

"What do you want, Corvin? I'm kind of busy."

"I did sense that."

"If you know I'm busy, then why are you calling me? I have things to do."

"You're leaving?"

"I didn't say that."

"You don't need to."

She wasn't sure how strong the psychic connection was for him, whether he could see her face or what she was doing. Or could he just sense her restlessness or her intent to leave? It took all of her focus to make her preparations. It shouldn't surprise her that he could sense that.

"You're going to Egypt?" Corvin demanded.

"If I am, it's none of your business."

"I should be there with you. You'll need someone who knows the country. Some of the language."

Though Corvin's language skills had proven not to be quite adequate the last time they had gone to Egypt. He knew some ancient Egyptian. He wasn't so good at the modern stuff.

"I'll be fine."

"Reg, it's too dangerous for a woman to go there unaccompanied."

"For a normal woman, maybe," Reg agreed. "But that's not taking my gifts into account. I can manage myself."

"Like you did when we went to see Kareem?"

Kareem had wielded part of the Witch Doctor's powers. And that, combined with his own natural gifts, had been too much for Reg. She had put a protective shield around herself and Corvin, but then had realized that she couldn't perform any magic from within that bubble of protection. She couldn't jump them back to Florida. She couldn't counterattack. It was a difficult lesson to learn—that a shield was not always the best solution and should not be her first line of defense. She needed to keep herself open to act, preserve her options.

"That's different. And I learned something from that."

"Yes. We both did," Corvin agreed.

"I'm not taking you," Reg reiterated. "Is that everything?"

"You're not thinking clearly. If you were, you would realize that this is a bad idea. You can't just go hopping all over the globe and expect to be able to handle whatever situation you put yourself in."

"Okay, gotta go now." Reg hit the red button to cut off the call. She watched the phone and waited for a moment, knowing that he would call right back. When he did, she rejected the call, sending it directly to voicemail. He tried one more call, and then a series of texts. Reg put down the phone and continued packing.

Reg made all the arrangements that she could think of. Francesca could come by and feed the cats. Reg took her date book over to Sarah and explained that she'd be gone for a day or two, but everything was taken care of and she didn't need to worry about taking care of Starlight or anything else at the cottage. Hopefully, that would keep Sarah from popping by the house while Reg was gone and discovering that Horace—a bigger and more dangerous Horace—was back once more. It was only for a day or two. Then Reg could get everything straightened out.

Even while she prepared herself for the leap to Egypt, Reg couldn't totally banish the problems that Horace presented from her thoughts. How was she supposed to keep him from entering her dreams—or anyone else's—in the future? Starlight had protected her from death by kattakyns twice now, but could she really expect him to always be keeping an eye on her? How could she keep Horace from returning to her house, no matter what kind of home she found for him?

She knew that she was avoiding the real question. Corvin had talked to her, back in the beginning when they first became aware that the Witch Doctor was raising draugrs, about the difficulty of fighting them. There were only a couple of ways to completely kill a draugr. Since they were dead already, most methods didn't have any effect on them. The Vikings had tried to bury bodies deep down underground, with a big tombstone over the grave, to make sure that bodies could not rise again. But that hadn't stopped them.

There was such a disconnect in Reg's mind between the kattakyns and the hideous draugr giants. As if they were two separate beings instead of two different physical forms of the same creature. She couldn't imagine using one of those methods on the cats that she had grown to love. Horace could kill her. It was part of his makeup. But she couldn't even think of hurting him.

She picked up her bag and closed her eyes, trying to calm the rapid beating of her heart and to focus her thoughts on Egypt instead of worrying about Horace. Horace would have to wait until she got back. Maybe if she let the problem simmer in the back of her mind for a couple of days, her unconscious mind would come up with an effortless solution all on its own.

Reg held the gems in the plastic bag in her hand, deep in the pocket of her skirt. With the other hand, she touched the rings, stroking across them with her thumb. She inhaled deeply, remembering the feeling and the smell of the drier air in Egypt. She remembered the heat of the sun on her skin. The pungent smells. The cadences of the language she couldn't understand.

And then she was there.

CHAPTER THIRTY

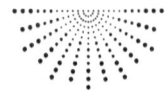

he heat and the dry air. The sounds of the voices around her. All as she had remembered and imagined them. And not all of it was from her previous visit to Egypt. Some of it had come to her in her dreams. She had been dreaming about Egypt since the time she had left and hadn't even realized it. Those dreams seemed almost more real than the memories.

Reg looked around, hoping for some sign of where she was supposed to go. There must be a reason the gems had brought her there. Some person she was supposed to talk to or sight she was supposed to see. There had to be something to lead her back to the origin of the gems or the rightful owners.

No one appeared to have noticed her materializing out of thin air. Had everyone blinked at the same time? Been distracted by something in a shop or stand? Or had they seen her, but denied the possibility of a human being appearing out of nowhere and had explained it away?

Whatever the reason, everyone around her went about their own business as if they hadn't noticed her, other than a tall Black man with a turban whose eyes remained on her for a few seconds. Reg walked around for a bit, looking at the store windows and street vendors, waiting for something to occur to her. She was beginning to get worried, thinking that she would not be able to find her purpose for being there. She fingered the rings, trying to decide on a course of action.

"A tour of the pyramids for madam?" a man asked, leaning in close and flashing a folded brochure in front of her eyes.

Reg startled and withdrew slightly, putting a little more space between her body and the man, feeling crowded. She looked him over. He gave her a big smile that showed several gaps between his teeth. Older than she was, brown-skinned, slender. He gave a little bow. "You would like to see the pyramids, would you not?"

"How did you know I speak English?" Reg asked.

He beamed at her. "You look American. Are you not?"

"Yeah. But I didn't know I looked any different from anyone else." Reg looked down at herself. She had changed out of her usual fortune teller garb, exchanging bright skirts and scarves for khakis and a loose white t-shirt with long sleeves. She knew it would be hot in Egypt, but the videos she had watched on sight-seeing in Egypt had advised that all women should wear long pants and sleeves so as not to attract unwanted attention from men who would see her bare skin as an invitation.

She didn't think that she looked all that different from the other women around her. She wasn't wearing any kind of head-scarf or veil, but she certainly wasn't the only one. Something about her, though, had given her nationality away.

"Well, yes," she admitted. "I am."

"You like to see the pyramids?"

Reg hesitated, not sure that was where she was supposed to go. But maybe this was the invitation she had been looking for. The sign pointing which way to go next.

"Tombs of the great pharaohs? Where they were buried with great splendor in preparation for the afterlife?" the man suggested.

Great splendor. Definitely a sign pointing toward the possible origins of the gems. If the rings were so ancient, then it made sense, didn't it, that they had come from a tomb? So many of the tombs of the kings had been raided over the years, stripped of gold and jewels and other finery. She'd even heard that it had once been in vogue to have mummy unwrapping parties.

Reg shuddered at the idea of a group of women nattering away and squealing as they pulled away the burial shrouds from a brown, desiccated body. How could such a thing ever have been considered proper?

"Yes," she told the man, who was still hovering, waiting for her answer. "That sounds very interesting."

He bowed, pleased. "My name is Ahmed, madam. I am very pleased to make your acquaintance."

"I'm Reg. Reg Rawlins. Good to meet you too. So where do we go? Do you have a car?"

"I will make arrangements for us to take a tour tomorrow. It is too late in the day to begin now. That would be acceptable?"

Reg looked at the sky. It was later in the day than she had thought. She had forgotten about the time zone differences.

"Yes. Of course. Do you have a card?"

He pressed the brochure into her hand. "All on here. Do you have a phone?"

"I do, but…" Reg pulled her phone out to look at it. As she had expected, there was no service provider named in the top corner. No service bars.

Ahmed stretched his neck to look at her screen. He nodded. "You need a SIM card." He pressed her shoulder to turn her around and pointed at what might be a grocer or convenience store. "You can get one there. Would you like me to help you?"

"Uh, yeah." Reg gave him a grateful smile. Despite planning ahead, she had not understood all the ins and outs of phone service when jumping across the ocean. She had hoped that her phone would recognize a service partner in Egypt and she wouldn't have to do anything. She could go into the store by herself, point at her phone, and hope that the owner charged her a fair price for whatever equipment was needed to make it work. But it would be better if someone local could help her out.

"Of course, madam." Ahmed bowed again. "It would be my pleasure."

Already, Reg was experiencing greater hospitality than she had when she had arrived there with Corvin. No one had approached her and offered to help then. The difference was probably Corvin. When people saw him with Reg, they assumed that she was taken care of. On her own, she would get more offers of help.

Probably more people trying to scam her too, but she was a psychic. She would be able to weed out the con artists. She had plenty of experience in that regard.

Ahmed walked with her over to the store and negotiated with the man at the counter. They argued back and forth about the price and, eventually, Ahmed told Reg the price. She took out the Egyptian currency she had purchased at the bank before leaving Black Sands and showed him, unsure of the denominations. Ahmed took what he needed from the bundle, handed it to the cashier, and returned the change to Reg.

The cashier displayed the SIM card that Reg had purchased and asked a question. Reg looked at Ahmed.

"He can install it for you," Ahmed said. "If you give him your phone."

Reg handed over her phone and watched the man pop out the SIM card drawer and replace her old SIM card with the new one. He carefully put the old one into the folder the new one had come in, patted it, and said something to Reg.

"To keep it safe," Ahmed said. "You will need it when you go back home."

"Thank you!" Reg received her phone and the folder back and put them into her purse. "You have both been very helpful."

Both men nodded and bowed. Ahmed indicated the brochure and pointed to the phone number on it. "This is my number. We will meet early tomorrow so that we have plenty of time to tour the tombs. You would like to see the pyramids *and* the Valley of the Kings?"

"Sure. Will we have time for both?"

"With an airplane ticket, yes."

"Oh. That sounds expensive." Maybe she could do just the

pyramids and then jump to the Valley of the Kings later if she needed to. She could find another guide there.

"No, not expensive," Ahmed assured her. He showed her packages listed in the brochure. "You see? Very reasonable."

Reg tried to breathe through her anxiety over spending so much. She had the money from the dwarfs. She didn't need to worry about the cost. It really wasn't bad for a full-day tour, including airplane tickets. And she could get everything done in a day and, hopefully by the end of it, have rehomed the gems, or at least she would know where she was supposed to take them. And then she could go back home to Black Sands.

And deal with Horace?

She pushed thoughts of Horace away. She could only deal with one problem at a time. Horace was safe in her house. As long as he stayed there, she didn't have anything to worry about. Maybe he would knock things down or break things while she was away. Maybe he would refuse to use the litter box. But he would be safe and so would everyone else.

Ahmed was looking at her face anxiously. "It is okay?" he asked. "Or you do not wish to go to the Valley of the Kings? You could catch a bus or rent a car, but it takes eight hours and would not be much cheaper than by plane."

"It's okay," Reg said. "It's perfect. What do you take? I don't think I have that much cash with me."

"You can e-transfer," he assured her. "Just text it to my phone number. You can use this currency converter." He took the brochure back from her, pulled a pen from his pocket, and wrote down a URL. "Just send US dollars. That is perfectly fine."

"Very efficient." Reg nodded. It was a good thing that she had deposited Gwythr's cash portion into her bank account before leaving, because she didn't know whether the bank would freeze the certified check for ten days as Gwythr had suggested. With the deposit, she knew she could make the e-transfer to Ahmed. "How early do we need to start?"

"Seven o'clock?" Ahmed suggested. At the look on her face, he quickly revised. "Eight o'clock? Nine?"

"Uh," Reg sucked air in through her teeth. It was still really early for her. But her body was on Florida time, so maybe it would be okay. And if she didn't sleep well before going, she could sleep on the plane halfway through the day. Have a little siesta. "Eight-thirty?"

"Eight-thirty." Ahmed agreed. "What hotel are you at?"

"I don't know yet."

He gave her the tolerant sort of look that she might get from Corvin when she didn't know something that he thought was basic magical knowledge, or from a foster mom who thought she was missing some vital life skill despite all the families that she had been through.

"How much you want to pay?"

Reg tried to come up with a reasonable price range. She didn't usually stay at hotels. Sometimes at a shelter or a hostel, a room to rent in someone's apartment. Whatever she could afford to get herself off the street. She made a tentative suggestion to Ahmed, and he nodded quickly. Apparently, she had not given a price that was so rock bottom low he thought she was crazy.

"You should stay at the Cleo," he told her. "Very clean, nice rooms, Wi-Fi, breakfast. I can meet you there and take you to the pyramids without having to go through traffic." He rolled his eyes. "You would not believe traffic in Giza."

Reg made agreeable noises.

"You want to go there now? I will get you a taxi?"

"Sure. Is there somewhere to eat?"

"Good restaurant. Some bars and clubs on the street." He spread his hands wide. "I would not recommend them for an unaccompanied lady. Best to stay in the restaurant. Good food. You will like."

"Egyptian food or American food?" Reg asked uneasily.

"They have some American. Plenty to tourists' tastes."

"Okay. Yeah. That sounds good."

He nodded and stepped out into the street, whistling shrilly and waving down a taxi. The car pulled over and the driver looked at them both.

Ahmed gave the driver rapid instructions Reg couldn't understand, but she did hear the word "Cleo" among the rest. Ahmed made a gesture in Reg's direction, rubbing his fingers together and looking expectant. Reg frowned. "What?"

"Your money? I pay him now, you don't have to negotiate when you get there. I get you fair price."

"Oh, okay. Thank you." Reg pulled out her money again, Ahmed stepping between her and the taxi to shield her money from the driver's view. He took a couple of bills and waited until Reg put the rest back away before turning to the driver. He dickered over the price for a few minutes and then handed the money over and shook hands with the driver. He turned back to Reg.

"It is all arranged. He will take you to the hotel. Get yourself a nice room. It is very reasonable. If you have any troubles, you call me." He indicated the brochure. "You have my number. I will deal with anybody who gives you trouble."

Reg smiled. "You've been so helpful, Ahmed. I will see you tomorrow."

CHAPTER THIRTY-ONE

*R*eg was relieved when the taxi pulled up in front of a hotel with Cleopatra splashed all over the signs and let her out. He did not demand any further payment. Two more marks in Ahmed's favor. He had been a godsend, eager to help her with whatever she needed.

She thanked the driver and nodded at him a couple of times as she climbed out of the car with her purse and her luggage and leaned down to close the door again. He seemed pleasant and satisfied with the transaction.

That just went to show Corvin. She could take care of herself without him, even in Egypt.

Reg walked through the lobby and approached the front desk. The desk clerk nodded at her, smiling, and waited expectantly.

"Do you speak English?" Reg asked, suddenly nervous.

"Of course, madam," he spoke with perfect British diction, "How may I help you today?"

"I need a room for the night. My... guide said that this was the best hotel." She smiled, hoping this would help her get a good rate.

"We are honored. What were you thinking, and how many nights?"

"I'm hoping just one night." Ahmed had said to get a good room, so Reg tried to envision what that might be. "Uh... queen bed?"

"We are happy to oblige." He tapped a query into the computer on the desk and scanned the screen. "We have the princess suite available. Always very popular with the Americans."

"That sounds expensive. I really just need a room..."

"You will be very happy with the princess suite. A queen bed separated from a sitting room and kitchenette. Jetted tub, very nice at the end of a long day of walking. Very good Wi-Fi signal in that part of the hotel."

It sounded very nice, but Reg was still worried about the price. He quoted her a number, and she tried to figure out what that translated to in US dollars. Sensing this, the man gave her the US price.

"Really? Well... yeah, that sounds really good. Is that all-in? All the room taxes or whatever?"

"Of course." He smiled. "Perhaps at that price you will be willing to spend more than one night with us?"

Reg smiled. "Maybe. I really don't know how long I will be yet; it depends on how things work out. Is that room available for a few days, if I end up needing it for longer?"

"It is. Shall I ring that up, then?"

Reg nodded. "Yes, thank you."

He did so, fingers working busily over the computer keyboard. He made pleasant small talk, asking her about where she was from and which sights she planned to see.

"It is your first time in Egypt?"

"No... I mean, it's my first time as a tourist. I was here before, but just for a few hours. I didn't get a chance to see anything."

He nodded understandingly. He printed off forms and prepared a folder for her with the room card key slotted into a special holder. As he handed it to her, his eyes strayed to her hand, looking at the rings. Reg touched them and tried to think of what to tell him. He hadn't actually asked anything, but clearly wanted to know how this American woman came to be wearing ancient

Egyptian rings. Reg wanted to tell him that they were not hers and she would be trying to find the rightful owner, but it didn't seem like the right time. She closed her mouth and said nothing.

"It has been a pleasure, madam. Please give me a call if there is anything you need."

"Thanks." Reg looked around, checking out where the various amenities, including the restaurant, were.

"The elevator is over there. Your room is on the third floor."

Reg nodded and headed in the direction he had pointed, not seeing the elevator alcove until she was practically on top of it. She pressed the up arrow and waited.

A man approached. Tall, very black skin, with a turban. His face was aged, but she couldn't be sure whether he was fifty or seventy. He looked as though he'd spent a lot of time in the sun. Reg glanced around, wondering why he was walking directly toward her. Maybe it was just for the elevator. Like Reg, he was going up to his room. But then she saw her duffel bag on his arm.

"Oh!" She looked at her shoulder and saw that she had her large purse, but had put down her luggage. "Thank you!"

He handed it to her and gave a bow. Reg studied him. He seemed very familiar. But how could anyone in Egypt be familiar to her? Other than Kareem or Ahmed. But it wasn't either of them.

"Thank you very much. I guess I wouldn't have gotten very far without this."

He didn't say anything, only nodded again, bowing very slightly. The elevator opened. Reg got on and nodded to him, feeling awkward. She had already thanked him and didn't know what else to say. Have a nice day? Thank you again? She didn't even know whether he could speak English. She felt like she should say something, but couldn't decide what it was before the elevator doors closed again, Reg inside and her helper outside.

Reg smiled and shook her head, and hit the button for the third floor. So far, her trip was going well. She had met some very nice people who had been more helpful than she could have asked for. She walked down the hall looking at the room numbers and found the princess suite a few doors down the hall from the elevator. Close enough to be handy, but hopefully not so close that she would be hearing it and all the conversations of people who got on and off the elevator all night long. The desk clerk had said that it was a popular room for Americans. Americans tended to be high-maintenance guests, and she expected that if the room were too noisy, they would have complained about it.

She used the card key to let herself in. It was a beautiful suite. As Ahmed had promised, it was very clean, as if the maid had just given it the full treatment, not a stain or speck of dust to be seen anywhere. The sitting room was lovely, furnished in sand and pastel colors that echoed notes of the desert. The furniture looked soft and comfortable, and there were a couple of paintings and pieces of decor that were there just for the pleasing effect. There was a large armoire which she assumed held the TV behind its closed doors, and the remote was not screwed into the side table that held a lamp handy for someone who wanted to read. The lamp was not screwed down either.

"Very nice," Reg murmured.

She opened the door to the bedroom, which continued the soft color scheme and tasteful decor. The bed and bedding looked comfortable. The coverlet and linens did not look like they had come from a bulk warehouse somewhere but, instead, as though they had been handcrafted just for that room. Reg was sure she would be very comfortable there. She put her bag down on the bed.

Her stomach was rumbling. She hadn't had much to eat that day, and was kind of getting tired of cake and ice cream. The restaurant had a grill and looked like it would have a good range of savory selections. The Cleo had been a good recommendation by Ahmed.

* * *

When Reg went down to the restaurant, she walked past the Black man who had retrieved her bag when she had forgotten it. He was just standing around the hotel lobby and, while he didn't have a name tag or anything else to identify him, she supposed he was probably security or maybe a concierge or other employee of the hotel. That would make more sense than his just being a guest or other passerby. She nodded to him as she went past, but he made no response.

In the restaurant, she ordered herself a drink and perused the menu, which had a combination of both local dishes and good old American and English classics. Hamburgers, fish and chips, pasta, grilled vegetables. Something for everyone. A waiter and waitress both waited on Reg, even though the restaurant was pretty full and they could probably have been used elsewhere. At least one of them. She certainly didn't need two people waiting on her.

She ordered a steak sandwich and, while she waited for it to be prepared, people-watched the other patrons of the restaurant. They were mostly tourists, as she had expected. Maybe a few who were there on business, but the overwhelming majority were tourists, mostly American and European. She tried to guess the stories of each of them, but it wasn't really fair, since she could not only see their auras and read their faces, but could also hear the inner thoughts of many of them. A place like that would have made a great location to pick up new clients. She would dress as an Egyptian mystic, offering to tell people about their ancestors who hailed from Egypt, and would tell them some great stories to make them feel good about themselves. She'd make a killing. Until the management caught on and kicked her out.

But she wasn't there as a psychic or a con. She wasn't there to read their stories or to make anything up.

Which made the ghosts who crowded in around Reg groan with disappointment, as they wanted her to tell their stories.

CHAPTER THIRTY-TWO

*R*eg eventually made her way back up to her room, where she watched a little TV until she thought she could fall asleep, and then lay in bed thinking about sleeping and restlessly tossing and turning. She watched some more videos on her phone, telling herself that it didn't matter what time she fell asleep. She would be able to have a nap on the plane anyway. It was just one time she was expected to get up early in the morning, and with the time difference between Florida and Egypt, it wasn't really even early.

But she kept thinking about the rings, warm on her fingers, and what she would be able to find out the next day. Would Ahmed lead her directly where she needed to go? Would she find a place in the pyramids that she was supposed to leave the gems? Or was she supposed to ask Ahmed or give them to him? He was the one who had shown up when she had needed to know where to go, and maybe all she had to do was to give the gems to him to be cleansed. He hadn't given her any signals that he was a practitioner of magic, but he might know a holy man who was able to cleanse the gems for him, or they might be cleansed simply by giving them to Ahmed, if he were the rightful owner.

But she didn't get the feeling he was the one to give them to.

They had provided her with a guide, but she didn't think he was the final destination.

Reg punched her pillow into shape and tried again to just let it go and float away into sleep. But she was so distracted by the unfamiliar place, the bed and sheets that didn't feel like hers, the lack of cats, and the noise of people walking up and down the hallway talking to each other. Even when they didn't speak loudly enough to disturb her, she could still hear random thoughts and found it very distracting when she was trying to empty her mind for sleep.

She had pretty much given up on sleep when she started to fall into dreams. Wild, restless dreams that made her feel unsettled and like she hadn't really gotten any sleep at all. She was finally in Egypt, but her dreams were still filled with images of walking the Egyptian streets or exploring the sites that she had only ever seen on TV or in books. How many times as a child had she wondered whether she would ever get to see anything like the pyramids up close? She had known that it was very unlikely, as a child with no family and no means. No education because she would never be able to pay for it. What kind of job was she going to get that would provide her with the money she needed to travel the world? There was always the possibility of marrying someone with money, but the thought had never appealed to Reg. She valued her independence too much and couldn't imaging fawning over a man and marrying him just because he had the means to provide her with the material things that she wanted in life.

She kept falling asleep, dreaming she was in the pyramids or some other tomb, and then waking up and finding out that she hadn't even begun her journey. It was frustrating to be so close and yet not to have started. She wished it was morning so that she could just get ready and meet Ahmed. She wanted to get started.

There was a heaviness on Reg's chest that she recognized and, even in the light state of sleep that she was in, it took her a few minutes before she could wake herself up to deal with it. She couldn't let him smother her in her sleep, getting heavier and heavier until the breath was crushed out of her.

Reg awoke and tried to turn onto her side to tip Horace off of her. She couldn't move. She ran her fingers through his fur and murmured to him, trying to coax him into getting off. If Starlight were there, he would have chased Horace off, but she had left Starlight back in Florida, thinking she would not need him in Egypt.

There was a loud knock on the door. Horace startled, leapt from her, and darted around the room looking for somewhere to hide. Eventually, he pushed his way under one of Reg's rumpled blankets and was still, his hindquarters and tail exposed. Reg chuckled at his hiding place. She got up to answer the door, wondering who it could be so early in the morning. She hadn't left a wake-up call, though maybe she should. It wasn't light enough yet outside the window for it to be time to get up. What, then?

She padded across the sitting room area to the hallway door and peered out through the peephole. There was no one there. Reg hesitated. Was someone waiting in the hallway for her to look out, in order to take her off guard? She stretched out her senses, searching for anyone close by, but could only sense the people sleeping in the next room on either side. No one in the hallway. No one lurking around with evil, predatory thoughts. She left the chain on the door and opened it a crack, and then as far as it would go with the chain on. She still couldn't see or sense anyone. There was no notice under or in front of her door. It was as if whoever had knocked on the door had simply walked away afterward, leaving no sign as to why he had disturbed her sleep.

It was lucky he had, though.

Reg put a "Do Not Disturb" sign on the door handle, closed the door, and bolted it. Then she returned to the bedroom. She gently uncovered the big black cat on the bed.

"Horace... what are you doing here, huh? You weren't supposed to come here to Egypt."

He started to purr, rubbing against her hand.

"Horace. You wanted to be at my house, so I left you at my house. I'll find you somewhere new. But you can't... follow me halfway around the world. You need to stay in the house, where it's safe." Reg looked around the bedroom. It wasn't exactly like there was anything dangerous there, but she couldn't help feeling like he had put himself in jeopardy coming back to Egypt. That was where he had lived with Kareem. That was where he had been taken advantage of, the powers of the Witch Doctor that were bound to him unwound and taken away. He had been robbed of something that was a big part of him. She didn't have any doubt that he might have been abused or neglected in other ways. Kareem obviously hadn't cared about him. He'd had cats before, but he hadn't shown any special affection or affinity to Horace. There was no sign that he put the cat before him in anything.

"I want you to be safe, and this isn't the right place for you. Do you understand? You shouldn't be here. And I can't leave you here in the hotel when I go out with Ahmed. You can't stay here."

Horace just purred and cuddled against her as closely as he could. As if by doing that, he could make up for the fact that he kept trying to kill her. She stroked and scratched and tried to let him know that she didn't hold it against him. He couldn't help what he was. But she didn't know what to do about him. There was no way that she could trust him. But she could never hurt him either. How could she protect him and protect herself and others from the dangerous draugr?

CHAPTER THIRTY-THREE

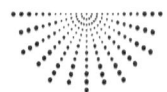

*B*y morning—real morning when it was actually light outside—Reg had made the decision to take Horace back to Black Sands. He would be safer there than in Egypt. She couldn't stop him from coming to her again if she fell asleep and dreamed, but she didn't think that would happen again before she returned home. She had every chance of being able to return the gems and rings to their source during the day, and then her quest would be complete. She could return home, knowing that she had done the right thing and no longer dealing with the disruption that the rings were causing. The money from the sale of gems to Gwythr would clear her account so that she would be able to buy whatever she needed. She would continue to work as a psychic, not necessarily because she would need the money, but because she enjoyed it. She liked working with people and helping to answer their questions and to make contact with the other side. It was important work and people appreciated working with someone with real talent, not just someone trying to take them for a ride.

She could jump Horace back to Black Sands, jump herself back to Egypt again without him, and then continue with her quest. No one would be any the wiser that Horace had returned briefly to Egypt.

It was too bad that cats were no longer worshiped in Egypt. Then maybe she could have just taken him to a temple there and made a new life for him with people waiting on him hand and... paw. Maybe he would have liked that and would have been convinced to stay there instead of following Reg. And they would love him because he was so big and friendly and had some powers, even if they were sort of dark.

But, no more cat temples in Egypt, as far as Reg knew. Maybe she could have Harrison take Horace back in time to sometime that was better for him. A time where he would actually like to stay. Maybe they could move all the kattakyns around in time and across multiple realities. That would be more likely to keep them from being reunited as the Witch Doctor than just trying to separate them in space, wouldn't it?

With Horace heavy in her arms, Reg closed her eyes and imagined herself back in her bedroom in Black Sands. She saw the picture in her head and focused on the smell of her room, the feel of the sheets against her skin in the heat of the Florida morning, the humid air tinged with the smell of the ocean.

She opened her eyes and released Horace into her bedroom. "You need to stay here now where it is safe. Understand? I don't want you back in Egypt again. It's too dangerous for you. You don't want to run into Kareem again, do you?"

She didn't even know whether Kareem still existed, or if Harrison had made him vanish from the face of the earth.

But she didn't want to take that chance, and she assumed that Horace wouldn't want to either. "You're safe here. And I'll be back. Probably tonight. Okay? You have to stay here until I come back."

Horace yowled unhappily. Reg went out to the kitchen to put a little food in both of the bowls. Francesca would still be coming by to feed them, but Horace could use a little treat. Because of the amount he needed for his larger body, if nothing else. She didn't want to starve him.

She put a little tuna in each of the bowls. She looked around. Where was Starlight?

"Star! Starlight! Come and eat."

She hadn't seen him in the bedroom. He hadn't been in his usual sunny morning spot. She had expected to see him in the living room window or hanging out with his bowl in the kitchen. But he wasn't in either place. The house felt cold and empty, not like it usually did.

"Starlight?"

She made a quick tour of the cottage looking for him, but there wasn't that much more to see. He wasn't in his litter box or hiding under the bed or the couch. The door to Reg's spare room was still shut like usual, but she opened it anyway just to make sure that he hadn't managed to get locked in there.

Where else could he have gone? Had he slipped out the door when Sarah or Francesca had been there? She couldn't imagine that either of them would have been careless enough to let him escape. There was no note telling her what had happened. He just wasn't there.

Reg made sure that she didn't let Horace out as she left the cottage to take a quick look outside.

"Starlight? Where are you, Star?"

There was no answering meow or sign of the cat. Reg looked through the underbrush, hoping to spot him hiding underneath, playing that he was a wild jungle cat. But there was no sign of him. Reg wandered into the garden. Sunning himself in a bright beam of sunlight in the garden? Seeing if he could fish anything out of the fountain or pond? There was no sign of him.

She reached out with her mind, calling to Forst.

Are you here?

Reg Rawlins! Forst pushed his way through some tall plants to reach her. *It is wonderful to see you. I thought... you were away.*

I was. I came back for just a minute because of the cats. But I can't find Starlight. You haven't seen him outside, have you?

No, Forst shook his head with certainty. *He is never outside.*

Yeah. That's what I thought. But I can't find him inside and there's no note to say that Francesca took him to her house or that he escaped. I don't know what to think.

You could perhaps call her on your device. Forst held his hand up to his ear in explanation.

Reg pulled out her phone to do just that. But there were no service bars. Reg stared at it for a moment before it made sense. The US SIM card was still back in Egypt in her luggage. She couldn't make any calls until she put it back in.

Oh, right. It isn't working right now.

Forst nodded. *Perhaps she will come here. I can watch for her.*

Would you? She must just have taken him to her house for a play date with Nicole, I think. Of course she wouldn't leave me a note, because she wasn't expecting me to be back in the time that he was gone.

Yes. I will watch for her. She will bring the cat back. If she returns and does not have him, I will ask her.

Reg knew how difficult it was for Forst to use his "outside words" and speak out loud to communicate with humans, so she knew he did not promise lightly.

You're a lifesaver. Thank you so much. I really appreciate it.

Forst smiled more broadly and nodded at her. *Of course. The cat is part of your family.*

Yes, he is, Reg agreed. *I wouldn't have left if I had thought that anything might happen to him while I was gone. I thought he would be safe at home with Francesca looking in on him.*

He is surely safe. He is a very wise creature.

That helped to reassure Reg too. The last time that Starlight had escaped, he had returned with an herbal remedy that she had needed. He had not been harmed. She was sure that if he had gone off, he must have had a reason, and he would intend to return to her safely.

But probably he was just hanging out with Nicole.

You're right. He wouldn't just take off and run away, she agreed with Forst. *He can take care of himself.*

He had powers, Reg knew. She didn't know what those powers were and why he normally didn't choose to use them, living with her just as a regular house cat. But if there were a need for him to use his powers, then he would, wouldn't he? He would protect himself and he would come back to her.

Reg's phone vibrated and she pulled it back out of her pocket to look at it. She knew it wouldn't be a call, because she was too far away from the Egyptian service providers. It was a calendar appointment she had added to make sure that she wouldn't sleep through the eight-thirty appointment with Ahmed.

You must go, Forst observed.

Yes. You're right. I have to get back there... to finish what I started.

Starlight will be fine. You go and be safe.

Thank you. I'll try not to be too long. Hopefully I'll be back sometime tonight.

Reg returned to the cottage. She had a feeling it probably wasn't considered polite to disappear in front of people. Though she hadn't told Forst anything about what her quest was or where she was going, she had a feeling that he understood exactly where she was going. Perhaps he had a better idea of it than she did.

CHAPTER THIRTY-FOUR

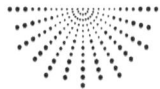

*I*n a few moments, Reg was back in her hotel room at the Cleo. She looked around carefully, making sure that Horace hadn't managed to return with her somehow and that Starlight wasn't there. Was it possible for him to dream travel as well? Or to hitch a ride with Horace? But she didn't see any sign of Starlight in the hotel room. He had not been there.

It was just her.

Reg tried to focus on the job at hand. She stroked the rings on her fingers, thinking about what she was there for. She would find the rightful owner of the rings and the other gems, and she would hand them over, and then return to Florida. Very simple. She was already well on her way to finding out what she needed to know.

Her phone vibrated again. Reg picked up her purse and headed down to the lobby to look for Ahmed. There was a continental breakfast spread in the lobby. Reg grabbed a muffin and a coffee to go. She wasn't a breakfast person, but she figured she'd better have something to sustain her. She took a bite of the muffin as she stepped out of the hotel to check the cars and taxis that were waiting outside. She thought of Harrison. Once again, she was having cake for breakfast. She smiled and shook her head.

"Madam Reg Rawlins?"

Reg looked around and found Ahmed. He gave her a brief bow.

"I trust you slept well?"

Reg rolled her eyes and shook her head. It felt like she'd gotten no sleep at all. "No, not well at all. It wasn't the hotel," she assured him quickly, seeing his head turn toward the Cleo as if he were going to give the manager a piece of his mind. "It was a beautiful room and, as you said, very clean and comfortable. It wasn't anything like that. I just had so much on my mind, and the time zone differences... my body didn't think it was time to sleep yet. And I normally sleep quite late. Or what normal people think is late."

"Perhaps... did you want to postpone, do something else today? And do the tour tomorrow?"

"No. I don't think so. I want to get it done as soon as possible."

Ahmed raised his brows but didn't ask her for her reasons. She supposed that most tourists probably didn't want to get everything done in one day. They probably spread the various sites out over a week or two and did what they felt like each day, doing less if they were tired and more if not. But she wasn't actually a tourist like he thought she was. She wasn't there for her own enjoyment. She had a job to do.

"As you say," Ahmed agreed. "We will begin, then." He looked at her muffin and coffee. "Did you want to finish eating first?"

"No. My stomach isn't really ready for breakfast yet, so I thought I would take it slow. Is it okay? Or you don't like food in your car?" She'd been at several foster homes where food was not allowed in the car. She could understand how parents didn't want to be cleaning up food ground into the upholstery. It didn't take much to make a big mess.

"No, it is fine. You may bring it." He nodded quickly. "Come along, I will show you the car."

Reg followed him to a small white compact car. She wasn't big on cars and couldn't tell whether it was an American or European brand. Or even something from China. When Ahmed opened the door for her, she saw that the interior was spotless, as if it had just come from the dealer. She slid into the passenger seat, regretting the fact that she had only picked up a napkin to catch the crumbs from her muffin and not a proper plate. She didn't want to get crumbs all over Ahmed's car. Even the floor mats were spic and span, and she didn't want to mess anything up.

"Wow, this is beautiful. Is this your car?"

It could be a rental. But Reg didn't get that feeling. "I own it with some other guides," Ahmed explained. "We share it, depending on who needs it on a particular day. Today I have you to take to the pyramids, so I get the car for the morning. When we go to the airport to go to the Valley of the Kings, one of my co-owners will pick it up and he will use it this afternoon for driving around an American couple here for their thirtieth wedding anniversary."

"That sounds like a good arrangement. It's so clean, I wouldn't have guessed that it was a shared vehicle."

Ahmed smiled. "Yes. We keep it very clean. Top working condition, too. No mechanical problems."

Reg thought about her own vehicle and nodded. Every time she had to go very far from the house with it, she always worried that it was going to break down at the worst possible moment. It was an old clunker and she'd put some money into it to try to keep it in good working condition. But it was a failing battle and she knew she would have to replace it soon.

"That's great. You probably put a lot of miles on it too."

"Yes, many kilometers," Ahmed agreed, correcting her subtly. "Now we should go. The pyramids will already be busy by the time we get there."

"Sorry." Reg shrugged. "I know you wanted to get there earlier, but I really don't sleep very well... I needed the extra time."

"Of course. I am not to judge. Different people follow different schedules. Maybe even some want to look at the pyramids at night. Who am I to judge?"

"Can you see them at night?" Reg asked, surprised. "I thought they closed at night. That's why we had to wait until today."

"They are closed," Ahmed agreed. "You can see them in the night, rising up out of the desert... but you cannot go inside." He paused, thinking it over. "It would be very expensive to get someone to open them up late at night."

But maybe if a person had enough wealth, they could arrange for things like that. Reg had never thought of using her money that way. It was strange to think of all the things a person could do with money, if they knew its power.

Reg put on her seatbelt. Ahmed opened the sunroof and pulled out.

It was a pleasant morning. Reg didn't know what the weather usually looked like in Egypt at that time of year, but it was a nice day, cooperating with her needs.

Ahmed chattered to her while he drove, pointing out landmarks and historical sites, filling her in on celebrity gossip, the political situation, and details of how he had gotten into the position of giving people tours. He was independent, clearly, and he obviously knew what he was doing.

Reg could see the pyramids in the distance almost immediately. They were stunning, rising up from the desert, as if they had grown there rather than being built by human hands. How had humans built something so massive without any machinery or blueprints? It was an impossible feat.

The rings on her hand were growing warmer. Reg rubbed them with her thumb, trying to keep them calm. It wasn't as if they were going to burn her. But they kept getting warmer.

"Can we go any faster?" Reg asked, trying to put the feeling from the rings into words.

Ahmed looked at her sideways. He thought she was just being impatient. He had no way of knowing how important it was to identify the proper place for the rings. They were ancient. They needed to be dealt with properly. They had waited a long time to be returned to their native country.

"Of course," Ahmed agreed, giving a nod. He pressed his foot down on the pedal and increased their speed. Reg watched the scenery race by outside her window, a blur of brown.

Traffic slowed as they got closer to the pyramids and Ahmed could not keep up his speed. He shrugged at Reg. "Now we wait."

Reg looked around at the gridlock. She should have gone early, as Ahmed had initially told her. "Maybe there's a back way?"

Ahmed eyed her. Like he would have kept going the way he was going if he knew of a better way?

"There could be," Reg said. "Sometimes there's a different way in. One that most of the tourists don't know about. An access road that the delivery trucks use."

"The pyramids are not Disneyland. We do not have concession stands."

"Staff parking? There must be security, a director or guide or something. They don't just leave the pyramids open for everyone to wander through without any supervision."

"No," Ahmed admitted. "But even if there is another route in, we will not be able to use it. They'll just tell us to turn back around and come back to the public entrance."

"I might be able to talk them into it." Reg kept her thumb rubbing across the rings. They gave her more confidence. And it was working with Ahmed, he was listening to her, considering what she had to say instead of treating her like some crazy American tourist. He wasn't just placating her; she knew the difference.

Eventually, Ahmed conceded. He pulled out of the long lane of traffic he was in and started scanning for roads that led to non-public locations. He knew where all the parking lots and ticket booths were; now he had to think differently. Think about the other roads he had seen and where they might lead to. If one of them would get them closer to the pyramids before the crowds, where Reg would then do her magic and talk someone into letting her in.

For no particular reason.

Just because she was going to talk them into it.

It was a pretty tall order. Reg was thinking through her approach, trying to figure out what she would say to them when they got there. *Please let me in because I have these powerful rings from five thousand years ago and I wanted to bring them home?*

CHAPTER THIRTY-FIVE

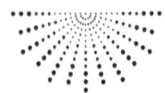

$\mathcal{A}$hmed looked in his rear-view mirror a couple of times. Looking back, Reg could see that another car had pulled out of the queue and was following them.

"Maybe security," Ahmed said. "Maybe coming to tell us to get back in the line."

Reg nodded. She watched through the window, but the glare of the sun on the windshield would not allow her to see the driver. If it were a security vehicle, the driver gave them no sign. He didn't flash lights or turn on a siren or honk his horn. Just followed them a car length or two back. Obviously following. Maybe it was just some other tourist who thought that if it worked for them, he could get in too. Someone willing to leave his place in line and take a risk.

Reg turned her attention back to the road. Many of the road signs she had seen had English on them as well as Egyptian, but the ones on the side road that Ahmed had taken did not. They were only in Egyptian, so she couldn't read them and give Ahmed advice as to which one to take.

"What do you think?" she asked. "Is there somewhere back here where we can get in?"

Ahmed shook his head. "Maintenance. Security. Why would any of them let us in?"

"Maintenance, try that. At least they're more likely than security to let us in."

"Really?" Ahmed shook his head. "They do not have the authority to let anyone in. Security at least has the ability to make their own decision on what is safe and who might just be breaking in to write graffiti or break into an off-limits area."

"You think so?"

He nodded.

Reg pressed her lips together, thinking about it. "Okay," she agreed. "Try that, then."

"What are you going to tell them? That you need to get in because…?"

"I don't know yet. I'm working on that."

Ahmed didn't express his disapproval out loud. He just drove until they pulled up to a gated lot. He looked at her.

"Just drive around the bar," Reg advised. "Get us right up to the door inside."

There were a number of smaller buildings at the base of the pyramid, out of the sight of the public. This one was clearly a security center.

"I can't do that."

Reg looked. "There's plenty of room to get by. And there aren't any of those spiky things on the road to pop your tires."

"We are not supposed to go in there."

"Fine. Stop here and I'll walk."

Ahmed looked torn. Eventually, he conceded and drove around the security gate, leaving the guard in the booth yelling after them in Egyptian. The following car performed the same maneuver and the two of them drove up to the doors of the building. Reg smiled weakly at Ahmed and opened her car door. "Wish me luck!"

"Good luck, Reg Rawlins." Accompanied by a head shake of disbelief. The gall of the American to think that she could just walk up to the pyramids and gain entrance based on her charming smile. Reg laughed at him.

The man in the car behind them got out as well. No passengers, only the driver. Reg studied him. It was the same Black man as had helped her with her luggage the night before when she had accidentally left it at the check-in desk in the lobby. The same man as had been watching her when she went to and from the restaurant later. And apparently, he had followed her all the way to the pyramids.

Reg looked at him. His eyes were intense and she was sure she had seen him before. Not just the day before at the hotel, but some other time. "Who are you?"

He gave a little bow and just stared into her eyes without blinking. He didn't say a word.

"You've been watching me. Following me. Who are you?"

He still said nothing. But Reg was not afraid of him. She knew she should be concerned about this tall, dark-skinned man who was following her everywhere. She didn't want to end up another statistic. Women who went to Egypt unaccompanied and thought that they could just act like they were back in the USA. It was a different country. A different culture.

She rubbed the rings, worried, anxious about what was going to happen next. But not at all worried that the man was going to hurt or abduct her. She knew that he was only there to watch over her. He wasn't there to cause her any harm. Just like Ahmed had appeared when Reg had touched the rings and wished that someone would notice her and help her out. There was a reason they were there. She had a mission to perform, and they were both there to help her.

She turned away from the tall Black man and to the door that they had stopped in front of. She pushed the door open and walked into the small, blue-carpeted lobby of the security building. A uniformed guard at the desk scowled at her.

"Who are you and what are you doing here? You can't just ignore all the signs and the gate."

Reg smiled as if he had complimented her. "Thank you. I'm glad I found this place. You will be able to help me out."

He looked uncertain about her reaction. "The public is not allowed to be back here."

"No. Not normally," Reg agreed pleasantly.

He looked at her, clearly wondering what this strange American was up to. Reg continued to smile, trying to think of what to say to him. She touched the rings, closing her eyes briefly.

"But I think you will let me through," she said confidently.

The guard stared at her. "I will let you through?" he repeated in a doubtful voice.

"Thank you."

He blinked at her. "What?"

"You said you will let me through. Thank you."

He walked around the desk to where Reg was, looking at her, then turned and motioned to a door on the other side of the lobby. "I will need to show you through. It isn't an area normally accessed by tourists."

"That would be great. Thanks. And can my guide come too—?"

The guard looked behind Reg and nodded. "Of course."

Reg turned and saw the tall Black man standing behind her. He had followed her into the lobby, quiet as cat's paws. Ahmed was still sitting in the car, waiting for her to come back out, or maybe to be thrown out by a couple of armed guards.

"No, I meant—"

It was too late; the guard was already escorting her to the back door. The other man followed close behind them.

"It's just that—"

The guard hustled her through the door into the dingy hallway behind. Reg had to walk briskly to keep up with him and was glad that she had worn comfortable shoes. They worked their way through a series of corridors without comment. Eventually, they emerged into a dark passageway built out of sandstone blocks. The guard closed the door behind them and escorted Reg around a rope security barrier to the other side, where members of the public were lined up to purchase tickets. He took her to the cashier.

"A special pass for Miss…" He looked at Reg inquiringly.

"Rawlins. Reg Rawlins."

He nodded. The cashier looked puzzled by the turn of events, but began tapping commands into her computer, and printed off a couple of security name tags to be attached to her lapel and that of her mysterious companion. Reg looked surreptitiously at the other tag to see what it said. While hers had her name on it along with the "special guest" designation that of the man merely said, "Escort."

"Don't you have a name?" she asked him jokingly.

He looked at her and didn't answer.

Reg didn't know what to make of the apparently mute man. She didn't feel threatened by him, but he had an obvious interest in her, having been helping and watching her since the previous evening. He had followed her there and presented himself as her guide when Ahmed had not believed that she would be able to get in.

When she tried to explore his consciousness to find out more about him, She found a closed door. While he let his feelings of interest and protectiveness toward her be felt, everything else was hidden. She couldn't identify him or what his intent was.

But he wasn't trying to deceive her or hurt her, as far as she could tell, so she would just have to accept that he had a reason to be there that would be revealed later. It was certainly something to do with the rings and the other gems. Maybe he was the one who was there to lead her to the rightful owner of the gems. She had believed that someone would show her the way, and he had attached himself to her.

With their visitor tags fastened to their shirts, they were ready to begin their tour of the pyramids. The guard nodded to them. "Okay… if you have any problems or questions, there are docents and security staff throughout the monument."

Reg nodded. "Thanks. You have been very helpful."

He blinked at her, looked at the cashier who had printed off their tags, and then retreated in the direction they had arrived. The cashier nodded.

"You can go ahead."

Reg hesitated. She thought she should probably wait for a tour guide to take a group of them through the pyramid. It didn't seem right to just walk in by themselves and start exploring. But the tall man touched her arm and guided her to a passage beyond the cashier, nodding toward it.

"We're supposed to go in there? You know... why I'm here?" Reg asked awkwardly.

He nodded again toward the hall. Reg walked with him.

"I've never been anywhere like this before," Reg said as they walked down the stone passage. "I never thought I'd be able to come somewhere like this. Just... rich people."

Her silent guide led her through a couple of public passages, then indicated an area that was blocked off with security ropes.

"I don't know whether we should go there."

He waved her on and, when she slowed, uncertain, he again took her arm and guided her past the security ropes and into a smaller passageway. The floor was sloped down. Reg gripped the man's arm, feeling a bit of vertigo in moving from the flat surface to the downhill.

"Are you sure we're allowed to go this way?"

He made no response. Reg didn't know why she was expecting him to, why she kept asking him questions when it was clear that he would not or could not answer. She wanted a response from him, whether it was telepathic, like she would converse with Forst, out loud, or some kind of gesture. But the only gestures that he made were to indicate that she should go on.

CHAPTER THIRTY-SIX

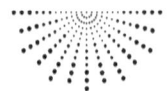

*I*t was quiet away from the public. No one discussing the pyramid as they walked through it or complaining about how long they'd had to wait in line to get a ticket and then had to wait for a tour guide as well. No crying children or raised voices.

Nothing at all.

But as they walked along, descending through the dimly lit passageway in silence, Reg could hear other voices.

Not from the tourists or their guides, or the staff or security personnel.

Other voices. Ghostly. Rising up through the back of her head and making the hair on her arms stand on end. Reg looked around.

Of course there were spirits there. A pyramid housed a burial chamber. Not just for the king, but also members of his household, favorite servants, soldiers. Whoever the king wanted to be with him in the afterlife. Someone would need to feed and serve him and protect him from harm. Things were no different in the afterlife the Egyptians envisioned than in one's first life. Except that the afterlife lasted much longer, and if a person was not properly prepared and equipped, it would be a long, torturous afterlife instead of the pleasant one that it could be with a little planning.

"Are there mummies here?" Reg asked anxiously. Her mind flashed through popular media, everything from Scooby-Doo mummies to those of graphic horror movies.

She had dealt with real life zombies; she wasn't so sure she wanted to contend with mummies as well. She was already holding the cursed gems. If they belonged to whatever king was interred in the pyramid, would he come and get them? Or could she just leave them as an offering in some small side chamber that no one would ever go into, hoping that they would remain safe there forever?

They couldn't be safe forever if she just hid them somewhere in the pyramid. Only if she gave them to the rightful owner personally.

She just hoped it wasn't a mummy.

In Africa, the rightful owners had been the villagers, the descendants of those who had originally mined or owned the gems hundreds of years before.

She really hoped that she didn't have to return them to the original owner whose tomb had been plundered. She wasn't sure how she would manage walking up to a mummy to hand them over.

The draugrs had stunk, rotten and vile. Would the mummies smell worse because they were older, or would the smell be gone by then, turned to dust centuries earlier?

Her companion was waiting for her to return her attention to him. Reg struggled to rein in her thoughts and pay attention to his answer.

It came, not in words, but in vibrant pictures that filled her mind. The queen and young prince following the soldiers carrying a large and colorfully decorated sarcophagus. It gleamed with touches of gold paint. Actual gold, Reg was sure, not just the craft paint like she got at Michael's. She couldn't see the man within the casket and hoped that she wouldn't. Hopefully, he was at rest in the bottom of the pyramid and would not be waking up to ask her for the gemstones and rings.

She wondered, briefly, if the rings had been stolen off of the fingers of the corpse. The idea gave her a little shudder of horror. But she didn't see the rings anywhere in the vision her guide had given her. She looked at the fingers of the queen and young prince and saw that they both had signet rings. But not the ones that Reg had on her fingers. She was glad she wouldn't have to put them back onto the shriveled black fingers of some desiccated corpse hundreds of years old.

"Do I have to see him? Talk to him?" Reg demanded.

One of the spirits was close by, doing all he could to impose himself on Reg's mind. "I am here. Why would you come here except to talk to me?"

"Umm…" Reg looked around, hoping for a quick way to get out of it. While she enjoyed the seances she did for her customers, she rarely actually channeled a spirit for her clients. When she did, it was always a bit of an unsettling experience, even though she brushed it off as perfectly normal when speaking with her clients.

"Don't delay," another told her. It was a younger, gentle voice, and she glanced around, looking for the owner.

She could see a younger man just at the edge of her vision, dressed very much like she had seen ancient Egyptians portrayed on TV shows. She knew that it was the boy who had followed the sarcophagus into the tomb in the vision from her guide, but he was older, a young man rather than a child.

"I just don't want to talk to the mummy," Reg clarified. I'll talk to *him*. She looked around, but could not see the ghost of the dead king. He was there, though; she could still feel him in her mind. "Just talk."

"It has been a very long time," the young man said.

"Well, yes, I would guess so. The rings and gems are very old. But I don't know… did they come from here?"

She closed her eyes and tried to expand the vision. Not just to see what the people were wearing on their fingers, but expanding to other chambers in the pyramid where the jewels might have been stored. They believed they could take their wealth to the afterlife, so it would be there somewhere. He would have wanted it all close at hand.

The young man shook his head slowly. "They were not my father's."

"Do you know where they came from? Were they from one of the other pyramids? Or from the other place that Ahmed is going to take me? The Valley of the Kings?"

"You will need to find out."

"You don't know? Do you recognize them?" Reg held up her hand, displaying the rings.

There was hissing around Reg, making her jump. She tried to see who the sound came from, but it seemed to come from various sources around her, not just one direction. She thought about the young man's father. The dead king. He wanted something from her. He wanted to get into her head. Because he wanted to use her voice and her body as other ghosts had? To be able to feel and speak again? Or because he wanted something else?

"You cannot command me," the old pharaoh's voice hissed.

"I wasn't... I didn't mean to command you," Reg explained. "I'm just trying to get these gems back to the place they came from and, if that's not here or one of the other pyramids, then maybe I'd better go on, not waste so much time here."

"You must come see me."

Reg rubbed her arms and neck, trying to get rid of the goose-flesh and the creepy, sticky feeling that someone was watching her every move.

"Why?"

"You come to my land and do not want to see me? I was the greatest of my time. You do not come here and command and not pay your respects."

"I didn't mean to be disrespectful. But I don't have a lot of time in this land. I am sure you were very powerful when you were in power here. It must have taken a lot of time and money to build these things." Reg looked at her guide, his black skin taking on a blue sheen in the dim artificial lighting. Why didn't they have stronger lights? Was it the cost? Would light damage the artifacts there? Other than the paintings on the walls, Reg hadn't seen anything left over from the time of the king. Was that because everything had been looted, or because it had all been locked up in a museum, safe from people who would use it the wrong way?

"You should come," the young man urged. He put his hand on Reg's arm. He was insubstantial, so she could not feel his touch, but she felt a sudden chill. Like the cold of a grave.

"I don't know. Do *you* think I should?" Reg looked at her guide. She assumed that he could see the ghosts and their whispered conversation.

He made a gesture to her, a sort of "Go on, then" urging her to continue down the sloping passage.

"I don't really like this. I don't want to stay here very long."

But she went. She and the guide walked close together. Reg was careful of every step she took. Didn't they set booby traps? She was pretty sure she had heard that somewhere. And what if she walked right into one because she wasn't being careful enough? She tried to sense ahead of her, both in space and in time, hoping that she could foresee any hazards that lay ahead.

Even though she was sure the lights were all the same all the way, she felt like the passageways were getting darker and more oppressive. "Is it much farther?"

If they could show her where it was, maybe Reg could jump herself there instead of having to go through all the hallways, taking so much extra time and energy.

The ghost and the guide just continued to take her down and down and down through winding passageways.

CHAPTER THIRTY-SEVEN

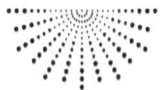

*T*here were locked doors, but her guide stopped at each, resting his hand on the doors, until Reg could hear the lock click open, and he would open it for her. The pyramid security clearly hadn't thought that they would have to deal with magical beings getting past the doors. Or maybe they had known that those who had the powers would still get through and didn't worry about it. If they could do nothing to keep people out, why go to a lot of trouble to try?

"We are here," the young man told her, stopping and looking around. Reg tried to reconcile the vision she'd had of the Pharaoh's burial with what she saw before her.

The room was bare, but for the hieroglyphics on the walls. Even those were faded and hard to read after so many years. Reg wandered around, looking for some sign of all the wealth and artifacts that had originally been housed in that small vault. It was so bare now. She hoped that the pieces were in museums or in display cases that people could tour in the public area of the pyramid.

"This is it? This is where the mummy was?" Reg asked.

A man stepped into the room, through the same entrance that

Reg and her guide had just used. He had apparently been following her.

At first, Reg took him for the ghost of the dead king. An old man. He looked ancient, like he'd lived a thousand years. But ghosts usually looked either like they had when they had died or were in their prime. They didn't keep getting older after they died.

She waited for him to hiss something at her, to confirm that he was the pharaoh who had been buried there, but he advanced, eyes fixed on her, looking as though he would prefer to take her head off. This wasn't a ghost who wanted to talk through her. He seemed to be very real, very much a physical being.

"Who are you?" Reg asked. She took a step back away from him and avoided him the best she could. He was spry for an old guy, but she managed to stay out of his reach, studying him, trying to evaluate him and to decide whether he was a danger to her or not.

"You don't know me?" he growled. "You can't even recognize me after a few short days?"

A few short days? Reg tried to picture him in her life. How had she known him? Was he someone who lived on her street? A client? Someone she'd sat next to in some public place who had decided that they were acquainted with each other?

"I'm sorry…" She looked at her guide and caught the flash of the young man's ghost in the corner of her eye. But she still didn't see the old ghost and couldn't figure out who the man was. "I know I should remember, but…"

"You stole my powers."

Reg stared at him. She hadn't stolen anyone's powers. She couldn't. Well, she could to an extent, but she didn't. She wasn't like Corvin, hunting down the weak and helpless and consuming their powers.

"*I* stole your powers?" she repeated, her voice challenging.

"You and your servants. All of you, ganging up on a helpless old man…"

Reg sucked in her breath. She studied the old man. She was getting an inkling, but it didn't seem possible. The old man who stood in front of her didn't look anything like the black-haired man they had originally met in Egypt when they had gone there to find out what had happened to Horace before Harrison brought him to the house.

Horace's old owner.

Kareem.

"It's not possible," Reg murmured. She couldn't see any of that man in this old man's face. He was utterly changed. He had seemed old when Reg and Corvin had gone to meet him. Not ancient, just like an old warlock, someone who had likely lived for far more years than he appeared to have. Witches and warlocks aged slowly. Sarah claimed to be hundreds of years old.

"Look what you did to me," Kareem complained. "Taking my power away from me. What did you think would happen when you had drained me?"

"I didn't... all I did was to defend myself. You were the one trying to kill the elf's child. How could you do something like that?"

"Why should the child of some other species be of any concern to me? I didn't care what happened to it. I was trying to gain leverage over you. It's your fault."

"My fault? I didn't attack you. You're the one who attacked me!"

Kareem spat. "You came to my home to show off your rings and to command me to tell you all I knew. You're the one who wanted the spark."

Reg bit her lip. She *had* wanted the piece of the Witch Doctor that Kareem had held. Not for herself, but to safeguard and make sure that no one could gather the pieces he had sent out to the kattakyns and re-form the Witch Doctor once more. She had been promised a thousand years. A thousand years before the binding spell would wear off. Longer still before the kattakyns could move around the world to gather together in one place. Multiple levels of complexity to make sure that the Witch Doctor would never be back in her lifetime.

But one of the pieces, the spark that Kareem spoke of, was

lost. They didn't know where to find it. Harrison had said that Kareem no longer had it, but he didn't know where it had gone. Kareem's words seemed to verify this. He was playing the victim because someone had stolen from him what he had taken from Horace.

And it was Corvin who had drained Kareem's power, not Reg. And Kareem knew that. But he needed someone to blame and Reg had returned to Egypt, giving him a target.

"How did you even know I was here?" Reg asked. She continued to stay as far away from Kareem as was possible. He didn't appear to be able to move quickly and, if his powers had also been drained enough by Corvin that Kareem was aging that rapidly, then Reg assumed he would not have the strength to wield any power over her. But she couldn't be sure. She still needed to be careful.

"Do you think I cannot feel your rings of power?" Kareem looked greedily at the rings on her finger. "Do you think I cannot recognize your aura when you come into my part of the world? You can't hide those things from me, even if I have been crippled by what you have done to me. I can still *feel* you."

Reg shifted uneasily. Her instinct was to throw up a shield around herself and her guide, to protect them against any imminent spell from the warlock. She had a feeling that, like a bird faking a broken wing, he was pretending to be far more pitiable than he really was. He wanted to take her off guard. When she wasn't looking, then he would attack.

But she had learned that maintaining a psychic shield around herself also prevented her from using her powers outside of that shield. She could not attack while she was defending, it was one or the other. She remembered the attack and defend exercise she had seen at the Spring Games. The defender had used a very small shield, which he could then move around to counter any move by the attacker. Could she do that? Defend with one hand and use offensive moves with the other? She didn't think that she was well enough coordinated to pull it off. Not without practice, which she didn't have. She was limited to one or the other.

"What do you want from me?" she asked Kareem.

"I want what you took from me."

"I didn't take anything from you. That was Corvin. The other warlock."

"He was in your service. He would not have been there or attacked me without you. You might not do your own dirty work, but that doesn't mean you're not responsible."

Reg wanted to argue it but, on at least one level, he was right. Corvin would not have been there if not for her. And he would not have had any reason to attack Kareem. He wouldn't have gone back to Egypt to question Kareem without Reg leading the way. He hadn't been too keen on going back.

Of course, that had changed recently. He had been angling to go along with Reg ever since he had fought Kareem. Did he know that Harrison had sent Kareem back to Egypt and he wanted to take the rest of Kareem's power? Or did he think that Harrison had done away with Kareem and that he wouldn't have to face the other warlock upon his return?

"How about you leave me alone, and I'll leave you alone?" Reg suggested. If she could negotiate a treaty with him, maybe he would be satisfied. "I'm not here to see you. I'm not doing anything to harm you. There's no need to start a fight."

Kareem shook his head, baring his teeth, which were few in number and looked like they were rotting out of his head. Maybe he was just grumpy because he had a toothache. "I am here to get what is mine," he said, looking again at the rings.

CHAPTER THIRTY-EIGHT

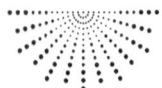

"*H*ow are these yours? I didn't take them from you. I didn't even get them from Egypt. I just brought them back here."

"They are not yours."

"No, I never said they were. But they are not yours either."

"You know nothing about my heritage. I am descended from the kings. I have more right to them than anyone else."

Reg hesitated. She looked out the corner of her eye at the ghostly young man, looking for some sign of agreement or disagreement. He looked at Kareem with disdain, shaking his head. "This warlock is not of our family."

Could he know that for sure? Or did he just figure that Kareem was disgusting and he didn't want the valuables being given to him?

But then, the ghost had not lain claim to the jewelry either. He had not said that they had belonged to him or his father, and Reg had not seen them in the vision. Someone might have stripped the tomb bare of everything else of value, but if the rings and jewels had not come from there, then Reg was wasting her time standing around having discussions with ghosts and warlocks who had nothing to do with her quest.

"Bring back my treasure," the old king's ghost whispered inside Reg's head. "You make things whole? Bring back what belongs to me."

"I don't have anything that belongs to you. I can't give you what I don't have."

"You must go find them. They have taken it all away. You must find it and bring it back."

"I can't," Reg insisted. "I have stones that must be returned to their rightful owners, but I do not have anything of yours."

"You see what they have done to me. You know it is wrong."

"Yes... it's wrong," Reg agreed. She pictured his sarcophagus on display upstairs in the public area, tourists gawking and taking pictures. Archaeologists taking pictures and doing special scans of the mummy inside. She wouldn't want her corpse to be treated that way. "But I don't have any authority over them."

"You have the rings. You can command."

Reg looked down at the rings. She ran her thumb over their surfaces. "You know where they come from? What they can do?"

Images flashed through her head too fast for Reg to be able to process them. She closed her eyes, bringing her hands up to her head as if she could physically block them from entering her mind. "No, no! You can't do that. Stay out of my brain!"

Another sharp hiss from the old ghost and the pictures stopped. Reg tried to recover. She couldn't process even part of what she had seen, it had been a flood of images and memories too complex to sort out.

"What was that?"

"You command an answer and then you command I stop. You don't know your own mind."

Reg rubbed her thumb between her eyebrows in the third eye position, a pounding headache making it difficult to think straight. "I'm sorry. I'm not commanding, I'm just... asking questions. I want to understand. But it's like drinking from a fire hose; it is too much."

"You want answers."

"Yes. No."

Reg's guide put his hand on her arm. She was distracted from talking to the old king's ghost. Had it all been in her head or out loud? Could the guide understand what had been happening, or was he lost at sea, trying to figure out if she had lost her mind. Kareem crept closer, his hand in his pocket, his manner furtive.

"You, stay back," Reg ordered. She focused her attention on the rings to make sure that this time it was a command, hoping that Kareem would be bound by it. "Don't come any closer."

She looked at the guide, deep into his eyes, wondering where she had seen him before. Because she was sure she had seen him before. She was sure he was someone she should know. There was a fleeting, familiar feeling that she was almost able to put her finger on, and then it was gone again. Reg groaned. "Who are you? Can you speak? What if I command you to speak?"

He shook his head. Did that mean that he couldn't or that she shouldn't command him? It was too hard for Reg to sort out. She should only ask one question at a time. That way maybe she could sort out the answers.

"Do you know where the gems came from?"

Steady eyes, an affirmative feeling, nothing else.

"Did they come from here?"

A slight turning away from her. Like a cat turning away from attention he didn't want. No, negative. Reg let out her breath in an angry puff.

Then what was she doing there? Why was she wasting her time climbing all the way down to the depths of the pyramid? She would not find a place to leave the gems, because they didn't belong there. Reg supposed that the Egyptians had, like all countries, gone through several different ruling families. Maybe related, maybe not, but whatever number of families there were, Reg was not in the right place.

Had he known that before they talked to the ghosts and had just followed her to keep an eye on her, or had he just figured it out like she had?

"Where should I go, then?"

As if an open-ended question was one that he would be able to answer. But Reg reached out with her mind, hoping that he would show her another vision or help her to understand another way. She closed her eyes to focus better. After a moment, a vision started to form, but it was dark and indistinct. Another tomb, another room somewhere. But where? There were not limestone blocks as there were in the pyramid Reg was in, but the room seemed to have been carved out of the rock.

Not one of the other pyramids, then, Reg decided. But then, where? The other site that Ahmed had told her he would take her on a tour of?

"Is this that Valley? The Valley of the Kings?"

An indecisive response. Maybe, but maybe not. No, but close. Yes, but not where she was thinking. Reg tried to sort through the feelings to pin one down, but that was as far as she could get. Yes, but no. No, but yes. She shook her head.

"Okay... so I'll go to the Valley of the Kings... at least it is closer."

The room around her was silent. Reg looked around at the occupants. Her silent guide. The ghost of the young man she could see out of the corner of her eye. She couldn't feel the old king's ghost, but she could still feel him there. He was unhappy with her decision to leave, and not to leave the rings and other gems there for him. All his treasure had been taken from him, and Reg felt sorry for him to be left with nothing, after all that planning and work to make sure that he would be well-supplied in the afterlife. But in the end, he was a ghost, not someone who could actually make use of all the amenities he had provided for himself. Or was he only a ghost because he had not moved away from that place, progressing along the appointed timeline for his afterlife?

And then there was Kareem. He seemed to have stopped when Reg told him to, but she didn't know how long the command would hold. Until they were separated again? Until she left the room? The pyramid? Forever?

He still had his hand in his pocket, close to whatever weapon he carried with him.

"What if I command you to stay here?" she suggested to him.

Kareem's watery eyes widened. "Taking my powers is not enough for you?" His voice was loud and querulous. "You would leave me here to die of starvation?"

Would he? It wasn't as though he had told her the truth from the beginning. It wasn't like he'd ever told her the truth at all. He'd even twisted what she knew to be the truth, what she herself had witnessed.

"Someone would come down here sooner or later," she suggested. "We could call in later and tell them to have a look."

"You can't do that!"

It did seem like a cruel thing to do, even if Reg was concerned about her safety. Putting someone else's life or mental health in jeopardy for her own convenience didn't seem right.

"Then…" She pressed her thumb against one of the rings. "I command you to stay here for one hour."

She looked at the tall, Black guide, seeking his approval. He gave no indication one way or the other. Reg hesitated, wondering if she had done the wrong thing. Too little or too much? Corvin had told her the last time that they needed to dispose of Kareem permanently. But he was too quick to disregard the lives of others. He took everything that was precious to a person and left behind the shell. What did it matter to him whether the shell survived or not?

She would see Kareem again if she did not do something to stop him permanently. But he was an old man now, ancient, with no more power that she could sense, other than the ability to feel her and follow her. And if it was actually the rings that he was following, he would stop when she divested herself of them.

Kareem swore and cursed in his own language. Reg didn't need a translator to understand his venom.

"Maybe you can keep the ghosts company," Reg suggested. "Maybe they could tell you where another treasure is located."

Kareem looked around the room, but was apparently unable to see either the old, dead king or his son. No powers.

Reg looked at her guide, and together they retreated from the tomb room. The unsettled vibe Reg had felt since arriving there gradually lifted.

Reg hadn't been thinking, as they had taken their downward path, that she would have to climb up the way she had come. Her leg muscles were burning before long, her breathing ragged and uneven.

"It didn't seem this steep when we were going down," she told the guide between wheezes.

He gripped her arm and helped her along, but he wasn't really providing any support, just urging her forward. After what seemed like hours, Reg stopped for a rest, leaning against one of the walls and breathing hard, wondering if the burning muscles would ever be the same again. She really did need to take up some kind of exercise routine and get herself into shape.

"What I wouldn't give to be back in Ahmed's car," Reg gasped out.

The man looked at her, eyes steady. As if reminding her of something she should know. Reg considered her statement and what he might mean by his mild reproof.

"Oh, brother." Reg couldn't believe that she was being so dense. There she was, trying to climb all the way up the passages of the pyramid, out of sheer habit. Because that was what she had done her whole life. Gotten herself from one location to another using her feet. She had covered many miles on foot, not always able to afford or "borrow" a car.

But she hadn't gotten to Egypt by walking.

CHAPTER THIRTY-NINE

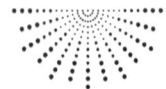

"*D*o you want me to jump you out as well?" she asked the man watching her with serious dark eyes.

He reached out and touched her hand. Reg thought about Ahmed's car, and where he had parked outside the security door. She didn't know whether he would still be there or whether he would have moved to a less obvious location to wait for her. Or whether he had just given up on the crazy American and decided to find another prospect. She switched her focus to the inside of his car, wherever it was. The spic and span surfaces, the smell of the carpet shampoo and the air freshener. Ahmed's reassuring presence, always eager to help her out.

Then she was there with him. Ahmed yelped and dropped the book he was reading, turning to stare at her wide-eyed.

"Sorry," Reg apologized. She wondered if she should try to explain the whole magic thing to him, then decided it would be too much. People tended to create their own version of reality when what they saw did not reconcile with their experience. If Ahmed did not have any experience with magical practitioners, he would just decide that he had been immersed in his story and hadn't seen her approaching the car, or opening the door and getting in. "Thanks for waiting around."

He blinked several times and shook his head. "You are back early if you went through a tour."

"We did our own behind-the-scenes thing. There's a lot to see in there, and we didn't have time for everything. What time is my flight to the Valley of the Kings?"

He produced a folder with the tickets in it. "It is an airbus; you can take the next one with available seats when you get there."

"Great! So we can go now."

"Yesss…" Ahmed drew the word out, doubt in his voice. Still trying to figure her out. She clearly wasn't behaving like the average tourist.

Reg looked around the car. Her other guide was standing outside the car. She didn't know where his car was or how far away from it Ahmed had parked. She opened the door.

"Do you want to go get your car, or come with us?"

He opened the back door and climbed in. Ahmed made a noise like he would object, then closed his mouth. Whatever the crazy lady wanted was fine with him. Better if there were someone else to deal with her nonsense. But he stopped and took a long, assessing look at the tall Black man before starting the car's engine.

"Who is he?"

"A friend."

Ahmed waited for more information, but Reg didn't have anything else to tell him. He looked at the other man, then back at Reg. "Does he have a ticket for the plane?"

"Uh… I don't know. I guess probably not. Can he get one there?"

Ahmed nodded. "It is more expensive."

Reg looked at the man. He didn't object to this. Did he have money, then? Or was Reg supposed to pay for his ticket? She shrugged, supposing that she had enough to cover it.

* * *

Ahmed guided Reg through the various queues and procedures to get them on the airbus to the Valley of the Kings, and Reg picked up a brochure about what they would see when they got there. She was absorbed looking through the pictures when she felt a familiar warmth. She straightened and looked around.

"Regina."

Reg stared at Corvin, taking in his self-satisfied expression. "Corvin? What are you doing here?"

"Looking for you. And now I found you."

"What do you mean? How did you get here?" Reg looked at her two guides, but neither of them seemed to have any idea where Corvin had come from.

Corvin raised his brows. "I flew."

"You flew here?" Reg repeated stupidly.

"How else would you expect me to get here when you didn't bother to take me along?"

"Well… I didn't expect you to get here at all. That was sort of the point."

Corvin looked smug. "And yet, here I am."

Reg couldn't believe that he had flown from Florida to Egypt to find her. Who did that? It was crazy.

"I don't know why you would do that. I'm just fine." Reg looked pointedly at her two guides. "I have people to help me out. We're making progress. I'm sure that by the end of the day…"

Corvin studied the two men. His eyes lingered on the tall Black man. He frowned. Reg felt immediately defensive of her guardian. He hadn't done anything but help her. He certainly did more than Corvin to make sure that she was kept safe. Corvin looked out for one person, and that was himself.

"You're going to the Valley of the Kings?"

Reg shrugged. "Seemed like a good idea."

"I don't see what you're going to find there. Everything has already been picked over. There are no more artifacts there."

"I'm not looking for artifacts." Reg looked at Ahmed and shook her head to disabuse him of any idea he might get from Corvin that she was there hoping to raid a tomb. She wasn't there looking for national treasures. She wanted to return the gems and rings she had.

Corvin and the guides measured each other. Reg got the idea that Corvin and the Egyptians didn't like each other, but Ahmed seemed to be willing to put up with the silent guide. Reg wasn't too pleased about Corvin being there. She had done her best to leave him back in Florida.

"Well... I can't stop you from going where you like," Reg said finally, "but you're not part of our party. I didn't invite you along."

"We're old friends. Why wouldn't you want me along?"

"Old friends or old enemies? You're not a part of this. I don't know why you think you should be."

"I'm just looking out for you..."

"You wouldn't come all the way here on your own dime just to look out for me. You're looking out for yourself. Like you always do. And you can look out for yourself somewhere else. Not with us."

Corvin could apparently see that he would not be able to get anywhere with her, so he shrugged. He would obviously not just turn around and go home. He could do the tourist thing all around Egypt if he liked; it didn't have anything to do with Reg. He could stay there permanently, for all she cared. Maybe that would be good for him. He could continue his studies of ancient Egyptian artifacts and whatever else he was researching and would be far away from Reg when she returned to Florida. So she didn't constantly have to be on her guard with him.

There were not assigned seats on the airbus so, of course, Corvin charmed the flight attendants and managed to get a seat just across the aisle from Reg. He smiled smugly at her, pleased with himself. Reg just closed her eyes and put her head back to go to sleep. She hadn't gotten very much the night before, and she had promised herself that she would have a nap on the flight.

She drifted off quickly once they were in the air, fatigue from her short night and long morning and the climb through the pyramid quickly taking over. She didn't awaken until a flight attendant shook her by the arm to tell her that they were landing, and she needed to put her seatbelt back on. Reg blinked sleepily and buckled up, then watched out the window closest to her, waiting for the plane to land. It took longer than she expected to complete its descent.

"You were talking in your sleep," Corvin told her. "And drooling."

Reg wiped her chin. She couldn't help herself. It was dry, no sign of drool. She shouldn't have reacted to him. "Talked about what?" she asked, keeping her voice casual and steady to signal to him that he hadn't thrown her off and she didn't really care what he had to say. She was just being polite, since she had to sit with him.

"You said something about Kareem. I couldn't make it out. Something like 'stay in bed' maybe?"

Reg's cheeks heated. She ignored her reaction, hoping that if she did, she wouldn't draw Corvin's attention to it.

"Oh. We saw him earlier. He asked about you." Reg decided to get in a little dig of her own. See whether she could get him off of *his* game.

Corvin's eyes widened, and he looked around. "He what? You what? Where?"

"At the pyramids."

"You saw Kareem at the pyramids."

"Yeah." Reg looked away from Corvin, watching the blue sky and clouds out the window.

"What did he look like? What did he say? After what happened, I thought that Harrison... I thought that we would never see him again."

"I guess Uncle Harrison just sent him back home. And... yeah, he didn't look too good. He was blaming me about you taking his powers. He aged... maybe because of that? Is that the way it works?"

"How much older did he look?"

"As old as anyone I've ever known. I don't know. A hundred. He didn't look good, but he got around okay. Followed me all the way down to the bottom to the tomb."

"He followed you."

"Yeah. Said that I should have known that he would be able to feel me there. And…" Reg tapped one of the rings but didn't do anything else to draw attention to it. She didn't want to get mugged when she got off the airplane.

"But he didn't do anything? Try to… harm you?"

"How could he? You took all his powers."

"Not all," Corvin hedged.

"How much did you leave him with? Not enough for him to do anything."

"If he followed you and the scent of those stones to the pyramid, then he still had some powers. What did you do? How did you get away?"

"I just commanded him. Apparently, people here have to obey when I tell them what to do, if I'm wearing the rings. I wonder if it works on everyone." Reg eyed Corvin. What should she tell him to do? Go away and leave her alone? Never try to trick her into giving up her powers again? What would be of the most benefit to her, if he had to obey?

"Don't try it," Corvin warned.

"Why not? You don't want to listen to me?"

"What would you tell me to do?" Corvin raised his brows suggestively. "I could give you some ideas…"

"I would be in charge," Reg said, "I wouldn't need any suggestions from you." She caught a glance from Ahmed and wondered if he picked up on Corvin's charms aimed in her direction. Her face warmed again. "Maybe I would just tell you to go home," Reg said, by way of example. Clearly, she and Corvin were not a thing. Ahmed could see that. They were not together and they were not discussing anything tawdry.

"And to wait for you, where…?" Corvin asked, still trying to embarrass her.

"No, to go to your home and to stay out of my life. I don't know why you think that you have any part in my life."

"I think that both of your companions have already figured out that isn't true."

"It is!" Reg insisted, flashing looks at the guides. "I do not have a relationship with Corvin."

Ahmed nodded and studied the air vents above him. The other man just looked at Corvin, unblinking. If only that were all it took to put him in his place.

The wheels of the plane touched down and, with one bounce, the plane settled on the runway and coasted, decelerating and then turning around to drop them in the right place. Reg's stomach lurched a couple of times with the plane's movement. After it stopped, she was happy to sit for a couple more minutes while the flight attendants organized their egress.

"So…" Reg rubbed her eyes and pulled out the brochure she had been looking at about the Valley of the Kings. "This whole valley in the middle of the desert, it's full of tombs of kings. A whole bunch of the pharaohs were all buried there."

Ahmed nodded. "They were not all kings. We do not know who all of them were. Some of them were lower in the government, or perhaps wealthy merchants. But to pay for a tomb like this and furnish it in the Egyptian manner, it did take a lot of money. Slaves and gold and all the trappings."

"And they were all buried here."

"Many were buried in this valley. But not all of them. As you saw, there were the pyramids, and there were many other tombs, most of which are probably gone now. But there have been 63 tombs discovered in Wādī al-Mulūk. And they are still looking for more."

"How could there be more that they haven't found yet? Aren't they… pretty easy to find with modern equipment?"

"No, not necessarily. Radar and other technologies do make it easier, but you have to tunnel through rock to find them. And much of this space is protected now; you can't just go out to the desert and start digging holes wherever you please. And any tomb that is discovered… they have to be properly documented and reported to the government, and you cannot just take whatever you find. Any valuable archaeological artifacts belong to Egypt and must be properly preserved in Egypt."

"That's fine, that's fine," Reg said, wanting to reassure him again that she wasn't out to rob a grave. "I'm not going to be digging around and trying to find one."

Ahmed looked slightly relieved at her reassurance. After the display that the crazy tourist had put on at the pyramids, insisting that she be allowed in through the back door, she might do almost anything. And he didn't want to be responsible.

"We will go on a tour of the tombs that are open to the public," he told Reg. "I have been here many times before, and I can tell you all about them. We can stay the rest of the day, and then go back to your hotel. If you want to see more tomorrow…"

"No, hopefully I'll be done today and I'll be able to head back to Florida tonight."

He gazed at her. Reg knew he was puzzled about what her purpose there actually was and what it was she had to do before returning home. She obviously didn't behave like the other tourists. She had something more going on.

And then there was this new American.

Ahmed flashed a look to Corvin.

"Ignore him," Reg said firmly. "I can't stop him from going wherever he wants to go, but he isn't with us."

"Yes, madam."

"You might as well call me Reg."

He nodded politely. The flight attendant reached their row. Reg and the others stood up to disembark together.

Outside the sun was bright. Reg put on a pair of sunglasses, but she wished that she were wearing one of her colorful scarves so that she could wind it around her head to keep the sun off and shade her eyes from the glare of the sand a little. Who knew that the sand could be so bright?

Ahmed led the way, and Reg and her guardian followed. Corvin stayed close, but he didn't try to get closer to Reg to charm her or make demands about what she was doing there or what she should do. She wasn't sure she understood why he was even there. The jewels had nothing to do with him.

CHAPTER FORTY

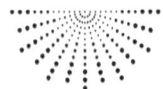

*T*he first couple of tombs that they visited were fascinating. Reg got to see some of the kinds of artifacts she had missed in her backroom tour of the pyramid. Beds and Coptic jars and decorated sarcophagi like she had seen on TV and in movies. More hieroglyphics on the walls. Ahmed told her what some of the depictions meant, and Corvin corrected him in a couple of cases, giving detailed explanations in his professorial voice about what they really said or meant, leaving Ahmed red-faced and sputtering over being shown up by an American. But Corvin was apparently not wrong; he just liked the longer, more detailed explanations, when Reg was fine with an overview even if it did gloss over a few points.

But as they went on, Reg's fatigue returned. The nap on the plane had not made up for the amount she had lost the night before, and after a while all the tombs and the displays started to look the same to her. Not only that, but in each one she had a fresh bunch of ghosts to deal with.

She didn't know why she hadn't foreseen this difficulty. She should have realized that all of these mummies who'd had their rest disturbed and their tombs raided would not be happy and would be looking for someone to complain to. Some of them just crowded in, wanting to tell Reg their troubles, and others wanted to dive right into her mind and take control of her. And she wasn't there to be channeling a bunch of disrupted pharaohs. She didn't have that kind of time.

Corvin could not only see her distraction, but could feel it when in close quarters with her. He probably felt as if he were climbing out of his skin too, absorbing some of her feelings.

"Can't you tell them to just leave you alone?" he asked impatiently. "Just block them out."

Reg rolled her eyes. "Is that what you did when you held my powers? Just turned it off?"

"Well… no," Corvin admitted, thinking back to it. "I seem to remember that some of them were fairly persistent."

Reg nodded. "And those weren't fresh new ghosts, either. Those were mostly old friends. They're quieter."

"But you must be able to suppress them somewhat."

Reg shook her head. "You know, I spent almost all my teenage years trying. And social workers and foster parents trying to get me to shut up about the voices and visions. And doctors trying to drug them to death. And you know what? They didn't go away."

As if to emphasize the point, one of the old kings seized her by the arm, putting so much energy into the motion that she could actually feel his fingertips restraining her, and he got in her face and tried to channel through her. Reg pulled back.

"I need… somewhere quieter," she told Ahmed. "I just can't do it here with so many of them around me."

There was a deep frown line between his brows. The tomb was filled with tourists, but the numbers were carefully controlled and people were not allowed to talk too loudly. And exactly what was it that Reg was trying to do? What made her so different from the rest of the tourists?

"I can't be in here," Reg insisted. "Let's go back out."

Ahmed nodded his agreement and led her out of the cave, back out into the bright desert sun, with heat waves reflecting off of the sand and stone. Reg covered her eyes, tears welling up and dripping down her cheeks.

"What is the oldest tomb?" she asked.

Ahmed motioned to the tomb that they had just come out of. But Reg already knew that wasn't the one that she wanted.

"No, not that one."

Corvin also shook his head. While he couldn't point out which tomb was the right one, he had placed the ring at 2500 BC or earlier, and none of the tombs they had seen were that old.

"That is the best I can do," Ahmed protested. "I am sorry if it is not what you would like, but I cannot take you to the undiscovered tomb."

Reg pulled her hands away from her face and looked at him.

"The undiscovered tomb?"

Ahmed shrugged. "There are other tombs out there. Maybe in this valley, maybe somewhere else in the desert that no one has seen in a thousand years because the sand buried it. Something from the ancient days may have been preserved by the gods and nature, but I cannot show it to you. If man has not found it, how could I take you there?"

Reg stood there for a moment, thinking about it. She scanned what she could see of the desert. Of course Ahmed couldn't show her anything but what was already known. And the rings and the gems in her possession had not come from any of the known tombs. She didn't think so, anyway.

Then how was she going to get there?

* * *

"Regina. Are you okay?"

Reg looked at Corvin, barely seeing him. "Yeah. I'm fine. Why?"

"Because you've been sitting here for... longer than I have ever seen you be still before. Do you have heat stroke? I could get you some water..."

"No. It's not heat stroke. I'm just trying to think."

"Don't try too hard," he joked. "You wouldn't want to burn anything out."

"Oh, ha ha," Reg snapped. "What I need is… somewhere I can be alone. Or just our group, anyway. I can't think with all these people coming and going. Their thoughts are like hamsters in a wheel. Add in all the other voices, and I just can't get everything sorted out." She ran her fingers through her thin red braids. "When we were in the pyramid, the old king there gave me a vision, but it was too much information too fast, and now I'm trying to remember it and sort through it all, but there's just too much going on."

"Let's see if we can find you somewhere quieter, then." Corvin strode away from her to go talk to some of the staff who supervised the tours through the tombs.

Reg put her face in her hands and rubbed her temples, trying to think through everything that was relevant to her quest.

In a few minutes, Corvin brought back with him a dark-complexioned, professionally dressed man with a look of concern on his face.

"You are not feeling well, madam?" he asked.

Reg opened her mouth to object, irritated that Corvin had told someone that she was having heatstroke instead of attending to what it was that she really needed. He projected a thought toward her to just follow his lead and not argue. Reg closed her mouth and considered.

"I think that if she just had somewhere quiet to lie down for a few minutes, she would probably be okay," Corvin suggested.

"Yes, yes; of course," the doctor agreed. "It can all be very overwhelming for someone who is not used to our climate. The heat, the brightness of the sun, the dryness of the air. Many tourists have problems going in and out of the tombs, alternating between the bright and the dark."

Reg put her hand over her eyes. "Yes," she agreed. "It gives me a headache, going back and forth."

Corvin nodded. "Maybe a bottle of water and somewhere she can lie down with a cold compress over her eyes?" he suggested firmly.

"Yes. Are you feeling well enough to walk a short distance?" the doctor asked Reg solicitously.

"Yeah, sure." Reg got up quickly, and then feigned a head rush, wobbling a little before straightening up again.

Corvin reached out to take her arm and Reg shook her head. Her guide took up the position instead. His touch was warm and soothing, unlike Corvin's, which always electrified her. They walked with the doctor, Corvin following behind, seething that the guide was the one at Reg's side. Ahmed followed behind him, uncertain about what he was supposed to do and staying out of the way of Corvin as much as possible.

There were several prefab buildings in a cluster, like the ones used at a school for overflow rooms or on a construction site. Not a trailer, exactly, but something similar. Reg was led to an infirmary, away from the hustle and bustle and much quieter than anywhere she had been all afternoon. She sat down on the bed initially; then, at the doctor's urging, she lay down with her feet off the end so that they wouldn't dirty the white sheets. The doctor retrieved a water bottle from a mini fridge and cracked the top. He handed it to Reg.

"Make sure you drink that. It's important to stay hydrated. You might not even feel thirsty, but you still need the water."

"Okay."

Reg knew if she drank too much water it would hamper her ability to kindle fire, but she didn't foresee the need to set fire to anything at the moment, so she wasn't too concerned. It was all for show anyway, since she wasn't really sick. She just needed some quiet and space to sort out her next step.

"Thank you." Reg touched the rings. "You can go now."

The doctor raised his brows and looked at her, confused by the dismissal. He didn't make any move to obey. Maybe because the infirmary was his domain, she didn't have any right to command him there. But Reg didn't like this apparent change to the circumstances, when everyone else had obeyed the requests and orders she had made while wearing the rings. She smoothed the faces and bands of the rings with her thumb, focusing her concentration on them. They grew warmer on her finger. She looked at Corvin. "How about you go back outside and give me some space."

He didn't move either. Reg didn't bother giving Ahmed a command; he would obey her whether the rings were still giving her additional powers or not. She looked at the other guide. He gazed back at her with clear eyes, unconcerned.

"Isn't it working anymore?" Reg asked him.

The doctor frowned at Reg's odd question and looked at the guide for his response.

The guide turned his face away slightly. *No.*

Reg sat up, worried. "Wait… why isn't it working anymore? What has changed?"

He couldn't answer those questions, of course. The doctor pressed Reg back, encouraging her to lie down again. "Don't exert yourself. Wait until you are feeling better, and even then, I want you to move slowly and be careful. Sometimes people don't realize how sick they are. You don't want to faint."

"Don't touch me." Reg squirmed away from him. "I'll be fine. I'll stay still; just leave me alone. I need to think. There are still too many people in the room."

"Someone needs to stay with you to keep an eye on you."

Reg pointed to the tall, Black guide. "You. Please."

Ahmed and the doctor prepared to leave. Corvin didn't look like he was going to.

"I need to think," Reg insisted. "When you're here, you interfere."

"How do I interfere? I'm not doing anything. I can be quiet."

"You still interfere with my brain," Reg pointed out. "Your charms and our psychic connection are too strong, too disruptive."

"You've never said this was a problem before."

"I haven't ever been in Egypt, surrounded by ancient ghosts, trying to figure out how to get to a tomb that has never been discovered before."

"Well…" Corvin cocked his head to the side slightly as he considered this. "Fair enough, I suppose."

"You're the most distracting. You need to wait outside, at least.

And don't hang around my window." Reg glanced toward the small window nearby. The shade was pulled down to keep the room from getting too hot or bright, but they could still see the outline of the sun shining through the blind.

"How long?"

"I don't know."

"How will we know when you are ready for us to come back in? Your... friend... doesn't seem to be too talkative."

"He can still come out and get you. Or I can come out. Once I've figured out what to do, I don't have to stay in here any longer. I'm not actually sick."

"I suppose not," Corvin admitted reluctantly.

Reg waited. Corvin let out an irritated sigh and left the room. Reg looked at the guide. He shut the flimsy door to the infirmary.

They were alone.

CHAPTER FORTY-ONE

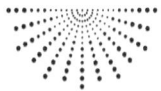

"*D*o you know what I am looking for?" Reg asked him.

He looked back at her, giving no indication one way or the other.

"I need to give these back," Reg said, indicating the rings. "And the rest of the gems I have from Egypt."

He expressed no surprise over this.

"I think that... I need to find an older tomb. These rings and stones are very ancient, and the tombs we have seen so far are too new. If I tried to leave them in one of the tombs we have been in, they would just be stolen. If we tried to give them back to the rightful owner... well, I don't think I've found the rightful owner yet, unless it is you."

He turned his head slightly.

"So I don't have anyone to give them to. If I give them to the wrong person, they might still come back to me, or they might cause a curse on the lives of the person I give them to, and that wouldn't be right. The stones have come to me, so it's my job to return them to their rightful place. Right?"

Yes. She could see that. She could feel that was right.

"I need to find an older tomb. Maybe... *the* oldest tomb. Do you know where it is?"

She got the feeling that the answer was much more complex than a yes or no.

"Can you take me there?"

Head turned. *No.*

Reg felt the frustration welling up inside her. She spun the rings on her finger, staring at them, focused, waiting for them to get hot.

"Take me to the undiscovered tomb," Reg commanded.

There was no flash of light. No sudden change to Reg's surroundings. The rings started immediately to cool.

"No! Take me to the tomb," Reg tried again. "Please. If that's where I need to go, then why won't you take me?"

But maybe the rings only allowed her to command others, not the rings themselves. And for some reason, even that ability seemed to have worn off.

If her guides could not take her, and the rings could not take her, then what was Reg left with? She couldn't take herself.

Or could she?

Reg closed her eyes partway, thinking about it. She could jump herself to places that she had never been before; that was how she had found the rightful owners of the previous bunch of gems. Ruan had taught her how to use her senses to see and feel and smell the gems and jump herself to where they had come from.

But when she had done the same thing with the Egyptian gems, she had jumped to the middle of the city and, when she asked for help, she had found Ahmed, or Ahmed had found her. The other guide had also found her, though she wasn't sure where or how she had picked him up. He had remained in the background at the hotel other than when he was needed.

Why hadn't she jumped to the tomb, so she could return the gems and jump straight home again? Why had she needed to find the guides instead? Was facing Kareem part of the quest she needed to fulfill before she was allowed to hand over the gems? Or meeting Corvin? Was he required for that part of the plan? She couldn't be sure what parts of all that had happened had been designed to bring her closer to the resting place or rightful owner of the gems and which were just things that had happened to occur along the way.

But now, all of that was past. She had met her guides. She had gone to the pyramid and to some of the tombs open to the public in the Valley of the Kings. And now she knew—or thought she knew—that she needed to go to an undiscovered tomb, one that was older than all the rest. One that was as old as the rings.

"Can I find the undiscovered tomb?" she asked the man who stood there silently waiting for her next question.

Cautious affirmation in his eyes. Why cautious?

Because she had said *find*? Maybe find wasn't the right word.

"Can I jump there? I don't need to dig it out or to find my way in through the front door, do I?"

A steady gaze, with a tiny fan of amused wrinkles in the outside corners of each eye.

"I can jump there. If I try to use the rings or the gems this time, I can jump there, instead of wandering around looking at all these modern artifacts. What about the others? Do I need to take everyone with me?"

He stood watching her.

"You. I need to take you with me."

A tiny nod, the strongest confirmation he had given her so far.

"And Ahmed? Do I need to take him?"

Less certain this time, but no head shake. Ahmed too.

"And Corvin?"

The guide lifted his head slightly and stepped back, as if he had just smelled something foul. He didn't like Corvin. But he didn't turn his head away. He kept looking at Reg, waiting for her to finish her questions and to take action.

"And Corvin," Reg sighed. Maybe that was why she had not jumped directly to the tomb the first time. Corvin had needed a day to follow her to Egypt, taking a plane instead of the instant jump that she had, because she had refused to take him along. "Well… I guess we should get ready, then."

He waited for her to make the first move. Reg went to the

door and opened it. She motioned for him to lead the way, but he hesitated in the doorway, looking out and then back at her. Reg supposed he was being chivalrous, letting her go out before him. Egypt seemed so far out of step with the society she had grown up in as far as women's roles were viewed. Dark ages. She rolled her eyes and went through the door ahead of him.

* * *

Reg looked around when they stepped out of the building. It was still just as hot and dry and bright as it had been earlier. She'd had a bit of a break from the sun and some of the water, so she was feeling pretty good. She didn't see the doctor or any others standing around outside. He might have been in another room inside or might be on call somewhere else in the historic site. It didn't really matter, as long as he wasn't there to witness her dematerialization.

As far as Reg could see, no one was watching or trying to listen in on what she was doing. Why would they? Everyone had their own jobs to do, or else they were tourists who wanted to see Egyptian artifacts, not some pasty-white American tourist who had succumbed to the heat.

"Well?" Corvin's voice was immediately inside her head. His facial expression was just as demanding. She wouldn't have had any trouble cold reading him even if she hadn't been able to hear his voice in her head.

"Okay. I have a plan," Reg advised.

Corvin looked expectant. Ahmed, somewhat nervous. He'd already seen her break all the rules at the pyramid site. She could only imagine the things he was worried she might do in the Valley.

"I don't know… if we all need to touch. But it might be the best, to make sure that no one is left behind."

This only ramped up Ahmed's anxiety. The other guide and Corvin seemed to take it in stride, unsurprised by the suggestion.

Corvin took one side, touching her on the shoulder so that

there was still a layer of clothing between them, rather than jolting her by touching her bare skin. The guide could have touched Corvin, but chose instead to take Reg's other arm, his hand resting lightly behind her elbow. Ahmed looked at them.

"You should come too," Reg told him.

He looked at the other two men. One on each arm. What was he supposed to do?

"You can touch one of them or get in closer." Reg stretched her hand for him to take.

Ahmed eyed the others, then gently took Reg's fingertips between his. Reg realized that the gems were in her pocket. Luckily not on the same side as Corvin and Ahmed; she still had the ability to move her other arm, as long as the silent guardian matched her movements and stayed in contact. He kept his fingertips on her as she touched the bag of gemstones in her pocket.

Without taking them out of her pocket, Reg found the edges of the mouth of the bag and gently opened the plastic zip seal. She reached in and touched the gems, trying to sense them as deeply as she could. She didn't want to display them to Corvin or Ahmed, so she couldn't see them, but she could feel them with her fingertips and her extra senses. And while she was not sensitive enough to be able to smell them as Ruan did, she thought that there might still be enough microscopic particles escaping the bag that her brain could process them, even though she couldn't consciously detect anything special.

She couldn't visualize the place she was to jump to, yet she could. She had seen the other tombs. She had a rough idea of what it would look like. A cave deep in the rock, rough-hewn walls, hieroglyphics and scenes on the walls. She didn't know whether there would be riches there already. She had to assume if it was an undiscovered tomb that it still contained whatever riches the mummy had been buried with. She pictured the beds and jars and other items she had seen on display.

CHAPTER FORTY-TWO

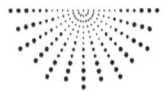

*I*t was suddenly difficult to breathe. Reg hadn't realized that she had closed her eyes. She opened them, expecting the bright Egyptian sun, and saw nothing. She could still feel the men around her.

Ahmed gasped. "What happened? Am I dead?"

"You're not dead," Reg assured him. She tried to see through the darkness. There had to be some flicker of light in the place that would allow her to see where they were. But it was as if her eyes were still closed.

"Where are we?" Corvin asked, his voice calm and even.

"In a tomb, I think," Reg explained. "The undiscovered tomb."

"That would explain the darkness."

Reg snickered. She looked around, still expecting to be able to see something. On TV when people discovered caves and treasures, there were always torches burning in holders on the walls, which lit by magic as they approached or had somehow remained burning for decades or centuries. She supposed that was just Hollywood taking a shortcut.

But if there were torches around...

Reg moved to free herself from the touches of the three men and held her hands close together, quickly kindling a small fire between them. After the total darkness, it was shockingly bright. Reg held it between her hands and looked around, shining it this way and that to get a better view of the cave they were in.

It was a little more roughly hewn than some of the tombs they had seen, but the walls were still covered with carvings, pictures, and statues. Reg wondered where they were geographically. Was the tomb within a pyramid? Buried under the sand for years? Or had it been carved out of the stone in the Valley of the Kings? In some other valley that had never been discovered? She could be anywhere in the world, but she assumed it was in Egypt. Or what had been Egypt millennia ago. Who knew what the geographical area of Egypt had been that many years ago? Reg didn't know whether they'd ever had an empire that had stretched across the known world, like the Roman Empire.

Corvin looked around at the hieroglyphics and scenes on the walls. When he stepped closer, his own shadow obscured what he was trying to look at.

"Can you get closer, Reg? Shine it over here."

Reg got closer to the wall and held the light so he could see the symbols clearly. She glanced around, looking for those torches in wall brackets that they had in all the movies. But there obviously weren't any. The dead king hadn't had enough foresight to ensure that he and his retinue would be able to see anything in the afterlife.

"This is... very ancient," Corvin observed, his eyes moving over the symbols and pictures, his hand just an inch from the wall as if to guide his eyes in a certain direction. "Archaic Egyptian."

"Well, that's good, isn't it? You said you studied ancient Egyptian. It was the modern stuff you had trouble with."

"Yes." Corvin looked uncomfortably at Reg. "But this is... even older than what I have educated myself in. My studies were of Middle Kingdom. Maybe one of your guides would be better able to take a crack at it..."

The silent guide remained so. Ahmed shook his head, looking at the wall. "I never made any study of the ancient tongues. This is... beyond me. Very obscure."

"It isn't gibberish," Reg objected. "It's just something that's hard to read. The pictures are pretty clear, though."

The men widened their viewpoints to look at the larger pictures that also told a story.

"They are not necessarily literal," Corvin warned. He studied the pictures. "In the Valley of the Kings, the earliest pictures were what was called the Book of Gates. But this is... not."

"This must be the king," Reg indicated one of the figures, sitting on a throne.

"Yes..." Corvin drew the word out as if he doubted Reg's conclusion.

"Well, he is, isn't he? He's on the throne. He has a scepter." Reg leaned closer in to the hand that was outstretched, pointing off in the distance as he gave an order. "And the rings. Look."

Nods from both Corvin and Ahmed. Reg looked at the other guide, but he seemed more reserved, not jumping right in to agree with her interpretation.

"This has to be the right tomb," Reg affirmed. "The rings are right there. This is the right place."

"But the right place for what?" Corvin asked. "What do you plan to do?"

"Well... I guess the first thing would to be to find the tomb. This isn't it." Reg looked around. There were several passages leading off from the room they had materialized in. There was no sarcophagus or any of the other trappings, so she must have to follow one of the passages to find it. They had landed in this anteroom so that she could see the rings on the wall painting and know that she was in the right place.

"*Then* what are you going to do?"

Reg scowled at Corvin. He was suddenly planning ahead? Now? It wasn't even his quest.

She went to each of the passages leading out of the room to look at the passageways and see whether there was any indication of which one she should take. A hieroglyphic that said, "this way" or a feeling pulling her in one direction. Maybe the rings would heat up.

They all looked very similar. But the floor sloped in one. Reg looked at it and tried to sense what was beyond. Did it lead to the tomb?

"The downslope suggests that this is the way to the tomb," Corvin said.

"We go down?" Ahmed questioned.

Reg looked at the passageway and turned her head to look at her guide. "Do you know where it is? You should lead the way."

"How would he know?" Corvin's voice was a growl. Was he jealous of the guide? Embarrassed because with all his studies about ancient Egypt, he still wasn't sure of himself?

Reg scowled at Corvin. "Don't be rude. So you can't read the old kind of writing. Nobody cares. You wanted to come along."

"I can read more than you think. *He* can't."

The guide didn't make any sign whether he agreed with this or not. At any rate, he wasn't going to read the writing aloud to Reg, and she didn't want to go through a whole long series of yes/no questions to try to figure out the interpretation.

"Do we go this way?" Reg asked.

The guide turned his face away from the passage.

"He doesn't know what he's talking about," Corvin insisted. "This is the only passage that slopes down; there has to be a reason for that. The tombs in the Valley were all at the lowest point. We should go look."

Reg shook her head. "We'll go where he says."

"That's not a wise choice."

"You don't know anything about him or whether it is a wise choice or not."

Corvin was insistent, hot anger pulsing behind his almost expressionless face. If she hadn't been connected with him and able to read him, she would never have guessed how angry he was. It seemed out of scale.

But the guy was probably jet-lagged. And humiliated that he couldn't do what he said he could do in the first place.

The guide moved away from them. Reg followed. Corvin and Ahmed didn't have much choice but to follow along, since Reg's fire was the only light. They went slowly down the passage, Corvin trying to read the signs and writing on the walls, trying to figure out the story that it told. Reg watched for the larger pictures, which gave her a better idea of whose tomb it was.

Corvin stopped when they reached one fork, putting his hand out to stop Reg from following the guide to the right-hand passageway.

"Look at that," he said sharply, pointing to an inscription on the wall. "I can read this one. It is a warning not to enter."

Reg looked at it. Of course, the symbols meant nothing to her. She looked at the guide. "Do we need to be worried about this? I'm not keen on getting trapped forever in someone else's tomb, you know."

The guide made a motion, inviting Reg to go forward, continuing in the direction he had chosen.

"Maybe it's just a warning to people with bad intentions," Reg told Corvin. "Like how the wards around my cottage will keep out someone who intends me harm. But not a friend."

"You're not exactly a friend with whoever is laid to rest here."

"But I am. I'm bringing back his rings and jewels. Why wouldn't he welcome me for that?"

"Reg…"

"He says it is safe."

"He doesn't know."

"He seems like he knows."

"You are too trusting. You can't believe that someone is safe and knows what they are talking about just because you think they look trustworthy. What do you know about this guy? Really know about him? Just that you met him here. You don't know anything about his family, where he came from, even his name. How can you trust someone like that? He has no past. He has no way to tell you anything. Why would you put someone like that in charge of your future?"

"I know him. He's not going to lead me into danger."

Corvin shook his head, huffing angrily. But he followed Reg as she continued down the right-hand passageway.

CHAPTER FORTY-THREE

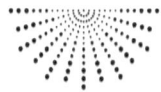

*R*eg had to admit that she was a *little* anxious following the tall Black man in the dark passage of the tomb. She didn't believe that he was leading her into danger, but she felt a little uneasy at Corvin's warning, and tried to reach ahead with all of her senses to determine if they were going to walk into a trap.

It wasn't like she and Corvin hadn't ever run into a trap together before. They did tend to run headlong into things.

"Do you sense anything?" she asked him quietly.

Corvin shot her a look. He looked ahead to their guide, then back at Reg. "No. Why? What do you feel?"

"Nothing, I just wanted to make sure. We should still be careful."

"You may be a little late on that."

"What do you mean?"

"We are stuck in the middle of a warren of caves, with warnings on the walls, and little air or light. It is sort of the definition of recklessness."

Reg was quiet, thinking about that for a while. She didn't like to be reckless, but it was something that had plagued her from childhood. Impulsive behavior. Doing things that parents had warned her against just to see what would happen. Thinking that she knew better and could control the outcome, only to find out that they had been right in the first place.

Some people learned from the mistakes of others. Some, like Reg, had to try everything themselves. She sighed and followed the guide, flitting like a shadow just at the edge of the light her fire cast.

He stopped before another doorway and waited for her. Reg and the others caught up.

"Is this it?" Reg peered into the room, brightening her fire for a moment to visualize more of the room.

It looked promising. There were more murals, a lot more hieroglyphics and, as they entered, she saw that there were dishes, furniture, and other practical items that the dead would need in the afterlife.

But as Reg entered and looked around, everything felt wrong and out of scale. She looked at Corvin and then looked around the room.

It was smaller than she had guessed. All of them inside would make it quite crowded. And the rectangular stone box sarcophagus was tiny. A prince who had died while still an infant? Reg stood still, feeling for any ghosts, for something to explain what they were seeing. She looked around at the pictures on the walls.

Corvin too was making a careful study of the symbols and pictures. Reg, looking only at the pictures, drew her conclusion before Corvin.

"A cat?"

She looked down at the small sarcophagus and saw that it also had a picture of a cat on the side and the wrapped bundle was about the right size. Reg got closer to the carvings on the side with her fire to look at the details of the cat picture. A cat which looked remarkably like Starlight, even down to the tuxedo vest markings on his chest. Reg gazed at it, a feeling gradually growing in her chest, warm and then hot.

"These hieroglyphs are about Bastet," Corvin advised. He pointed at a couple of pictures and inscriptions. "Defender of the king and goddess of the sun." He indicated several of the pictures on the wall. "Pictured as a lioness, as a god with a cat head, and as a domesticated cat." He shook his head slowly. "I did not know that cats were domesticated so early."

Reg looked back down at the sarcophagus. She raised her eyes to look at the other figures on the walls. Were they all representations of Bastet? Or were some of them another cat? Maybe this was the tomb for the king's cat, a beloved pet that he had promoted to a god.

"Was Bastet always a female god?" she asked Corvin.

"That's a strange question. She was generally portrayed as a lion or a woman, yes."

"Who are the other figures? Are they all Bastet?"

Corvin looked around at them. "Perhaps some are the king. Others are probably servants or members of the family."

Reg looked at her guide to ask him his opinion. He seemed to know more about the ancient Egyptian than Corvin did, despite Corvin's bragging. Living in Egypt, he had probably been taught in school and been exposed to other myths and histories that Corvin hadn't studied. She opened her mouth and then closed it, looking into the guide's face.

Something had changed. The guide's appearance had visibly shifted since the last time she had looked him in the eye. Reg knew that it had to be just a trick of the light. He hadn't actually changed; she was just having one of those moments when something familiar suddenly seemed different and alien. It had happened more than once before, and she had been told that it was perfectly normal. Just one of those little brain hiccups, like deja vu.

Corvin noticed Reg's distraction and looked back at the guide. He too stopped and studied the guide, frowning.

"A trick of the light." Corvin didn't say it out loud, but inside Reg's head.

Reg raised her fireball higher, so that the light struck the guide directly in the face instead of underlighting it.

But Corvin was wrong. It wasn't a trick of the light. The guide's face had morphed into something much more feminine.

Reg recalled Harrison's amusement over her difficulty with the idea that Starlight had been Bastet in a previous incarnation. Reg couldn't understand how a female goddess could have become a male cat. And one occasion, when Starlight had leaped to Harrison's defense, he had taken the form of a warrior, a full-sized man, instead of a cat. Harrison was amused that Reg had a hard time recognizing Starlight in another form or not understanding how fluid his physical identity was from one life to the next.

And then there was the time that Harrison had appeared to them as the proto-goddess Eostre. Sarah had been perfectly willing to identify him as a female goddess instead of a male immortal, since that was the form he had taken, but Reg could hardly wrap her mind around it. People were individuals. They didn't shift between species and genders and names.

Only, apparently, they did. She should have known that from her early days in Black Sands, when she had discovered that the fairies changed children of other species—both human and pixie, as examples—into fairies. Not just that they adopted them and treated them as if they were members of the family no different from anyone else, but actually used magic to transform them into something completely different. Calliopia had completed her transformation to a fairy, and would never again be pixie, even though she had taken a pixie mate.

All those different things should have prepared Reg for the fact that her guide was now clearly a woman rather than a man. Still tall and Black, with much the same lean body shape as he—she—had had before. But an identifiably feminine face. Reg looked around the room, taking it all in, trying to put all the pieces together.

"Is this... this is the tomb of Bastet," Reg suggested.

Corvin looked at her, rolling his eyes. "I highly doubt that. If there was an actual Bastet, and she wasn't just an invention of the people, then she was an immortal, and wouldn't have had a tomb."

But Reg looked back at her guide, a handsome woman watching her with clear, perceptive eyes. No longer two brown eyes, but one blue and one green. Suggesting that changing form from man to woman was not the only shift she was capable of. "You. Are you Bastet? Is this your tomb?"

The woman's gaze was approving, but she still gave no audible answer.

"Can I call you Bastet?"

There was no indication that she should not or that it would be considered sacrilegious. Corvin was still doubtful about the whole thing. But he didn't know Reg's previous relationship with Bastet. Reg was just starting to make the connections. Why Starlight had not been home when she went back to Florida to return Horace. Why her guide did not speak. How she had known where the tomb was and that Reg would be able to jump there.

Reg looked down at the small mummy again. If Bastet had been an immortal who sometimes took the form of a cat, then how had she died? Reg didn't even want to think further along this path, like how Bastet had then been reincarnated, and if so, how many times, and whether she still had power in each of those forms that would allow her to change her form. Was her death really a death, or just leaving behind one previous form?

Reg shook her head. She would not think about all those questions, or she would remain in that tomb for the rest of her life trying to sort it all out in a way that made sense.

"Do I give the rings and gems to you, then? You could have told me that before."

Bastet turned her head to the side slightly. *No.*

"Then the picture we saw to start out with in the first room, that was not you?"

No.

"The person in that picture was a man," Ahmed pointed out. "It was not Bastet."

Reg liked the way that he said *Bastet*. Even though he was speaking English, it had a slightly different intonation and pronunciation from when Reg had heard it used before. More intimately familiar.

"But…" Reg indicated Bastet. Ahmed had surely not missed her transformation from a man to a woman.

"And I am not so sure," Corvin said slowly.

They all looked at him.

"Sure of what?" Reg asked.

"The king with the rings on his finger… I was not sure, when we looked at it, that he was a man."

"He looked like a man," Reg objected.

"But there were subtle variations from the traditional Egyptian depiction of a king."

"He had a beard."

"But when women took the throne in Egypt, even as regents, they often wore a fake beard as a symbol of their authority. A beard on the picture does not necessarily mean that it was a man. Also, he was painted with yellow ocher."

Reg looked at the pictures of Bastet on the wall. The skin tone was yellowish. "So…?"

"Typically, men were painted with red ocher, and women with yellow ocher."

Reg considered this. "Well… okay. Maybe the king was actually a queen. But it wasn't Bastet, because Star—Bastet says that we are not to give them to her."

"Do we have to go to another tomb?" Ahmed suggested.

"No, I don't think so," Reg disagreed. "The picture of the queen at the beginning had the rings. There must be someone else interred here in a different room…"

She looked at Bastet, who watched and waited with crystal-clear, steady eyes.

"Is there another room?" Reg inquired. "Or a ghost or somewhere else to leave an offering?"

There was no disagreement. *Yes*, then.

"We keep looking," Reg told the others.

"What about the downward passage? Now that we have seen this room, maybe we can take that one. We know that a tomb is most likely to be at the bottom of that passage."

Reg looked at Bastet. "Will you lead the way? Is that the one we are supposed to take?"

Bastet stepped toward the doorway.

CHAPTER FORTY-FOUR

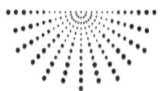

*R*eg walked with Bastet, since she was the one with the light. Bastet could, presumably, see in the dark, but it seemed to be polite for Reg to walk with her to share her light. Both of the men seemed to be feeling a little put out by the events of the day. Finding that their other guide was a woman as well as or instead of a man. And that she was Bastet, which neither of them fully believed. Ahmed was somewhat superstitious and was therefore more likely to believe that one of the ancient gods might have appeared to them. While Corvin had seen other immortals like Harrison, Weston, and the Witch Doctor, he didn't have much faith in the idea that their guide was Bastet. Why not? Because she was in the form of a woman? Because he thought that she was less in some way than the immortals that he had previously seen? He was the one who was studying ancient Egypt, so it seemed like he should be the one most excited to see her. He hadn't given any good reason for rejecting the idea that she might be Bastet.

They reached the intersection that met up with the down-sloping passage and stopped at the head of it. Reg looked at Bastet, not sure why they had stopped. Bastet looked at the walls.

Reg held her light up and looked at Corvin, wondering whether he would be able to interpret this inscription.

He cast his eyes over it, mouth pressed into a thin line.

"Can you read it?" Reg prompted.

"It is not as clear as Middle Kingdom would be to me. The syntax has changed, and some of the glyphs are different… but the meaning is fairly clear."

Reg looked at him, waiting.

"The tomb is cursed." Corvin said it as if Reg should have figured that out already. And maybe she should have.

"But so was the one for Bastet, and we were safe to go in there."

"Maybe. But," Corvin looked grudgingly at their guide, "that could be because we went in with Bastet, if that's really who it is. But going farther than this… unless *he* is also going to turn into someone else, we may be inviting a curse upon ourselves. And your whole purpose in coming here was to rid yourself of the cursed stones."

They both looked at Ahmed, as if he might morph into the pharaoh who was entombed there. Ahmed just blinked at them and shook his head.

"I am who I said I am," he objected. "I am not one of the ancients." He sounded somewhat peeved that they would even think it.

Reg shrugged. "If Bastet believes we are safe to go down there, then we can go."

Bastet was at the head of the group, waiting for them to follow. Corvin still hesitated. Ahmed did not look too keen on going down to a cursed tomb either.

"I do not believe in curses," he said. "Yet… why would one take the chance?"

"You two can stay up here, then," Reg said. "In the dark. Bastet and I will go down and deal with this, and then we'll be back."

"Or you won't," Corvin pointed out.

"I will be."

"Do you know what you are going to find down there?"

Reg looked at the pictures on the walls. She looked at the floor that sloped down into darkness. She closed her eyes and reached out her senses, trying to identify anything that was ahead of them. She should look for traps. She should think ahead and consider the matter before going on.

There would be ghosts. She could feel more than one entity ahead. She'd always had trouble differentiating between the dead and the living, but she thought it was pretty obvious that anyone else there in the tomb was going to be dead. No one else had entered the tomb in millennia.

She searched for other magic, wards or triggers that might have been placed to await their arrival. Bits of magic that she couldn't understand or account for.

But the place was laced with magic. She could see it woven through the hieroglyphics written on the walls. At the doorway of every passage and room. Imbuing the objects that had been left there to accompany the dead in their afterlife. And of course, in the mummies themselves. Everything was awash in magic, and she wasn't accomplished enough to understand it.

"There is a tomb," she said finally. "A very old one. And I'm going to go down for a visit." She looked at Bastet. "And hopefully, with an old friend along, the Pharaoh won't mind."

Corvin and Ahmed looked at each other, neither one willing to say that they refused to go, but at the same time, reluctant to join. Maybe Corvin had learned something from their past adventures. The Corvin she had met when she first arrived at Black Sands would already be halfway down to the tomb, ready to see what magical artifacts he could get his hands on. Of course, it was that propensity that had landed them both in trouble in the past.

"Let's go," Reg said to Bastet.

Bastet stepped forward. She had a smooth and silent gait, seeming to skim over the stone floor like a ghost. Reg might have thought that she was a ghost, if she hadn't been so substantial. At least now she knew why the guide had seemed so familiar to her. She had seen Starlight transformed into a man once before, but she couldn't remember enough details of his appearance as a soldier before to know whether he had put on the same face as her guide, or if it was just his manner and his aura that had been familiar.

Reg didn't say anything else to Corvin and Ahmed, but she could hear them following her. So they had decided that they didn't want to stay in the pitch black after all. She wondered which of them had been the first to step forward to follow her. Or whether they had counted to three and stepped forward together. She shook her head.

There was not a square foot of the wall that was not covered with carvings and symbols. They were not as bright as the walls in the tombs she had visited in the Valley of the Kings, but they weren't as brightly lit, and maybe the ones in the Valley were cleaned regularly too, to keep the colors bright. Or maybe they even touched them up. Or maybe the pigments that they'd had available when this ancient tomb had been painted just hadn't been as bright or well-wearing as the ones several thousands of years later in the Valley of the Kings.

Corvin was murmuring something behind her, or maybe whispering inside her head. She wasn't sure which and she didn't want to turn to look at him. A spell? A lecture? Reading aloud the symbols that he could interpret?

"Is it far?" Reg asked Bastet, even though she knew that she wouldn't answer. She just wanted to hear her own voice for a minute. It was small in the dimly lit, cavernous space. There was the whisper of an echo, trailing off into the distance. Reg could no longer see the ceiling above her, unless she made her fire brighter, and she didn't want to do anything that would startle or upset any entity that remained there after so many thousand years.

The pictures on the walls were not particularly cheery. They detailed the wars that the Pharaoh had apparently fought, orders given, slaves managed, goods traded. It had been a powerful and wealthy empire, if the pictures were to be believed.

CHAPTER FORTY-FIVE

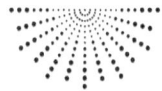

*T*he slope of the floor suddenly changed, and Reg stumbled for a moment before she got reoriented. It had, she thought, evened out, so that she was now walking on the level instead of a downslope. She waited for the men to catch up and, once more, they surveyed their surroundings.

"You're sure you should go on?" Corvin asked once more.

"What else am I going to do? Give the gems to you?" Reg challenged. "This is what I came here for. I don't even understand why you are here. You didn't have to come to Egypt or to come with me to the tomb."

Corvin grumbled, but it was not loud enough for Reg to make out the words, and she was sure that if she heard them, she would be even more angry with him. What right did he have to show up and tag along with them and then to complain about what they were doing? He could have stayed in the Valley of the Kings and looked at the other artifacts. Maybe he would find something that still retained a small amount of magical powers that he could suck up.

She looked back at Corvin suddenly. Was that it, then? All the artifacts that had been on public display for the last century had been long-since drained of any special powers they might have had. But the artifacts in a tomb like this, that had lain undiscovered for thousands of years? It could be filled to the brim with powerful objects that Corvin would want to drink.

"You aren't to touch anything," she told him firmly. "If you have any concerns about the curse being real, then you won't take the chance of touching anything and having the mummy come after you, or catching some ancient disease and dying next week."

"I'm not touching anything," Corvin said mildly, his mouth curling up slightly in the corner.

Reg wished that he didn't look so cute when he was being oppositional. She kept her gaze as hard and unyielding as she could, channeling all of those foster moms that she had been exposed to who could freeze a hardened juvie hood in his tracks with one look.

"That means taking anything from here. Even powers that you can suck out from three feet away. You are not to take anything from here."

He cocked his head slightly, looking not the least bit cowed by her attempt at sternness. "What about the air that I breathe? I suppose you want that back too."

Reg shook her head. "If you get cursed because you're stupid and can't keep your hands off anything with magical powers, that's on you. Not on me. Everybody here is a witness that I told you not to take anything. You're the one who forced your way on this trip. So you'd better be on your best behavior."

He was still smiling. "I'm always on my best behavior with you, Regina."

Sheesh, even in the middle of a thousands-of-years-old tomb, he still poured on the charm, figuring he could cloud her mind and sway her into doing whatever he wanted to.

Reg turned away from him and continued down the passageway, faster than they had been walking before. Bastet looked back and picked up her speed as well, looking a bit spooked that everyone was suddenly moving so fast behind her. Reg let herself slow back down gradually. She didn't want to be scaring anything in the tomb.

* * *

There was a boom far off down the tunnel, as if something big had just been dropped or a big door closed tight. Reg's step faltered. She looked at Bastet for her reaction.

"What was that?"

Bastet took another step along the passage, indicating that she would continue. Reg hesitated. Whatever was down there, it sounded pretty big. Most ghosts were not able to manifest that strongly. It took a lot of energy to be able to move objects in the physical world, and most ghosts did not have enough energy stored up over time to do much more than appear or make a few noises. Even coming to a seance to speak through a medium like Reg took an enormous amount of energy and they probably had to be saving it up for a while before they could make another appearance.

"What is it?" Reg asked, hoping that Bastet would give her some sign or reassurance. Reg studied the walls around her, raising her fireball to study some of the ominous-looking pictures.

But Bastet did not answer or make any sign. She just waited, taking another step and looking over her shoulder for Reg to follow her. Just like Starlight often did when trying to lead Reg step by step to his empty food dish. *Come on. Come on. This way. Another step...*

Reg wanted to be sure that she wasn't going to *become* someone's dinner this time.

She kept walking, her heart pounding hard, scenes from every mummy and horror movie she had ever seen flashing through her brain. All of the *don't go in there* moments. She had mocked heroes and heroines who seemed to lose all brainpower and walk into the most dangerous situations possible without regard for their own health and safety.

And there she was, acting like she was one of them. Walking toward something big and powerful in hopes of appeasing it with a bit of jewelry.

"I sure hope I'm not going to regret this."

"So do I," Corvin intoned dryly.

"Okay. So I am getting a little nervous now. But what are we going to do? Turn around and go back now? Then we'll be cursed for sure. I brought the gems here to offer them to the rightful owner, I'm not going to back out now."

Shhhh!

Reg wasn't sure whether it was a command to be quiet or just a puff of wind that raced down the corridor making a rushing sound. But it sounded like the shushing of Mrs. Perth, a high school librarian who had been out to get Reg. She had always been within hearing whenever Reg had said a word in the library, acting like she was the noisiest, most disruptive student in the school. Mrs. Perth peered through her old granny glasses down her long, bony nose while she hushed Reg and gave her a fierce, quelling look.

Reg wondered whether Mrs. Perth would have had any effect on Corvin, or if he would just have turned on the charm and she would have melted into an old-lady puddle at his feet. She stifled a giggle.

Regina! The rebuke from Corvin was inside her head. He hadn't dared to voice it aloud.

Giggling after being quieted by an ancient mummy was probably not the brightest thing she could do. If she wanted to stay on the good side of this pharaoh, then maybe she should guard herself a little bit better.

Sorry.

Bastet looked back again. That same beckoning, overly-patient look. The humans were being too slow again. The humans were likely to let a cat starve if they didn't get a little bit of encouragement. Maybe a nip on the ankles.

Coming. Reg directed this reassurance at Bastet, following at a slightly quickened pace to make up for lagging and giggling. It was just because she was nervous. Plenty of people giggled and got silly when they were nervous about something. She remembered one girl going into hysterical laughter and tears before the big final exam in... one of the classes that she'd managed to fail before aging out of foster care and leaving it all behind.

Her feet were too loud in her own ears. She could barely hear Corvin and Ahmed, and could hear nothing at all from the cat-footed Bastet, but her own feet sounded like a giant stomping down the hall. Ruan would have called her a buffalo. Or maybe an elephant. Humans were so clumsy and noisy, and Reg Rawlins worst of all.

She was almost laughing by the time they reached the end of the hall. But keeping in mind that girl who had eventually had to be taken off to the nurse's office to recover from her hysterics, Reg kept it under control and was careful not even to smile.

CHAPTER FORTY-SIX

*T*he doorway before them was open. Reg had half-expected it to be shut, after the big boom. Slamming the door before she could get to it. Sorry, Miss Rawlins. Try again in another century.

But maybe it had been the door slamming open. Maybe that *shhhh* had been the rush of fresh air as a ventilation shaft was thrown open so that they wouldn't run out of oxygen before they finished their quest. Who could tell? That boom might very well have been a good thing.

There was a chanting coming from the dark room beyond the doorway. Reg stopped and listened to it.

She didn't know any Egyptian, modern or ancient. Maybe this was where Corvin's knowledge of conversational Middle Kingdom would come in handy. Hopefully there were enough words that were still the same between Archaic and Middle Kingdom that he would be able to get their mission across to the angry mummy waiting for them.

"Reg?" Corvin prompted.

"Yes?"

"Are you going in?"

Reg glanced back at him. "I was hoping you could translate that."

Corvin looked around at the walls. "The inscription?"

"The chant."

Corvin looked at her blankly. Ahmed didn't give any sign that he could hear the chant either.

"There's…" Reg motioned to the room. "A…"

"A chant," Corvin repeated.

"You can't hear it?"

"No. Not me. Must be something you are picking up psychically."

"Dang." Reg tried to discern the individual words or sounds so that she could repeat it back to Corvin with some accuracy.

He put his hand lightly on her shoulder, giving her a jolt. Then he closed his eyes. Reg realized there was no need to repeat the chant back to him. She just needed to channel it to him. Their shared bond was close enough that it didn't take any extra energy for her to do so. It seemed like the natural thing to do.

Corvin's head went up as he listened and tried to make it out. He shook his head. "I don't… hear any words. It might just be a meditation chant, empty sounds to try to clear the mind. Or it could be something that I'm not familiar with. Sumerian, maybe, or some offshoot of archaic Egyptian that I've never heard before. I assume there were probably different accents and dialects in different parts of the land. They didn't have the same communication abilities that we have now. Populations that were isolated developed language along different paths and became more distinct—"

"Yeah, I don't want to hear it, professor," Reg said, stopping him.

Maybe when Corvin got nervous, he switched into intellectual mode to cover his anxiety. He looked at her for a moment, face red with anger or the light from the fire. Then he nodded. It was not, of course, the time for a lecture on the way that languages developed.

"Do we go in?" Reg asked Bastet. That's who she should have

spoken to in the first place. At least Bastet could understand the language of the time. "Is it... a prayer? Something that we shouldn't interrupt?"

Bastet stepped into the doorway and looked back. She looked into the room, and then back behind her again. The same behavior as cats around the world when presented with an open door? *Do I go in? Do I stay out?*

Reg waited, trying to curb her impatience. She had asked the question; she should wait for the answer. It was only fair. Whether it took Bastet a million years to make the decision or not.

Eventually, of course, Bastet stepped into the room, and took short steps into the darkness, then looked back at Reg, waiting for her to enter as well. She hadn't set off any booby traps and hadn't been immediately struck down by whatever entity was down there. So far, so good. Reg stepped into the room. She too remained herself, not turned into a beetle or a toadstool. Always a good sign. This seemed to encourage Corvin and Ahmed as well, and they stepped in behind her.

Reg paused. In a horror movie, that would be the point at which the big stone door closed behind them, once they were all in the trap. But no door closed.

Reg enlarged her fire slightly so that they would be able to see around the room without having to go any farther. Get the lay of the land and decide on their next step.

The walls were adorned with many carvings and pictures, as they had been in the rest of the tomb. Studying the pictures, Reg thought that these ones were more discernibly female. Despite the fact that most of the pictures showed the Pharaoh with a beard, the face was more feminine than Reg had initially perceived. And the skin tone was yellow ocher.

"Do we know... the name of the Pharaoh?" Reg asked in a low voice. It would be best if they could address her with the right name and titles. Ghosts liked that. To know that they were remembered after their deaths and that their lives had not been so insubstantial that they were immediately forgotten.

Corvin was studying the walls. He swallowed and looked at

Ahmed, as if expecting him to speak up. But Ahmed had said that he didn't know ancient Egyptian.

"Bastet?" Reg prompted, hoping that now that they were in the final chamber, it would all be revealed. Just because Bastet was drawn as a lioness, that didn't mean she really couldn't talk. Why would something as powerful as a god be unable to speak aloud? And if she chose not to speak aloud, then why didn't she at least put the answers into Reg's head?

"Mer..." Corvin started, and for a moment, Reg thought that he was trying to say *meow* or *purr* to communicate something to Bastet. Maybe in legend she could only communicate in cat speak. "Mer-neith," Corvin finished finally.

He stopped. He looked at Ahmed,

"Merneith?" Ahmed's eyes widened. "This is not Merneith."

"That is what the cartouche says," Corvin insisted.

"Who or what is Merneith?" Reg demanded.

I am Merneith.

CHAPTER FORTY-SEVEN

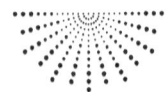

*R*eg whirled around, looking for the source of the voice that resonated down to her breastbone. She felt suddenly lightheaded, as if her blood were no longer reaching her brain. She reached out to steady herself on the nearest shelf.

She hadn't really taken stock of her surroundings, and pulled back immediately after steadying herself. There was a raised box beside her, similar to the one that she had seen in Bastet's tomb, but bigger. A huge stone box that presumably held the mummy of the Pharaoh. Not something that you stuck your hand into. She hadn't touched anything disintegrating inside the box, but all the same, it probably was not good etiquette to stick her hand into someone else's casket without permission.

"Merneith?" Reg looked around. Looking for a figure, for the shape of the spirit somewhere nearby.

She was glad to see that Corvin and Ahmed looked just as shaken as she felt. That at least meant that the voice was outside her head. The manifestation was not limited to only her.

"Do you want to show yourself?"

"Who disturbs my rest here?"

"This can't be the tomb of Merneith," Ahmed insisted.

Reg glared at him. She didn't ask him "Why not?" but it was certainly implied.

"Scientists have already found *two* tombs of Merneith. This would be a *third* tomb."

"How could she be buried in three different places?"

"She couldn't," Corvin said. "I mean, she could—part of the body in one place and part in the other, but the Egyptians were pretty keen on keeping the corpse intact, for obvious reasons."

"So, what...? One was the main house and one was the summerhouse? So she could go on a little vacation?"

"No," Corvin smiled at that, despite how tense they both were. "More like one was a red herring, a big, obvious tomb, and the other was where she would really be entombed, where no one would find her."

"A secret tomb."

"Yes." Corvin nodded quickly. "Long entrance passageways that could be collapsed or filled with stone once she was interred, and all the slaves who had been used to build the secret tomb would be... disposed of so that they couldn't tell its location."

"But why a third?"

Corvin shook his head. "I never heard that Merneith had three tombs. It's news to me, too."

"But you said that the... name tag said Merneith."

"It does."

"Then... were there more than one? Maybe it was a common name back then."

"Who disturbs my tomb?" the resonant voice demanded again.

"Well, whatever Merneith she is, she's certainly cranky," Reg observed. She looked around, hoping again for a physical manifestation to address her remarks to. "Merneith. I apologize for disturbing your rest."

"Who are you?"

A wind hissed through the tomb, cold and biting, snatching Reg's breath away so that she couldn't answer at first.

"I am Reg Rawlins. I have come looking for the rightful owner of these rings and stones."

There was no response. Maybe the ghost was thinking this over. Reg looked at the others, eyebrows raised for any suggestions.

"I am here with Bastet," she said. "Bastet said that it would be okay for us to come down here. You two are friends, right?"

"Bastet?" the voice repeated. "After so many years?"

There was another wind, and this time the ghost did manifest, appearing near Bastet. A tall, dark-skinned woman with rough-hewn features. She was not wearing the fake beard, and had markings on her face emphasizing her eyes.

Reg bowed her head slightly and tried to look small and insignificant. Which wasn't too hard. She was feeling very small and insignificant.

"Merneith. It is an honor to meet you."

Merneith did not have eyes for Reg. She saw Reg but immediately discounted her. Her eyes skipped past Corvin and Ahmed as if they weren't even there and fastened on Bastet.

"Bastet!" She reached out and touched Bastet's cheek, then laid her face alongside Bastet's for a moment in greeting. Not quite a kiss, but not the barely-touching bussing of cheeks that Reg had seen in the society set either.

"The rest shall go!" Merneith ordered. Wind pushed through the room, driving them the way they had come.

"No, no!" Reg protested. "We came here on a mission!"

"Your mortal affairs are none of my concern," Merneith waved this aside. "I care not."

"Don't you care about these?" Reg held her hand out, displaying the rings.

Merneith stepped closer, looking at the rings, the shadows on her face dancing in the flickering of Reg's fire. Her nose cast a long, dark shadow. Reg tried not to stare at it.

"I was hoping these are yours," she explained. "I have been trying to take them home. There was a mural in the first room we arrived in. I think it was you, with these rings on your finger. They're yours, aren't they?"

Merneith held out her hand. In her hurry to remove the rings, Reg scraped her finger. They were just a bit too tight around the knuckle. She was surprised that Merneith, such a tall woman, would have such narrow fingers.

Reg handed them over to the ghost, and neither of them anticipated that the ghost was not solid enough to take them. They fell to the floor.

"Stupid mortal!" Merneith shrieked. "You disrespect me by throwing them on the floor! I would have killed anyone who did such a thing to me in life!"

"I'm sorry! I was just trying to hand them to you. I didn't mean to." Reg's stomach tightened. She felt like she had as a little girl when Norma Jean would scream at her for something she had done, something that was rarely within Reg's control and, more often than not, actually Norma Jean's fault. Merneith shouldn't have put her hand out to receive them if she wasn't material enough to hold them. Reg had just obeyed her command. "Do you want me to pick them up?"

"Imbecile! Of course! You would just leave them lying on the floor in the dirt?"

Reg bent swiftly over to retrieve them. She looked around the room. "Where would you like me to put them? Do you have a chest or a bowl or something you would like them to be in?"

"Look at this place," Merneith growled. "I spent years building the tombs, decorating them, furnishing them, getting everything just right. I made sure that only my closest family members would know where my body was really laid to rest."

Reg looked at the mummy in the sarcophagus, her skin crawling. "Yes, that seems like a very smart thing to do."

"Do you think so? Do you really think so?" Merneith's voice rose in a shriek.

Reg winced and looked around at the others. Couldn't one of the men who knew more about Egypt and its history and traditions step in to help her? But Corvin and Ahmed both seemed frozen.

Bastet stayed close to Merneith, gazing at her with clear eyes, exuding calm and reassurance. Reg wasn't sure that the feeling was helping at all. Merneith seemed pretty worked up about something.

"I'm sorry. I don't know what happened."

"Does this look like the place you would like to spend eternity?"

Reg looked around at the room. It was very old. And despite the richness of the carvings and paintings around them, there was little of value in the room. Some Coptic jars set into a niche in the wall. A few broken dishes and a goblet. No piles of food or treasures. And Reg hadn't seen the bodies of dead slaves on the way in, slaves who might have been intended to protect the tomb or to serve Merneith in her afterlife. No family members. No other sign of another soul, other than the mummy of Bastet.

"What happened?" Reg asked. Maybe there had been an earthquake and the tomb had been buried. Maybe there had been war or an outbreak of plague and Merneith had died at a time when it was inconvenient for everyone to complete the arrangements that Merneith had made, having to compromise by just laying her mummy there alone, with no ceremony, wealth, or company.

"You want to know what happened?" Fury sped across Merneith's features, making her flicker in and out several times as she tried to stay in control.

The broken plates spun and flew around the room like they were in the middle of a whirlwind. Reg and the others put their hands up in front of their faces to try to prevent sharp bits of debris from cutting their skin. Reg tried to think of a way to dampen Merneith's anger. Like Bastet, she did the best she could to exude feelings of calm and comfort that Merneith would be able to feel and absorb. Positive energy to replace the negative energy. Merneith had been there for a long time, stewing over what had happened to her. She'd had hundreds of years to work herself up into a lather.

"I do want to know," Reg confirmed. "Do you want to tell me? I'm sorry it's so painful…"

"I am not hurt. I am not a weeping woman. I am a king!" Merneith shouted. "I am the greatest king this country has ever known! Not a queen," she said, her voice lower, threatening, "not a regent to someone else. I myself was the king. The first of my sex that this world has ever known. And the best, the most powerful, the most effective king in the history of humankind!"

Reg widened her eyes at Corvin and Ahmed, who knew more about the history, encouraging them to step in.

"Even now, thousands of years later, your name is still known," Corvin assured her. "Five thousand years, and the world has not forgotten."

Merneith looked at him for the first time, nodding proudly.

"You were the first," Ahmed agreed, his voice a little squeaky and breathless. "The first reigning quee—female ruler in recorded history. Even today, women cannot hold the type of powerful position that you did. Which you administered so well."

Reg bowed her head, hoping that would suffice to demonstrate her respect for Merneith. She was astounded that in all she had heard about Egypt, she had never heard of this woman. A king in her own right? Ruling a powerful country five thousand years ago? Why was her name not spoken in every girl's ear? Instead, they heard of Hatshepsut. Cleopatra. And in modern time, the Queen of England. Where were the other female rulers?

Had they removed Merneith's name from history? Ahmed seemed to know who she was; he was the one who had said she had two tombs. So her name couldn't have been wiped out, like she'd heard other rulers' names had been.

"They stole from me," Merneith addressed Reg again, her anger seething. "My own closest family members stripped this tomb. Took my gold and my rings of office and my gems of power." She shook her head, quaking with anger. "Can you imagine such treachery?"

No wonder she was so angry. They stripped everything that she had managed to keep for the afterlife, and then had forgotten all about her, burying the tomb so that it would never be found, and their treachery never revealed to anyone but the dead Merneith.

Reg looked around and found a bowl that was nearly whole. She put it on the edge of the stone box that held Merneith's body. She reverently put the two rings into it. She reached into her pocket and pulled out the baggie of gems.

Corvin's and Ahmed's eyes got very wide. Neither had known the extent of what she had when she'd said that she needed to return the stones to their rightful owner.

Reg held the plastic bag in the direction of Merneith for a moment. Then she slowly poured the gems into the bowl. Everybody watched the stream of jewels flowing into the bowl, covering up the rings.

"These were wrongfully taken from you," Reg said. "I return them to you, to do with as you please, to comfort you in your afterlife."

Merneith's eyes glowed more brightly than Reg's fire, which she was juggling around as she tried to restore everything to its rightful order.

"You have done well," Merneith admitted. "You have come far to restore this treasure."

"Yes. All the way from Florida."

The name obviously meant nothing to Merneith. But then, Reg hadn't expected it to.

"You must do more," Merneith announced.

CHAPTER FORTY-EIGHT

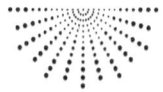

$\mathcal{U}$h-oh.

Reg did not get a good feeling in her stomach when Merneith said that.

She had pretty much expended all of her mental energy getting the gems back to Merneith. She didn't want to do anything else.

"Why do I need to do more?" she asked. "Haven't I done more for you than anyone else in the last five thousand years?"

"You have returned what is mine. But you also made use of them."

Reg grimaced. She looked at Corvin, who raised an eyebrow. She had, in fact, used the rings. She had done it unintentionally to begin with. She had slipped them on in a moment of distraction and had activated them by returning to Egypt to talk to Kareem. On returning to Florida, she found that the rings and the gems had changed. Still, other than the different feeling she had around them and the dreams of returning to Egypt, they had not made much difference in her life.

Each request and demand she had made since going back to Egypt had been fulfilled. And that wasn't Reg. A few people might be kind to a tourist from the States, but not everyone. They wouldn't all go out of their way to do what she asked them to, no matter how strange.

That wasn't Reg's power. That was the rings. Merneith's power, even after thousands of years.

"Okay," she admitted cautiously. "I used them a little. But not that much. Just a few times, to help me to find you."

So what Merneith asked of her could not be too big. It had to be reasonable, in proportion to what Reg had done with the rings. Which had really been for Merneith's benefit anyway. Maybe the rings wouldn't even have worked if it hadn't been for Merneith's benefit.

"You must bring me a body."

"What?" Reg recoiled, her mind filling with pictures of zombies, blood sacrifices, children or animals on an altar. She wasn't doing anything like that. No matter what Merneith asked of her. She wouldn't commit violence to some innocent.

Merneith's eyes went over each of them in turned, examining each member of the party as she evaluated their strengths and weaknesses. Reg's stomach clenched. Did Merneith expect her to sacrifice one of the members of her party? The scenario was getting worse and worse.

"No," Reg told her, before she could make any suggestions as to how the bargain would be struck. "You can't have anyone from my party. I'm not doing anything to harm anyone."

"Harm?" Merneith repeated. "I ask you to harm no one."

"But you said... I don't know what it is you want." Reg didn't want to put words into the ghost's mouth. With her luck, suggesting that she'd thought Merneith meant a blood sacrifice would make her think that it was a good idea. And it wasn't. It definitely wasn't.

"I have been a wanderer all these years," Merneith told Reg. "I need a home."

"Isn't... this your home?" Reg looked around. "Maybe we could bring you a few things to make it more comfortable."

"This no home for my *sah*. I need a receptacle. A *khet*. To be able to hold my being. Like this one." She motioned to Corvin.

Reg turned wide eyes toward Corvin. "I'm sure you would enjoy possessing Corvin, but... isn't there another way? I can't really leave him behind here."

She remembered asking Bastet whether she should take Corvin along, and her affirmative answer. Had Bastet known that Merneith would ask for his body for her to inhabit? Bastet still said nothing, just watched and listened to her old friend.

Reg was still having a hard time wrapping her mind around the idea that her cat Starlight had been an Egyptian god and had known this first queen of five thousand years before.

"Before Bastet died, we had a bargain," Merneith told Reg. "She promised me that I would be able to use her cat form."

"Use it... how?"

Merneith let out an exasperated sigh that the living humans were being so stupid. "She would allow me to join with her, when my body died. We had a plan."

"But that deal was with your Bastet," Reg said sternly, getting an inkling of what Merneith was talking about. "You cannot use my cat."

That was all she needed, some ancient queen stomping around the house in Starlight's body. Reg thought the cat demanding now; how much more demanding would he be with this woman's ghost inhabiting him?

"No," Merneith agreed. She gave a little bow of her head instead of arguing as Reg had expected her to. "I understand my bargain was not with Bastet's current incarnation."

Reg sighed with relief. One disaster averted. What was it that Merneith wanted her to do? To provide her with someone else who would make room for her? Perhaps Reg herself? Reg already had enough voices in her head. She couldn't make room for another person, especially one with as strong a personality as Merneith.

"So, you want me to..."

"You must bring me a cat," Merneith said simply.

Reg looked around as if there might be kittens playing around her feet like in the statues of Bastet. Obviously, there were no cats in the tomb, or Merneith would not be asking for one. Cats were still much beloved in Egypt; surely it wouldn't take Reg long to find one and take it back to her. Although she felt a little queasy at the idea of leaving a kitten shut up in the tomb with the ghost. Who would take care of it?

"It cannot be just any cat," Merneith warned.

"I don't know about this," Reg said. "I'm not really good at matching up cats and their owners."

She'd tried to help with that once, and look at how it had turned out. Horace had ended up with someone who had unbound the piece of the Witch Doctor attached to him and had traumatized him. Kareem had been exactly the wrong person to match a kattakyn to. Who knew if the damage done to Horace had been permanent, or if it were something he would eventually get over? Reg had no idea how she would find Horace a home if he was just going to keep coming back to her in her dreams.

"It must be a cat who was willing to be joined with me," Merneith went on, ignoring Reg's protest. "Like Bastet agreed to."

"How... would you do that?"

"I don't know whether any of us have access to that kind of magic," Corvin warned.

Ahmed just blinked at them, maybe considering the word magic, and what he had seen and experienced that day. The people who had stepped into his world were very different. He would probably decide never to have anything to do with anyone who might potentially be magic again. He'd been through a lot.

"I can do this," Merneith told Corvin with a shake of her head. "I do not need *your* magic."

The first woman to rule a country, and Corvin still thought that she needed his help. Reg rolled her eyes. At least the next time he insisted he had to do something for Reg, she would know it wasn't personal. He just thought that all women were helpless.

"How will you know...? How will you talk with this cat to make sure that it doesn't mind?" Reg asked haltingly. "I can communicate some with cats, but that's a pretty difficult concept. I'm not sure how I would communicate that with it, or how it would tell me that it was okay with the idea." She paused. "Not all cats are Bastet."

"Bastet will help. Perhaps she already knows a candidate. She surely knew she would be coming back here and has been looking for a suitable host."

Reg turned her gaze to Bastet. Maybe she could talk to the queen in a way that Reg could not. Maybe their previous relationship and a shared language and culture years ago would allow them to communicate much more freely than Reg.

Bastet looked Reg in the eye and cocked her head to a slight angle.

Reg licked her lips, thinking. She had that awful feeling of having forgotten to answer everything on a test. No matter how she had done on the portion that she had completed, she would fail it anyway. What was the question? Or what was the answer that she already knew but didn't know she knew?

CHAPTER FORTY-NINE

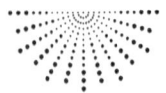

*R*eg tried to keep her gaze steadily on Bastet's eyes, to communicate all of her feelings and to pick up the slightest changes in Bastet's.

As Reg stared, Bastet suddenly seemed to be melting, shrinking down to a fraction of her size and folding over into a shape that Reg recognized. Her Starlight.

Reg bent over to pet him as he rubbed against her leg. Corvin made a choking noise. "Your cat?" He took in Reg's demeanor. "How are you not surprised by this?"

"I already knew," Reg pointed out the obvious.

"You knew? How could you know? When did you know?"

"I found out… through a client. And Uncle Harrison. A little while back."

"You knew that your cat was Bastet."

"Or had been… yes."

He shook his head in amazement. "This is… unbelievable. So, you will leave him here, so that he can be joined with this spirit."

"No. Didn't you hear? She already agreed that she didn't have any contract with Bastet in this form."

"But…"

"No, Corvin. Starlight is not staying here. He's coming home with me."

Corvin considered this. "Your other cat, then?"

"I don't have another—you mean Horace?"

He waved a hand. "I don't bother to learn their names. What point is there in that? Cats don't answer to their own names."

He looked at Starlight and didn't say, "Stupid creatures," but Reg heard it in her head. She glared at him. The worst part was that she knew that he knew the cats' names. As many times as he'd heard Reg and others refer to Starlight, he had never mentioned him by name to her. It was always "the cat." And he certainly knew Horace's name after all of the back and forth to Egypt.

"She wouldn't want Horace," Reg said slowly. "He's been… quite a problem lately. Because of… what he is. You know."

Corvin thought through the issues. Eventually, he shrugged. "Maybe he's just the thing for her. He could grow or shift on her command. And he's used to being joined with another entity. Maybe part of the reason he's having so much trouble is because he doesn't know how to govern himself by himself. He needs that… other prompting."

It would solve two problems at once, if Horace were amenable to joining with Merneith. Reg could be more sure of getting out of the tomb, with Merneith's anger sated and demands met. And she would have found another home for Horace. He wouldn't keep traveling back in her dreams if he were somewhere he was happy. He couldn't very well lie on Merneith's chest until she smothered, since she was already dead. It was a win-win solution.

If it worked.

"Maybe," Reg murmured. "Should we try? Should we tell her… *you know?*"

"I think she'll probably know what he is once we bring him. I don't think we'll need to tell her anything."

Reg kind of liked the idea of not having to tell Merneith anything. Just to give her the cat, say, "Nice meeting you," and go back home. Well, probably jump Ahmed back home, then pick up her stuff from the hotel, and then go home. Corvin could catch the plane back to Florida. And Starlight would, of course, jump with Reg. All neatly fixed and tied up with a bow.

"I have a cat who might agree to your plan," Reg told Merneith. "I don't know for sure. I will have to talk to him first. And if he doesn't want to…"

"Then you will need to find me another," Merneith said archly.

Reg couldn't help raising her brows in disbelief at Merneith's cheek. It was one thing to ask for help, but it was another to try to order people around when she didn't really have any authority anymore. She had been dead and gone too many years to just pick up where she'd left off.

She wanted to mouth off to Merneith, to declare that she had never agreed to do anything for her, that Merneith already owed Reg for bringing the rings and gems back to her, not the other way around. There was no reason for Reg to serve her.

Except, of course, that she was stuck in a small room with a ghost that had been gaining in power for five thousand years and appeared to have built up some pretty good reserves. All she had to do was to take the last of the air from the room, and Reg would be dead. The atmosphere was already pretty thin. And there were four of them breathing it. Well, three and a half, now. Starlight would not need as much oxygen as Bastet.

"Go get this creature, then," Merneith said impatiently.

Reg could just imagine if she had to retrace all of her steps that day, and even to fly back to Florida to fetch Horace and bring him back. As far as Merneith knew, Reg might have to do all of that to bring Horace back. It wasn't exactly a simple process.

But Reg didn't have to do all that.

There was no proper furniture in the room, and Reg's legs and feet were killing her. Walking for so long, in and out of tombs, her flat feet slapping against all of the stone floors of the passageways, Reg's feet felt as though they'd been beaten to a pulp.

She sat down on the floor, with Merneith's stone box behind her. She needed to get comfortable. Or as comfortable as she could be. The stone wasn't particularly forgiving to her sitting bones or back, either.

Reg arranged herself the best she could and closed her eyes. She didn't have her crystal ball this time, which she always found helpful when doing a call. She wondered whether she would need Corvin's help to extend her range. She'd been able to jump back and forth between Florida and Egypt, and it shouldn't be that much more difficult to call Horace that far, should it?

Starlight rubbed against Reg and settled into her lap, rubbing against her encouragingly. Reg pressed him down gently until he snuggled into her lap. She slid her fingers through his fur and felt his warmth and encouragement, the little bit of an extra boost that she got whenever they joined their psychic powers together.

She wondered whether he had been holding back on his powers to avoid overwhelming her. It seemed like he had quite a bit more power than he had previously shared with her.

But she put all of that out of her mind. Those were considerations for another time. Another day. She needed to focus on only one thing. Horace. The pure-black cat back at the cottage. She pictured her home. The inside furnishings. The place where Starlight would have been snoozing and looking out the window if Reg had been home instead of jumping all the way to Northern Africa. The various places that Horace sometimes settled down to go to sleep, or things that he regularly got into or knocked over when he was out of control.

Then she saw him. Sitting right in the middle of the kitchen island. Where, of course, cats were not supposed to be sitting. Except that it was true that she sometimes let Starlight get away with it if he really wanted to look at something or talk to her, or if she were busy and couldn't be bothered to go over and move him off.

"Horace," Reg whispered. *"Come."*

He was, perhaps, more startled than Ruan or Corvin would have been. They could at least have understood what she was going to do and prepared themselves. But a cat had no way of understanding what was going to happen. Reg saw the world in a kaleidoscope through Horace's eyes, everything upside down and wonky, racing through space, and then eventually falling into the darkness at Reg's feet.

Reg reached out to pet and reassure him immediately. "It's okay, Horace. I know that was scary, but it's done now."

Horace pressed his furry cheek against Reg's hand, and then looked around, trying to figure out what had happened. He tensed, fur standing on end, as he looked at his surroundings and the people around him. Reg felt his terror at being back in Egypt. Back to where Kareem was. With Corvin, the soul-drinker and others that Horace didn't know. He was glad to see Starlight, but even he didn't look and feel like he was supposed to. Something had changed in him.

"It's okay," Reg assured him, reaching out both hands to try to corral Horace before he bolted. If he escaped, they might never be able to find him again. "It's okay, you're safe here. No one is going to hurt you. And if you don't want to stay after I tell you everything, then you don't have to. I'll take you right home before anything else. Just like I did last time. Remember how I took you back the last time?"

He hissed and spat, not liking her hands so close to him. He wanted to know that he had an escape route, but it was blocked off, not just with her hands but with fire. She was really serious about keeping him in that dreadful place.

Reg hadn't even thought about how the fire would scare him. It hadn't bothered Starlight, but then, he'd seen her playing with fire plenty of times with Davyn. She couldn't put it out, or they would all be plunged into darkness. Reg pushed the fire away from her, finding a slight depression in the floor where it nestled naturally. Horace relaxed a bit with the fire farther away.

"It's okay." Reg stroked him, trying to calm his fear and the anger that would naturally result from it. A being who had been abused would expect more abuse and would try to use the defenses he had learned in the past before he could be hurt again. Reg scratched his jaw and ear. "You're safe. You don't have to worry.

I'm just going to tell you why you're here, okay? And if you don't like it, I'll take you straight back home."

Horace didn't move. He wasn't calming down as much as she had hoped, but he was definitely not on such high alert as he had been previously. Cautious and guarded, but not terrified.

She supposed that was progress.

"There is a ghost here," Reg explained. "A very old ghost. You see the symbols on the wall and the pictures? That is her. Merneith."

Horace wasn't particularly interested in the pictures. He could smell the ghost. And he'd probably smelled other ghosts around Reg at other times. It wasn't as if she managed to stay away from them all the time.

"Merneith is Starlight's friend."

Starlight got up from Reg's lap and he moved around Horace, going slowly and being careful not to do anything that would startle him. Horace bumped faces with Starlight, and the two of them sniffed and snuffled and groomed each other. Reg waited, wondering how much Starlight could convey to Horace through these actions. She knew it wasn't the same as direct language, but there was much that could be conveyed about their feelings with these social behaviors.

"Merneith has a problem. And you have a little problem. And I wonder if the two of you might be able to solve each other's problems."

Horace was calmer. He looked at Reg, waiting for more. She was glad Starlight was helping.

"Merneith has been a ghost for a long time and wants to rest in a body. She needs to be anchored. And you... have been in this body, but you are maybe missing that part of you that Kareem took away?"

Horace's alarm returned, his fur puffing out as if electrified.

"No, it's okay. Kareem is not here. And he won't come here. If he showed up here uninvited, Merneith would send him away. She's a very powerful ghost. She wouldn't let him hurt you anymore."

Horace calmed a little, but was still on edge. He didn't like even the mention of Kareem's name. Reg determined to proceed without mentioning it again.

"You have been feeling bad ever since he did that, and Harrison brought you to my house, hoping you would feel better there."

And he kept returning to her house, even though it was not the right place for him.

"I am hoping that you would feel better, more whole, if you were joined with this ghost."

Horace began licking his fur back down again. Reg sat there and listened to him and tried to feel his feelings as he groomed himself, thinking of all that Reg had said and Starlight had explained. The two men watching were impatient, shifting and sighing and acting like if they were restless enough, it would hurry along Horace's decision. But a washing cat could not be hurried.

Eventually, Horace stopped and was still. He sat like a statue, looking at Merneith's ghost.

"I think he is ready to try," Reg said. "But if he doesn't like it, then you have to leave him. I'll look for another host for you."

"He is a fine specimen," Merneith observed, noticing how large Horace was, Reg was sure. As Corvin had said, if Horace could grow and shift for her, that would probably make her very happy. She didn't actually have to protect herself from anyone in the outside world, because no one but Reg had discovered her tomb since it had been sealed, but it would probably make her feel better to know that she could grow Horace to monster size to protect her if she so wished.

CHAPTER FIFTY

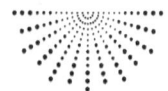

*M*erneith faded from sight. Reg continued to follow her progress by feel, as she moved slowly across the room toward Horace, taking care not to startle him by simply jumping in and taking over. Gradually, the two auras began to merge. Reg was waiting for the finish line, the point at which she could tell that Merneith had snapped into place and the two of them were one. But it was so gradual that she couldn't detect the line. Horace-Merneith looked around, surveying the room with his physical eyes.

Reg and the others waited. Horace-Merneith didn't start racing around the room like a devil-cat, or attack anyone, or puff out again and try to shake the ghost loose. He seemed to be contemplating the new feeling of being joined to the ghost, and the ghost of being joined with a physical body after so many millennia of waiting, neither in a big hurry to judge whether it would work or not.

"How is that?" Reg asked, prodding for some reaction.

Horace-Merneith looked at her, but didn't answer audibly. Reg waited some more. Horace began to walk around, picking his way delicately like the floor was wet. He walked over to Starlight, and the two cats rubbed against each other, bumping heads, rubbing cheeks, sniffing, and eventually grooming each other.

Reg couldn't feel any anger or alarm coming from Horace-Merneith. The cat's fear and anxiety seemed to have subsided, and the ghost's anger at the world with it. The combined entity seemed to be calm and satisfied with the state of things.

Horace-Merneith left the mutual grooming and jumped up to the edge of the stone box, where Reg had left the bowl of gems and the rings. Reg's breath quickened in anticipation. Now that the stones had been returned to their rightful place, they should no longer be cursed. If Horace-Merneith decided to give her any of them, Reg would be set for the next time that she wanted to negotiate with the dwarfs for more cash. Or she could choose to have them set in jewelry and wear them. Maybe she would make a ring of her own.

Horace-Merneith nosed at the gems, shifting them around. Eventually, he turned away from the bowl and Reg heard a slight *tick* as something hit the stone floor. She brightened her fire and brought it in closer. There was a large, sparkly diamond beside the sarcophagus. Reg picked it up, displaying it to Horace-Merneith.

"You dropped this. Did you want me to take it?"

Horace-Merneith sat on his haunches and looked at Reg. She reached out to touch his thoughts, now a strange mixture of catly feelings and Queen Merneith's words. She felt the calm *yes* answer, which reassured her that the diamond was meant for her.

Horace-Merneith bent down over the bowl once more. Twice more, he delicately picked out a gem with his lips and dropped it, though he deposited it directly into Reg's palm instead of on the floor. Then he sat up again and looked away from Reg.

That is all.

Reg nodded. She took in a deep breath, still feeling like she wasn't getting quite enough air, and let it out slowly.

"We will go, then, and leave you on your own." Reg looked around. "You will be okay here? Are there... mice? How will you eat?"

Horace-Merneith shook his head quickly, making the ear-flapping sound that always made Reg giggle. She wasn't sure whether that meant that the entity wouldn't need to eat, or that there was food present or he would find it somewhere else, but it didn't seem to be of concern, and wasn't any of her business.

"Okay... well, I'll be going home, then. I hope that everything works out the way you are hoping."

With the return of some of Merneith's riches and the emblems of her office, and a body to anchor her once more, hopefully she would be happy. Reg had done her part and received her payment.

Reg picked Starlight up. He snuggled comfortably in her arms. She looked at Corvin and Ahmed. "Ready to go back home?"

"Where will you take me?" Ahmed asked anxiously.

"Where do you want to go? Back to the airport where you left your car?"

Ahmed nodded. "That would be most gracious."

"Okay. Sounds good."

"Are you forgetting something?" Corvin prompted.

Reg frowned at him. "What?"

"You received three gems. There are three of us. Doesn't it seem logical to..."

Reg couldn't believe his gall. "Are you serious? You expect me to give you one of the gemstones?" She shook her head. "You were not even invited to come along. You weren't supposed to be here. You just took it upon yourself to fly to Egypt and track me down. That's your own business. And Ahmed..." Reg looked at the guide, hoping that she was not offending him. "I paid him for the tour already. I e-transferred his fees last night."

"I'm sure he wasn't expecting to be dragged to some remote tomb where he faced danger and—"

"I didn't drag him. He didn't have to come with me. And he wasn't in any danger." Reg chose to suppress the memories of Merneith throwing her dishes around the room in a whirlwind. Or the warnings and threats in the hieroglyphics on the way to the room. His life hadn't ever been in any *real* danger. "I'm sure he is glad that he got this education. What other guide has ever actually visited Merneith's third tomb? The one where her body really rests?"

Reg looked over at Ahmed, and he didn't object. He, at least, didn't seem to be angling for what was rightfully Reg's.

Reg glared at Corvin, daring him to try again. He shook his head, face red with suffused blood. "I came all the way here to protect you—"

"From what? Heat stroke? You could hardly even read most of the inscriptions. You didn't protect me from anything. Bastet-Starlight is the one who led and directed me, not you. And he doesn't care about jewels. I'll take him home and give him a tin of tuna. That will make him happy."

CHAPTER FIFTY-ONE

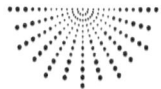

*R*eg jumped with everyone back to the airport so that Ahmed could pick up his car and carry on with his day. Probably to go home and have a good stiff drink.

Reg turned her attention back to Corvin. He was still angry, his mouth set in a scowl and the red flush still visible on his throat. She considered whether she should just leave him there and let him find his own way back to Florida. Sixteen hours in an airplane should give him plenty of time to cool off.

"You're not leaving me here," Corvin warned, catching the edge of her thoughts or reading her expression.

"I could, you know. You came here on your own. You can go home the same way."

"You're not that cold-hearted."

Reg would like to think that she was. She looked after herself first and, if Corvin was a threat to her, then why wouldn't she just leave him behind?

But she knew that she had stepped in and saved him before when others would not have. Standing up for him in spite of what he had done to wrong her. Taking him home after he'd been ensorcelled by Norma Jean, at her own peril. Other times when her friends had said that she had too much to do with Corvin and should stay away from him.

She was too warm-hearted for her own good. She'd been able to justify looking after herself first in other situations, but for some reason she couldn't leave Corvin alone.

"Fine. Where do you want me to take you?"

"Back to your place would be nice." Despite his anger at her not sharing her wealth with him, he couldn't help but fall back into the familiar pattern of engineering opportunities to charm her whenever he could. His voice was once again a low, intimate purr.

"No. Starlight and I will go home after we drop you off."

She felt as if she were taking a school child home after a particularly long field trip. The whole adventure in Egypt seemed a little distant and surreal.

"What about dinner?" Corvin suggested. "You could drop the cat off and then you and I go out to eat."

He knew he could often tempt her to go out to eat. Reg might have to start eating at home to try to break the pattern. She resisted the offer. "Not today, I need to spend some time at home…"

She didn't know why she always felt like she had to give him a reason. He never accepted her excuses anyway. Unlike Damon, Corvin wasn't a diviner, but he had a direct connection with her brain, and he could often tell when she was lying.

"Now that you've dealt with the gems and the other cat, why do you need to be anywhere? You've had a long day and should just be giving yourself time to relax."

"I am. At home, with Starlight."

"I want to hear all about what happened before I got to Egypt. You running off like that, I missed all of the first day…"

"Later. Tonight, I'm at home. Now, you want me to take you somewhere, or leave you here?"

Corvin grumbled. "Fine. Back to my house, I suppose. I really couldn't tempt you with something to eat? Some nice fresh fish? A walk on the beach?"

Reg just shook her head. He knew how dangerous the beach was. "Back to your house, then."

She touched his arm, remembered all of the sights and sensations of his house all too quickly and, in a moment, they were back there. Corvin leaned in toward Reg, so close that she could feel the warmth of his breath on her cheek, the smell of roses already strong. He was really laying on the charm, trying to ensorcel her the moment they arrived, while he was in his own territory.

Reg's mind immediately started to cloud. She pictured her house, pressing her face down into Starlight's fur to block out Corvin's pheromones. It took a few seconds for Starlight to focus her enough that she could make the jump, and then she was finally back at home.

Just Reg and Starlight. No other psychics, witches, or warlocks. No other cats. Just the two of them.

CHAPTER FIFTY-TWO

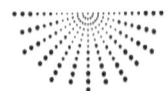

*R*eg awoke to the sounds of Sarah banging around in the kitchen late the next morning. At least, she assumed that it was Sarah. It could, of course, be Harrison. He didn't usually bother with the cupboards, since he could just materialize whatever he wanted. But he had been known to rummage through the fridge from time to time.

Reg rolled herself out of bed and was rubbing her eyes with her fists as she walked out of her bedroom and into the kitchen.

"Morning," she greeted croakily.

Sarah turned around to face Reg, smiling pleasantly. "You're back. I wasn't sure."

"Oh, sorry, I guess I should have called you yesterday. I didn't really think about it."

"No need. It isn't like it is a long trip to get here!"

Reg chuckled. Just across the back yard. Not too far at all. She caught Sarah looking around at the floor suspiciously.

"Just Starlight," she told Sarah. "Only one cat. As promised."

"Well, good. I'm very pleased to hear that. You got Marian to hold on to the other one, then?"

"Well, no, he wouldn't stay there. I'll have to give her a call and update her on the whole thing. But I found someone... elsewhere to take him. That should be the end of it."

Reg was pleased with the way things had turned out. Despite all odds, she'd been able to find a permanent home for the large, misbehaving cat.

With just one cat again, and more cleansed gems in her possession that could be sold, everything was perfect.

No more worries.

CHAPTER FIFTY-THREE

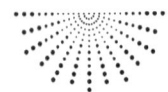

*R*eg was studying her client's hand, focused not only on the fine lines that mapped its surface, but also on Susan Petrovich's aura and emotional state, and what Reg could gather from her clothing, face, and the way she talked. There were no helpful spirits attached to her to tell Reg part of her story, so it was mostly what Reg could read and speculate from what she could see.

The woman's hands were thin and strong. Not calloused, but they felt like she had done a lot of physical labor in her lifetime.

"You are a hard worker," Reg speculated. "Goal oriented." This, based on her strong, determined aura. Reg had met people like that before. People who rose up from the mire and made a way for themselves. They found an escape and pulled themselves up out of poverty and other adverse circumstances they were in.

"Yes," Susan agreed crisply in her strong, Russian-accented voice.

"You will—"

Reg was seized suddenly with emotion. A jubilant, exultant feeling that thrilled all the way through her body from her heart outward. She gasped at the shock of it and was disoriented.

She was sure that it hadn't come from Susan. Reaching out to

Starlight, Reg knew that it hadn't come from him, either. He hadn't captured some disgustingly wonderful prey that he was thrilled about. He was still on her bed, snoozing peacefully. Reg expanded her search, trying to identify what direction the triumphant euphoria came from.

"Miss Rawlins?" Susan inquired, sounding like she was very far away. "Is everything okay? What's going on?"

"Something…" Reg gave Susan's hand a squeeze and pushed it away from her. "We'll have to reschedule. Something… unexpected has happened. I'm so sorry. I'll call you later."

There were more questions and expressions of concern, but they just flowed right past Reg. She was too focused on the rapture and where it was coming from. Susan made her way out and was gone. Stumbling over her own feet, Reg got up and retrieved her crystal ball from the shelf. She didn't even get back to the coffee table with it, just stared into it, searching for the answer to her query.

She had been staring into its depths for some time when her phone started vibrating in her skirt pocket. Reg set the crystal ball back down gently into its place on the shelf. She searched through the folds of her voluminous skirt to find her phone and pulled it out. With numb fingers, she tried to swipe to answer the call before it went to voicemail.

"Hello?"

"Reg, it's Davyn." There was hesitation in Davyn's voice. Reluctance to tell her what he had called to say. "I just wanted to give you a heads-up that the tribunal reconvened to rule on Corvin Hunter. And it was decided—"

"I know," Reg interrupted, not needing to hear the rest. "He has been reinstated to the coven."

Did you enjoy this book? Reviews and recommendations are vital to making a book successful.

Please leave a review at your favorite book store or review site and share it with your friends.

Don't miss the following bonus material:
Sign up for mailing list to get a free ebook
Read a sneak preview chapter
Other books by P.D. Workman
Learn more about the author

Sign up for my mailing list at pdworkman.com and get
Gluten-Free Murder for free!

PREVIEW OF
MISSING POWERS

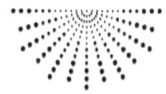

REG RAWLINS PSYCHIC INVESTIGATOR #16

CHAPTER ONE

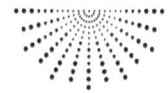

*R*eg met with Davyn for her lesson on firecasting in a forested area outside of Black Sands. The woods in Florida were a beautiful, lush green. Davyn wore his usual black cloak, hood pulled up over his head so she couldn't see much of his face. He had been selecting different areas for her to practice in each time they met lately, which she supposed was to help her be prepared to use her craft in whatever circumstances she found herself in. He did seem to prefer remote outdoor locations. Easier to avoid detection. Less danger if her fire got out of control. Assuming that she didn't accidentally start a fire that was too big for Davyn to control. She worried about things like that sometimes. She'd had at least one experience where he had been unable to stop her and didn't want to experience that again.

"How are you feeling today?" Davyn asked. It was a routine question, but Reg felt something different from him. Not the usual concern of a mentor for the young, red-haired firebrand he was training, but something more. Deeper. His dark eyes were piercing under the hood of his cloak.

She looked at him, trying to mask her curiosity about his emotions. He would reveal himself sooner or later. If there were something wrong, she would find out. But she didn't want to pry into his personal life. There were things about Davyn Smithy she didn't want to know. Reg gathered her red box-braids in one hand and pushed them back, over her ears and shoulders.

She shrugged casually. "I'm fine."

"Got a good sleep? Hydrated?"

"Yeah. All ready to go."

Davyn started to form a fireball between his hands, cupping the glowing ball. Reg mimicked him, calling on her own fire. She tried to mimic every movement he made and every change he made to his fire. Bigger or smaller, warmer or cooler, changing in color. It was a routine warm-up exercise.

"I just wondered… how you were handling the news about Corvin."

Reg grimaced and kept her focus on her fire, which immediately flared at Corvin's name. She calmed it down again and watched Davyn's fire closely for any changes. He would be examining her to see whether she could maintain her focus when he distracted her with talk about her archenemy, the warlock who had once stolen her powers but then given them back to save her, something unheard of for his kind. The warlock who would like to take them back again, and this time keep them for himself. It would be one thing if she and Corvin were just enemies and she could keep a wall between them. But having shared her powers and part of her consciousness, Corvin was bound to her in a way that couldn't be dissolved. They had helped each other out of sticky or dangerous situations. They had dated and flirted, and Reg couldn't help but be tempted every time he tried to charm her.

But she was strong. She had learned to use some of the powers that she had never realized before she took up residence in Black Sands. She could hold Corvin off. Usually. If she wanted to, she believed she could overcome him. But she didn't want power over him. She didn't want to destroy him or take his powers or to drown him in the depths of the ocean.

Usually.

There were times…

But she tried to suppress those impulses.

"Corvin being allowed back into the coven doesn't affect me," she told Davyn, keeping her eyes on his ball of fire. "I knew that he was going to be allowed back in sooner or later. I don't like it, but I always knew that Corvin being shunned by his coven was only temporary."

"You think it is too soon."

"I don't think anything. It isn't anything to do with me. I'm not the one who brought charges against him in the first place. What you people choose to do with him is your own business."

Davyn was part of the tribunal that had judged Corvin and imposed the sentence on him for his attacks on Reg. For breaking a promise and trying to wrest her powers from her without her consent. They didn't care about the time that he *had* taken her powers because, in their eyes, she had consented to it—but of course Reg hadn't. She hadn't understood anything about what he was or what he was capable of. She had no idea what she had been agreeing with. She hadn't even understood anything about her powers. She had thought that the voices in her head were just that, voices in her head. Not that she was really hearing the voices of those around her, both living and dead.

Corvin's silencing of those voices when he took her powers had been terrifying. Reg didn't know how the people around her could walk around with empty heads, hearing only their own inner voice. To her, the silence had been like a cacophony. Overwhelming and terrifying.

"Focus," Davyn prompted quietly.

Reg looked at her own fire, growing smaller and darker. She instantly fed the flames and it burned brightly.

"I'm ready to play. Can we get on with it?" Reg asked impatiently.

"I just want to make sure that you're ready. That you're not too distracted."

"I don't care what Corvin does or what the coven does with him. He can do whatever he wants. It doesn't have anything to do with me. Let's just play."

Throughout Reg's childhood, her various foster parents, teachers, and leaders had always warned her not to play with fire. It was too dangerous. They said that she couldn't control what happened once a fire was started. A fire could get bigger, jump to a new location, hurt someone. Even hurt Reg herself. Fires were dangerous tools; not for children, not something to play around with or experiment with.

But now, with a firecaster for a mentor, Reg *was* allowed to play with fire, and it was one of the best parts of her week. If Davyn would just stick with the lesson and stop trying to distract her with talk about Corvin.

Davyn gave Reg a tolerant smile. His concern was still there, under the surface. Maybe he was doing more than trying to distract her this time. Maybe he really was worried about her mental state and how the news of Corvin's reinstatement in the coven had affected her. But it wasn't time to think about Corvin or about Davyn's concerns. It was time to play.

"What is your fire drawn to here?" Davyn asked. He closed his eyes for a moment, then opened them and looked around.

Reg mimicked him, closing her eyes and reaching out with all of her senses, trying to identify what things attracted her fire. Her fire was like a separate entity, a different Reg that dwelt inside her, with its own agenda. She knew it was part of her, but was sometimes surprised at its strength of will and how it could be so different from her conscious desires. She opened her eyes.

"There is a crow's nest in that tree," Reg nodded to an ancient tree that towered over them. "Very big. Lots of sticks that are as dry as a bone."

Davyn nodded.

"And... deadfall, over here..." Reg indicated an area where she could see the trunk of a tree that had fallen years ago. There were other remnants of the tree scattered around it. Wood that had been there a long time and had time to dry out.

"Yes," Davyn agreed.

"Dried mosses," Reg closed her eyes, trying to envision everything clearly in her mind's eye and to feel the stirrings of her fire. "Other birds' nests, little ones."

"What would you choose to burn?"

Her mind went again to the crow's nest. It was huge. So much tinder. But she was hesitant to choose a nest. She could see that it wasn't abandoned, but was still in active use. She couldn't tell if there were any eggs in it, but it was home to at least one bird. She turned her mind back to the deadfall.

"The fallen branches over there, I guess. I could gather them together. Make a nice bonfire."

A warm feeling in her chest, her fire responding to the idea. *Bonfire. Bonfire was good.*

"Why did you discount the nest?"

"There's something still using it. The bird. I don't want to burn up its home."

"There is other wildlife here. Smaller. Less visible. Did you consider the creatures that might live in the deadfall?"

Reg shook her head. "Bugs? Termites in the wood or maggots underneath? Gross. No. I don't care about those."

"Is that the only life that would be affected?"

"Yes." Reg focused on the dry wood again, checking her premise. Was there only insect life? What about mice or squirrels making a home in a hole in the trunk? Woodpeckers drilling for the bugs? She couldn't feel anything else and shook her head. "I don't feel anything else."

"You always need to be aware. Sometimes, there is more there than you can see."

CHAPTER TWO

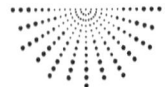

*I*s there something else?" Reg asked, a little impatient. "Did I miss something?"

"There might be other kinds of creatures that you are not aware of."

"Like what?" Reg thought about Sarah's garden. There had been a number of visitors there. "Like elves, you mean? Are there elves or some other magical race out here?"

"I don't feel anything either," Davyn admitted. "But you do need to be aware when you enter a new environment. If you burn a tree attached to a tree sprite, or that elves have made a home in, or some other being, you could end up in a lot of trouble."

Reg glowered at him. "So, this is just a safety lesson?"

"Safety is important. Not just your own, but of other creatures too. You don't want to end up cursed or the target of a malevolent force, do you? I've been trying all along to teach you how to use your fire responsibly. Firecasters... can be very dangerous and tend *not* to have good control. There's a reason for the expression 'a fiery temper.' Not only can that lead to the firecaster's early death, but also to a certain amount of prejudice from other practitioners."

"You're not like that."

"Prejudiced?"

"No, I mean, you don't have a temper. You're never out of control."

He shrugged. "You can master it. But mastering your fire is a lot easier than mastering yourself. There are a lot of things that can trigger your temper or distract your focus. It's much easier to let your fire burn than to keep it confined or put it out."

Reg nodded slightly. She'd had more than one experience where it had gotten away from her. But it was hard to see Davyn ever losing control. He always seemed very disciplined and calm.

"So... can I burn some of the deadfall, then?" She motioned to the trunk and branches. She ached to get a really good fire going. The warm-up exercises were fine for a start, but she wanted to ignite a nice big fire. She wasn't allowed to practice by herself, only when she was under Davyn's supervision. And that made it way too long between opportunities.

"Go ahead," Davyn agreed, nodding. "But keep it to the log and the larger branches. Don't let it spread to the undergrowth."

That was a little tricky. But Davyn knew that she was good at small, targeted fires. Reg focused on the log to start with. It was very big and dry, and she was excited about setting it blazing. Davyn stood nearby but didn't give her any instructions. She didn't have to make it burn with a blue flame or rise to a certain height. Davyn was allowing her free rein. Almost. She couldn't allow anything else to catch fire, but other than that...

The wood started smoldering. A thin column of black smoke rose from the surface. In a moment, it was blazing merrily away like a log in a campfire. The flames warmed Reg's face and hands and, even though it was already quite warm outside, Reg enjoyed the almost-scorching feeling she got from standing close to it. An ordinary person would not be able to get that close to it, but Reg didn't have to worry about being burned. She could tolerate any fire as long as she was concentrating.

Reg let her mind drift as she watched the fire. She wasn't taking her focus off of the fire. She was just allowing the back of her mind to work through some other things. Watching her subconscious thoughts as well as the flames.

It was Davyn who had brought up the subject as Corvin, as he often did, knowing that it was a good test of how well Reg was able to focus on her work. That and Davyn's... *friend* Julian Sabat, someone Reg had known when she was still a child. A tormentor that she was not interested in having back in her life. Bringing up Corvin or Julian was a great way to raise Reg's blood pressure and pull her attention away from her fire.

But Julian was not in town. He had work to do with Magical Investigations. And Corvin being reinstated back into his coven—maybe that was a good thing. Being shunned by his coven, he had no one to keep him company or focus his attention on, other than Reg or non-practitioners in the neighborhood. The other covens supported Davyn's and Corvin's coven by not having anything to do with him. Now that he was going back to his own kind, he would have other things to do, other people to talk to, and he would leave Reg alone.

Hopefully.

She told herself that it would be okay. She did not need to worry about late-night calls or dinner invitations from Corvin.

"Reg." There was a hand on her arm. "Regina."

Reg turned her head toward Davyn and looked blindly in his direction for a moment before she could see his face or the rest of the forest around her. He had lowered his hood so she could see more of his handsome, clean-shaven face and dark hair. And over in the deadfall, a pillar of fire rose straight out of the log toward the sky. Not a campfire, but a solid pillar of fire that looked like something off of some sci-fi TV show. Reg pulled back, but her fire was happy where it was. Happy to be allowed to play, to pull in deep breaths of oxygen and grow and strengthen. Davyn tried to use his fire to contain Reg's. Like stopping a forest fire with a back burn so that there was no fuel left for it. Reg fought the anger that flared up in her at Davyn's interference.

"Wait. Just let me."

Davyn withdrew his hand from her arm, but she could tell

that he was still cautious, eager to step in and contain Reg's fire before it could get beyond his control.

Reg thought about the little fire in her hands when she started an exercise, encouraging her fire to shrink down and not to consume the wood so quickly. She breathed slowly, trying to cut down the amount of oxygen it was sucking in.

"Come on," she murmured to herself. "Just a campfire. Not too big."

The wood crackled. Reg reached out, letting the fire warm her cold fingers.

"Just take it easy."

She didn't know whether she had said the words to the fire or whether Davyn had said them to her. Maybe both. Maybe they were that synchronized after the warm-up exercises.

"A nice calm fire."

The pillar of fire that had seemed to be reaching directly for heaven gradually shrank down until it was closer to the size of a campfire. A large campfire, to be sure. But there was nothing wrong with a campfire.

"Good," Davyn approved, relaxing his stance. "That was quite the display. You'll attract unwanted attention with a fire like that."

"We're out in the middle of nowhere," Reg dismissed. "No one would see it."

"We're not that isolated. And it can still be seen from the air." Davyn raised his eyes over the treetops. Reg had to concede that it had certainly been high enough and large enough to attract the attention of someone in the air. What would they do? Call in those firefighters that jumped out of airplanes to fight forest fires? What were they called? Fire jumpers? Smoke eaters?

"No one saw it."

"Were you aware of its size?"

Reg hesitated. It would be easy to tell him that she had known it was that big. That she realized what she was doing and had it all under control. Davyn was not a human lie-detector like Damon Knight, but he would probably know she wasn't telling the truth.

"I... lost track for a minute."

"You need to work on that. When you're kindling or tending a fire, it's not a good time to daydream, however hypnotic it might be."

"I wasn't *daydreaming*." Daydreaming would imply that she was thinking about something she liked, not that she was thinking of her enemy, worrying about how things would change when he went back to the coven. It would be good, wouldn't it? It would be good not to be Corvin's sole focus in life.

"Bring it down," Davyn told her, jerking his chin toward the fire. "There is more to tell you."

* * *

Missing Powers, Book #16 of the *Reg Rawlins, Psychic Investigator* series by P.D. Workman can be purchased at pdworkman.com

ABOUT THE AUTHOR

P.D. Workman is a USA Today Bestselling author, winner of several awards from Library Services for Youth in Custody and the InD'tale Magazine's Crowned Heart award, and has published over 90 mystery/suspense/thriller and young adult books, including stand alones and these series: Auntie Clem's Bakery cozy mysteries, Reg Rawlins Psychic Investigator paranormal mysteries, Zachary Goldman Mysteries (PI), Kenzie Kirsch Medical Thrillers, Parks Pat Mysteries (police procedural), and YA series: Tamara's Teardrops, Between the Cracks, and Breaking the Pattern.

Workman loves writing about the underdog, who the reader may love or hate. She has been praised for her realistic details, deep characterization, and sensitive handling of the serious social issues that appear in all of her stories, from light cozy mysteries through to darker, grittier young adult and mystery/suspense books.

> P. D. Workman, does not shy from probing the deep psychological scars of childhood trauma, mental illness, and addiction. Also characteristic of this author, these extremely sensitive issues are explored with extensive empathy, described with incredible clarity, and portrayed with profound insight.
>
> — —KIM, GOODREADS REVIEWER

Some of Workman's titles have been translated into Spanish, French, Portuguese, German, and Italian.

Workman began writing at an early age and is a prolific reader as well as writer. She is also passionate about teaching and learning, expresses her creativity through art and cooking, and loves exploring the Calgary parks and green spaces where the Parks Pat Mysteries are set. She was a legal assistant for many years and has done extensive charitable work.

Workman was born and raised in Alberta, Canada, and is married with one adult son.

* * *

Please visit P.D. Workman at pdworkman.com to see what else she is working on, to join her mailing list, and to link to her social networks.

* * *

If you enjoyed this book, please take the time to recommend it to other purchasers with a review or star rating and share it with your friends!

facebook.com/pdworkmanauthor

twitter.com/pdworkmanauthor

instagram.com/pdworkmanauthor

amazon.com/author/pdworkman

bookbub.com/authors/p-d-workman

goodreads.com/pdworkman

linkedin.com/in/pdworkman

pinterest.com/pdworkmanauthor

youtube.com/pdworkman

Find P.D. Workman's books at

PDWORKMAN.COM

Scan the QR code below